Readers love *In the F*
by ETHAN STON

"Mr. Stone has tailored a story filled with plot twists and emotional turns that kept me sitting on the edge of my seat."

—Dark Diva Reviews

"This book is amazingly good. The action was so nonstop I felt as though I'd been strapped into Colby's 1956 Corvette and hurtled at maximum speed around a Formula 1 course."

—Reviews by Jessewave

"Ethan Stone pens a thought provoking, suspenseful tale of one man's rise above his past. Hop on for the ride with Ethan Stone and *In the Flesh.* At the end, you will see the makings of something wonderful."

—Sensual Reads

"This is one of those stories that draw you in slowly, but once you're in you find it hard to put the book down. I will definitely be looking for more stories from this author."

—The Romance Studio

"The writing and unique voice of the narrator keep the story moving and always engaging. As the first book in what is likely to be a series, *In the Flesh* is a hit."

—Long and Short Reviews

Flesh & Blood

ETHAN STONE

DSP PUBLICATIONS

Published by
DSP Publications

5032 Capital Circle SW, Suite 2, PMB# 279, Tallahassee, FL 32305-7886 USA
http://www.dsppublications.com/

This is a work of fiction. Names, characters, places, and incidents either are the product of author imagination or are used fictitiously, and any resemblance to actual persons, living or dead, business establishments, events, or locales is entirely coincidental.

Cover content is for illustrative purposes only and any person depicted on the cover is a model.

ISBN: 978-1-63216-880-1
Digital ISBN: 978-1-63216-881-8
Library of Congress Control Number: 2014953891
Second Edition June 2015
First Edition published by Dreamspinner Press, April 2011

Printed in the United States of America
♾
This paper meets the requirements of
ANSI/NISO Z39.48-1992 (Permanence of Paper).

This book is dedicated to my son. Thanks for putting up with me
and my endless hours in front of the computer.
I love you with all my heart.

Acknowledgments

I OWE words of gratitude to several people.

To my amazing group of readers: Laura, Dawn, Amy, Mary, and Anne.

To the Ladies of DOS for the incredible support and words of encouragement.

To everyone who read *In the Flesh* and pointed out what was good and what wasn't so good. I hope I did better this time.

Prologue

HOW THE hell did I end up here? I kept asking myself that question, and the answer was Colby Maddox—the man I love. But it was still very surreal. He and I standing next to each other, dressed in expensive tuxedos, while that all-too-familiar tune played on a nearby organ. The church was large, with high ceilings, glittering columns, and shimmering stained glass windows. Not my normal type of place—not a place I would choose to get married in—but, once again, I was there because of Colby. He grabbed my hand right then, and I looked into his eyes. I could see the love for me, and I knew I was a goddamn lucky man to have him in my life, even if he did make me dress up for this event.

He looked toward the back of the church and smiled, and I followed his gaze. The bride came down the aisle—Colby's soon to be sister-in-law, Cassandra. She was marrying Colby's younger brother, Danny, who had straightened out his life thanks to Cassandra. She wore a lacy white dress that I'm sure was very old and very expensive. Her groom to be was at the altar, anxiously waiting for her to get there. He was likely even more anxious for all the festivities to get over so he and Cassandra could consummate—that's a ten-dollar word for fuck. But their wedding night would be special because, according to Colby, while Danny wasn't a virgin, Cassandra was. I tried to remember when I was a virgin and swallowed the bile that rose in my throat. I was young when my virginity was taken from me with force and hate. I didn't wish that on anyone, and I hoped Cassandra and Danny's first time together was everything it should be—sweet, tender, romantic, and explosive.

I'm sure the wedding was gorgeous and elegant—everything weddings should be. But I didn't really pay attention to the ceremony. Shortly after we sat down, Colby reached out, his large hand engulfing mine. I wasn't a small man—six foot two and built—but Colby was even bigger. He was my height but seemed twice as wide. He was a big man with a big heart. He also had another organ that was large. At one point in my life that would've been all that mattered and all I cared about. Not that I didn't care about that now, because I did; it just wasn't my top priority.

I focused on our connected hands. Colby was a light-skinned African American, but even his light-dark skin stood in sharp contrast to my lily-white flesh. Flesh was a major part of my life, and not just because it was my last name. Cristian Flesh was the name I selected many years ago when I left behind my past. Both my first name and last name have specific meanings. The last name was because that was how I was choosing to live—in the flesh. I wanted sex and as much of it as I could get. I didn't want emotions or attachments, and I concentrated on getting fucked as often as possible. Until I met Colby.

And that was what brought me to this big house on the hill in San Francisco. Colby had saved my life in more ways than one. I had been charged with a murder I didn't commit, and Colby helped clear me of the charges. But he did more than that—he taught me there was more to life than just sex, even great, mind-blowing sex. Somehow the big guy got past the rules and walls of my life, and I fell in love with him.

Before I knew it, the ceremony was over. Danny and Cassandra were kissing. And everyone was laughing and applauding.

AFTER THE reception, and after Cassandra and Danny left for their honeymoon, we all returned to Colby's parents' house.

The men—Colby and me, his brother Ted, his father, Theodore, and his sister Melody's husband, Blaine—were in the library drinking cognac. Apparently that was something rich people did on a regular basis.

"Colby tells me you're a cop," Ted said. He'd been making snide comments to me since I met him, and I had the distinct feeling he didn't like me.

"Yes," I said. "A homicide detective, actually."

"You have a good arrest record?"

"Pretty good," I said, unsure where he was going.

"Do you arrest a lot of black people?" Now that was an odd question.

"Yeah," I answered. "I suppose so. Never really thought of it."

"Of course you don't."

"What does that mean?" I was getting angry.

"Now calm down, Ted," Theodore said. Ted leaned back, but I wasn't done.

"I want to know what he meant," I said. "Because it seems as if Ted doesn't like me."

"You're not as stupid as you look," Ted sneered. "You're right. I don't like you."

I got up, and Ted did the same. The rest of the men stood—ready to step in if the fight got physical. I had no intention of that happening. Ted was a slight man, and I could fold him in half and stuff him into an envelope if I wanted.

"And why don't you like me?" I asked. "Because I'm gay? So what the fuck if I like to suck dick and take it up the ass. Deal with it."

Ted looked honestly shocked at what I said. "Being gay has nothing to do with it," Ted said. "My brother is gay, and I love him to death. I have nothing against homosexuality."

"Then what is it? Why don't you like me?"

"Because you're white. I don't like you because you're a white cop."

"That's why you don't like me?" I almost laughed.

"It's a well-known fact that Caucasian police officers trample on the rights of my people."

"Ted, knock your shit off," Colby said. "Do you really think I would be involved with a racist? Do you think a racist would get involved with a black man?"

"Well...." Ted hesitated.

"Damn, for such a smart man you can be a fucking idiot, Ted," Colby said. "Just for the record, Cristian has never treated me as less than equal. Actually, he tells me all the time that I'm a far better man than him. And it drives me crazy. He doesn't think whites are better than blacks or any other race. He's a good man, and I love him."

Ted was speechless, but Theodore spoke up. "Forgive my eldest child," he said. "He can be a bit dense. And his opinions are not the same as the rest of the family. Cristian, you are more than welcome here any time."

"Thank you, Theodore."

"I need some fresh air," Colby said. He took my hand, and we strode out of the library, not speaking until we got to the stables.

"I used to come here for peace and quiet," he said.

"You couldn't get peace and quiet in that huge house?"

"There was always someone around. So I'd come here and climb up there." He pointed to a ladder that went to a loft. He climbed up, and I followed him. It was a small loft with some blankets and other supplies. He spread out a couple of blankets and lay down on them.

"I'm sorry about Ted," he said.

"You don't have to apologize for your brother. At least he's honest about his feelings. I can respect that."

"He just drives me nuts with his holier-than-thou attitude and arrogant comments."

"Thanks for standing up for me," I said as I crawled on him.

"That's my job as a boyfriend." He smiled.

"I need to repay you."

"Oh?" He grinned again. "What did you have in mind?"

"Oh, I don't know." I slid down his body until we were face-to-crotch. "Maybe a blowjob."

"You don't have to repay me, but I'm not about to turn down a BJ."

"I didn't think you would." I opened his jeans, and his cock popped out. Not wasting any time, I quickly went down on him. I swallowed his entire length and started my best Hoover impersonation. Before too long, Colby was arching into my mouth and shooting down my throat.

THE NEXT day the Maddox clan had a huge formal lunch. I'd never heard of such a stupid thing—getting dressed up in tuxedos just for lunch. And the food wasn't even that good. Sandwiches so tiny I would've had to eat two dozen of them to be filled. They also served crackers and fish eggs. Goddamn fish eggs!

That night I felt claustrophobic. I needed to go out.

"Sure, I'm up for a night on the town," Colby said when I told him.

"No, I need some alone time, big guy. I'm sorry."

"No," he replied. "It's okay." He was saying one thing, but I knew he was feeling something different. He was hurt, but I didn't know what else to do.

I went to a nearby gay bar, a quiet place where you could actually have a conversation with someone. I talked to a few guys and danced with a few others. I was invited to join several men in the back room or at their places, but I turned them all down.

"So what's the deal?" the bartender asked after I had rejected yet another man.

"What are you talking about?"

"Just wondering why you keep saying no to all these good-looking men. You got a boyfriend at home?"

"Yeah," I replied.

"Does he know you're here?" I nodded. "So you guys have an open relationship?"

"Yeah, we have some rules, but he's given me permission to have sex with other guys if I want to."

"And he fucks around too?"

"Well, I told him he can if he wants to. But he doesn't. Says he doesn't need to."

"Sounds like you have an ideal relationship," the bartender said.

"Yeah, Colby's great."

"I think you're extremely hot, man. I'd love to fuck you." He winked.

"You're pretty goddamn good-looking too," I said.

"So you want to fuck?"

I looked at him and chuckled. "Yeah, I want to."

"Great. It's my break time. Let's go to the back."

I grabbed his hand. "I want to," I repeated. "But I'm not going to."

"What do you mean?"

"Since I've been with Colby, I haven't slept with another guy."

"You have an open relationship, but you don't play around? What's the fucking point?"

"The fact that I can is enough for me. Colby gives me what I need. If sleeping with other men was forbidden, I'd have a hard time with it. I'd feel the need to break the rules just to make a point. Colby knows that about me. That's why I love him."

“Sounds weird to me, but whatever works for you.”

I paid the tab and went back to the Maddox house. Colby was in bed, but I knew he wasn’t asleep. I stripped and climbed in next to him, pressing my body to Colby’s. He wrapped his arms around me.

“Feeling better, bello?” Bello was his nickname for me. It means *beautiful* in Italian. Even after all this time, I still didn’t see how he could consider me beautiful.

“Much better.” He kissed my neck, and I felt warm all over. He didn’t ask me if I’d fucked someone else—he didn’t have to ask, because he knew the answer.

Chapter 1

"THE WEDDING was okay, I guess," I said.

"Come on, Cris. I need more details than that." It was around 4:00 p.m. on Monday, and I was sitting at my desk at the Reno Police Department, being grilled by my partner, Alexandra Luther. Everyone calls her Lex. I had no idea why she chose to take her husband's name when it gave her the same name as a comic book character. I guess love makes you do stupid things. She was the total opposite of the other guy. The *Superman* bad guy would tower over her five-foot-six frame, and he'd probably love to have her long black hair on his bald skull. My Lex was slightly chubby, though she had slimmed down in the past few months.

"What kind of details?" I asked.

"What did the wedding dress look like? Were the vows sweet? How did the cake taste?"

"Fuck, Lex, I don't pay attention to shit like that."

"What kind of fag are you if you don't pay attention to those things?" she asked, laughing.

"I'm the kind of fag who doesn't care about those things," I answered.

"What did you pay attention to at the wedding?"

"I paid attention to the fact that Colby was there and held my hand during the ceremony. I paid attention to Colby standing up for me when his older brother bad-mouthed me. I paid attention when Colby and I fucked like rabbits all over that huge place."

"TMI, Cris. Jesus Christ, I don't want to hear about your sex life." She grimaced.

"What kind of fag hag are you if you don't want to hear about my sex life?"

"How many times do I have to tell you—I am not a hag."

"Flesh! Luther!" Chief Gary Brunson boomed from the door of his office before he stepped back inside.

"We're being beckoned." Lex smiled. "You want to make him stew and wait a few minutes?"

"No," I replied. "He'll blame me."

"I know." She grinned.

"Let's go," I said, smiling.

"Have I told you how much I like seeing you smile?" Lex said.

"Aren't you used to it yet?"

"You've been with Colby for a while now, but I had years of your constant frown before that."

I ignored her comment, and we stepped into Brunson's office.

"What's up, Chief?" I asked.

"Clayton Shaw is in the hospital. He's unconscious. He was beaten with his own cane."

Clayton Shaw was part owner of the Legacy Casino—one of the largest casinos in the area. Clayton was openly gay and fit the description of a silver fox. He was forty-five with a full head of gray hair and the beginning of a gut. He was also smug and arrogant and walked with a fancy cane—as an affectation because he thought it made him look cool, not because he needed one. I'd run into him a few times at the gay bars and the bathhouse. He'd propositioned me a few times, but his body reminded me too much of certain things in my past. But my past is something I don't talk about. That's rule number six.

"We got a suspect?" I asked. Though Lex and I were homicide detectives, we also handled cases that involved a lot of publicity.

"That's your job," he answered. "Go." His eyes turned to the computer screen, which was his way of dismissing us. We didn't have to ask where we were going—Shaw's place was well-known to everyone in the area. He lived in a gated community called Arrowcreek, which was located on the eastern foothills of the Sierra Mountains and had amazing views of Reno and the Truckee Meadows Valley. Homes there started in the mid-$200,000 range and ran into the two millions.

Lex rode with me as I drove my faded blue 2005 Jeep Liberty Sport to Shaw's place. I'd seen it before, but it still took my breath away. It was gorgeous in an ostentatious sort of way. The mansion was built in Tuscan style, with curved windows and an arched gate that led into a large central courtyard. In the center of the courtyard was a statue of a golden woman that was also a fountain.

Uniformed officers were already there, and one of them led us through the front door, up a curved staircase to the master bedroom, and into the attached bathroom. The bedroom had a small leather love seat and a king-size four-poster bed made of dark oak. The bathroom itself was almost as large as my entire apartment. It had sinks on each side as well as floor-to-ceiling cherry cabinets. At the far end of the room were a large, deep sunken tub and a huge shower.

Lex and I went to the tub—the scene of the crime. It was still filled, but the water wasn't clear—it was red. There was also blood all over the outside of the tub, the floor, and the wall.

A CSI tech named Cherry was there collecting blood samples.

"Find anything yet?" Lex asked.

"I'll be running tests on the blood as soon as I get back," Cherry answered. "I have the weapon bagged already. I'm hoping we'll find a fingerprint on it."

"Why would the attacker leave the weapon behind?" Lex asked.

I shook my head but didn't answer. I surveyed the room, trying to picture how the crime had taken place. The first guess would be breaking and entering. Maybe Shaw was taking a bath when the intruder broke in, not knowing anyone was there. That theory didn't make sense for a couple of reasons. The first was that Shaw's place had a state-of-the-art alarm system. The second reason was that nothing had been stolen. Even the dumbest thief wouldn't ignore the valuables downstairs and come upstairs to the bathroom.

I didn't have to verbalize my thoughts to Lex, because I knew she was thinking the same thing.

"It couldn't have been an intruder," Lex said.

"Whoever it was had to have been invited in," I replied. I turned to the uniformed officer who had escorted us in. "Where was the victim located?" I asked.

"Half in and half out of the tub, sir," he answered.

"And the wounds? Were they on the front of the body or the back?"

"All over, Detective. My guess would be the perp first attacked the vic as they were facing each other. And the beating continued after the vic had been knocked unconscious. I would say the perp stood on the side of the tub while he beat the vic."

"Can I see the cane?" I asked Cherry. She grabbed the bag and handed it to me. The staff was made of a light oak, and the handle was a single deer horn. The point of the horn wasn't very sharp, but with enough force, it could've been used as a stabbing weapon. Based on the blood on the cane and the handle, it looked like that was exactly what it had been used as.

"What time did the attack take place?"

"Approximately 3:30 p.m.," Cherry answered.

WHEN WE got to Renown Regional Medical Center, we learned Shaw was in surgery and probably would be for at least several more hours. A nurse pointed us toward Shaw's younger brother, Dale. Dale was the other co-owner of Legacy Casino.

"Mr. Shaw," I said as we approached him. "I'm Detective Flesh, and this is my partner, Detective Luther. We're investigating your brother's attack."

"I don't know what I can tell you. I wasn't there, and I haven't spoken to my brother for months."

"I understand, Mr. Shaw, but you might know more than you realize."

"I'll do whatever I can."

"Do you know anyone who had personal issues with your brother?"

"I'd be at the top of the list, right up there with my wife."

"You guys had a falling-out?" Lex asked.

Dale Shaw chuckled ruefully. "More like a major blowup. His… sexual habits caused me some problems."

"You had a problem with his homosexuality?" I bristled.

"No, Detective. It's not that I had an issue with what gender he had sex with. It was the age of his partners that bothered me."

"Exactly what do you mean, Mr. Shaw?"

"Please call me Dale. I hate being called Mr. Shaw."

"Dale," Lex spoke softly. "We need to know what happened between you two."

"I have an eighteen-year-old stepson named Austin. I consider him my son because I've raised him since he was eight. He told us last year that he was gay. It was a shock, but we encouraged him to be safe and be happy. He's a good kid and didn't rush into sex with the first guy who offered it."

"What does this have to do with your brother?" I asked sharply. Lex hit me on the shoulder—her way of telling me to shut up. She's one of the few people who can get away with that sort of thing.

"Go ahead, Dale," she said.

"I had Austin talk to Clayton because I thought my brother could help Austin out. I never thought my brother, my own goddamn brother, would do what he did."

I had a sinking feeling in my stomach that I knew what had happened. Family was supposed to love and support you, but I knew from my own experience that family could also hurt you and rip you to shreds.

"Your brother slept with your son, didn't he?"

Dale couldn't say a word. He bent his head, and I could tell he was crying.

"Oh Lord," Lex murmured with a hand over her mouth.

Dale lifted his head and wiped the tears from his face. He nodded. "Yeah, my brother slept with my son. He took my son's virginity, Detective." He looked me in the eyes, and I didn't look away, though it hurt me to see the raw pain there. Neither Lex nor I said a word, giving Dale the time it took to collect his thoughts and continue speaking.

"He took Austin's virginity. Such a special thing, and he took it. Then he stomped on Austin's heart. Austin loved Clayton. He thought sex meant love and commitment. Clayton treated Austin like just another trick, another one-night stand to be discarded like a used condom."

"How is Austin now?" I asked.

Dale met my gaze again. "He's fine now, but he wasn't when it first happened. He tried to kill himself. Thank God he failed. He's healing now. Healing emotionally and physically, but Clayton took something from Austin that he can never get back."

"Did Clayton apologize for hurting Austin?" Lex asked.

Dale shook his head. "He doesn't think he had anything to apologize for. He said Austin was eighteen and not related by blood."

"Unbelievable," I muttered. I hadn't thought much of Clayton Shaw before, and now I thought even less of him.

"Why are you here?" Lex asked. "If I were you, I wouldn't give him a second thought."

"Clayton is still my brother," Dale said. "He and I went through a lot when we were young. All we had was each other. It's hard to forget that, so when I was told Clayton might die, I couldn't stay away."

"Where were you at three thirty today?" Lex asked.

"I was in meetings most of the day," he answered. "The first meeting started at nine. I work with my wife, Sarah, and she was in most of the meetings with me. She joined me around ten. We were still in a meeting when I got the call about Clayton."

"Can anyone corroborate your story?" I asked.

"Several people, Detective," he replied. "I had meetings with employees and contractors regarding an expansion we're planning. My personal assistant, Serena, can get you the names and numbers of everybody I was with today." He handed me a business card. "She'll be in tomorrow at eight."

I cleared my throat. "We need to talk to your wife, as well as Austin."

"Austin?" he asked. "Why him?"

"We have to look at all suspects," Lex said.

"Don't worry, Dale," I said. "I'm sure he didn't do it. I have to speak to him so I can clear his name."

"I just don't want him to get hurt any more than he already has," Dale said.

I approached Dale and stood a few inches away, and I put my hand on his shoulder. "I'll talk to Austin, and I'll make sure he doesn't get hurt. It won't be an interrogation; it'll just be two men talking. I promise."

"Thank you, Detective." He gave us his address, and we agreed to meet him there in fifteen minutes. He lived in the same upscale subdivision of Reno as Colby—Damonte Ranch.

As we drove to Dale's place, I could feel Lex's eyes on me.

"Why are you looking at me like that, Lex?"

"You constantly amaze me, Cris. You can switch from pissed-off cop to almost a human being so quick, it makes my head bobble." To accentuate her point, she wiggled her head. I tried to keep a straight face but didn't manage and let out a chuckle.

"Almost a human being?"

"You know what I mean, Cris. I've been with you for so many years, and I'm only just starting to see the real you."

"Well, don't get used to it. It could change again without warning." If Colby left me, and I didn't know why he hadn't done that yet, I would be back to my old self again. And if that happened, I would never open up again.

When I saw Dale's place, I was amazed at the stark contrast between the two brothers. I knew enough about the Shaw family to know they each had the same amount of money. Dale's house was large but not extravagant.

The sun was setting as we arrived at the same time as Dale, and we followed him up the path to his front door. It opened before we got there, and an attractive woman with long brown hair stood inside. Dale greeted her with a kiss.

"Sarah, this is Detective Flesh and Detective Luther. Detectives, this is my wife, Sarah."

Lex and I shook hands with her, and she greeted us with an icy glare.

"Where were you today, Mrs. Shaw?" Lex asked after we walked into the living room and sat down.

"Dale and I were both in meetings today," she answered. "We own a real estate agency, and we spent all day at a meeting with our sellers. We're planning to expand to selling commercial properties."

"Who was there?" Lex asked.

"I met with a few accountants around nine. Then I joined Dale for meetings with some of our employees and contractors."

"Where was Austin today?" I asked.

Sarah turned to face me. "Why do you need to know where Austin was?" she snapped.

"Just standard procedure," I said.

"Austin didn't do anything," Sarah said loudly.

"I agree, but that doesn't change things."

"Don't you think he's been through enough?" Sarah asked.

Dale stood up and rushed to his wife. He put his arm around her. "It's okay, Sarah. Let Detective Flesh talk to Austin." Dale looked at me. "He's upstairs in his room."

I headed for the stairs, and Lex stood to follow me.

"I got this, Lex," I said. She eyed me questioningly but didn't argue.

Upstairs, I saw four bedrooms with one door closed. I knocked on the door.

"Austin," I called out. "My name is Detective Flesh, and I'd like to have a conversation about Clayton Shaw. May I come in?"

There was a moment of silence before a tentative voice called out, "Come in."

I opened the door and stepped in.

The overhead light was out, but a small desktop lamp illuminated the room enough for me to see Austin. He had shaggy, curly brown hair and a look of sadness that I knew well. He was sitting on his bed, wearing a pair of sweatpants and a white T-shirt.

I sat down in a computer chair.

"Is Clay okay?"

"He's still in surgery."

"I hope he doesn't die," Austin said.

I didn't like what I was hearing. I didn't want to have to arrest the kid. The idea of not arresting him even if he did confess came to mind, but I knew I couldn't ignore a crime.

"Did you do it?" I asked.

Austin glanced at me. I expected either an adamant denial or a tearful confession, but that wasn't what happened.

"I don't know," he said in a voice just above a whisper.

"What?"

"I don't remember. As soon as my parents left this morning, I started drinking whiskey. I was hungry and went out to get some food. I parked in front of Clayton's house and thought about confronting him. I wanted to tell him that he's a monster for what he did to me. I sat there in my car and drank more. The next thing I remember is standing in the shower. My skin was wrinkled, like I had been there for a while. I don't know how long." Austin bowed his head and cried almost silently. I sat next to him and put my arm around him.

"Don't worry, Austin. We'll figure this out."

"But what if I did it? What if he dies? I'll go to prison." I wanted to say that wasn't going to happen, but I wasn't going to make a promise I wasn't sure I could keep.

I stood up. "Look, Austin, I can only promise you one thing: no matter what happens, I will be here to help you. I'll talk to you soon."

I left the room and rejoined Lex in the living room.

"I have all I need for now," I said. "We'll be in touch."

We walked to the car but didn't get in.

"What do you think?" Lex asked me.

"Unfortunately, that kid is the chief suspect."

"Are you going to let your personal feelings get in the way of the investigation?"

"Have I ever done that before?"

Lex snorted. “Yes, you have made very stupid decisions based on your personal feelings. You went to save Gabe at an empty building, *and* you went to Donner Pass to find Colby—both without police backup. It’s like in the movies when the stupid blonde goes out into the dark garage, even though she knows there’s a killer on the loose.”

I shrugged. “Yeah, I could be considered too stupid to live based on those actions. Sometimes I think with my heart and not my head,” I said, laughing.

“Thanks for making my point,” she said.

“Okay, I promise I won’t let my personal feelings interfere. Can we go now?” On the driver’s side, I said, “Hey, Lex, will you—”

“Will I drop you off at Colby’s place and take your car back to the station?” she said, as if she had read my mind again.

I nodded and smiled at her.

“Have fun,” she said when she pulled up to Colby’s place.

“I plan on it.” I hopped out of the car. I wanted to surprise Colby, so I rang the bell.

“Bello!” he said when he opened the door. “What are you doing here? Why didn’t you use your key?”

“I wanted to surprise you,” I said. He leaned forward and kissed me.

“What a great surprise,” he said. We kissed again. His arms wrapped around me and enveloped me in an all-consuming hug. We remained like that for a minute before I realized we were still standing in the doorway.

“Hey, big guy, it’s not that I don’t like doing what we’re doing, but I think we should take this inside.”

Colby laughed and dragged me into the living room. He was wearing a pair of thin pajama pants, and I could feel his large erection pressing against my leg.

“Damn, baby,” he whispered in my ear, “I’ve been thinking about you all day.” He slipped his tongue into my ear, then traveled down to my lobe and my neck. Pressing his teeth into the dip between my neck and shoulder, he bit gently. A shudder ripped through my body, and he bit down harder, sucking as he did so. I knew there was going to be a mark in the morning, but I didn't care.

"Colby. Oh God, Colby. Fuck me. Please, fuck me." After talking to Austin, I was full of memories I didn't want resurfacing. I wanted—needed—Colby to fuck me so hard I forgot it all. Thankfully, Colby wanted the same thing I did.

"Yeah, I'll fuck your ass," he said. "I'm going to fuck you hard." He took my mouth with his again, owning it as his tongue pressed against mine. It was gone sooner than I wanted it to be. I tried to keep the precious contact by sliding mine into his mouth. He closed his lips around my tongue and sucked it in. I practically melted and might've slipped to the floor if his big arms weren't wrapped tightly around me.

In a lightning-fast move, Colby spun me around and pushed me against the wall. He pressed his erection against my ass as he bit my neck again.

"Get naked," he ordered. I unbuttoned my shirt and removed it and my T-shirt. He kissed down my back and stopped just above my ass. I had my belt pulled out of the loops, the top button of my jeans open, and was poised to do the rest, but Colby's big hands were on mine and holding them still. With his lips pressed against my lower back, he slowly undid each button. He worked himself lower and lower with each one, kissing and nipping at the exposed flesh.

He tugged my pants to my ankles, grabbed my hips, and pulled me toward him. I put my hands on the wall to steady myself as he spread my cheeks and gently licked from the bottom to the top—his tongue only brushing against my hole. Just that slight touch was enough for shivers to rack my body and my cock to totally harden.

"Ohh Lord," I murmured. Colby reached around, gripped the bottom of my shaft, and slowly stroked it, squeezing out drops of precome. He ran his thumb around the head, and I moaned again. He pressed his tongue against my hole, this time more firmly than before. I pushed back, reveling in the sensations. He licked around my hole and nipped at my cheeks before once more trying to tongue fuck me.

"Colby, fuck, I need you in me. Please."

He stood up and whispered in my ear, "I love it when you beg. Don't move." I stood there and stroked my shaft as I waited for him to return. He was back right away, and I could feel he was naked when he pressed himself against me. I heard him snap open the lube and jumped when a finger coated with the cold liquid touched my hole. Colby and I had stopped using condoms early in our relationship, the first time by accident, but we'd both been tested since then.

"Relax. I won't hurt you," he said. I knew he wouldn't hurt me, but I still liked to hear him say it. One thick finger slipped in, and I arched backward to get the digit deeper inside. Colby slid the finger in and out until he hit my gland. He rubbed my prostate as he chewed softly on my neck. When I moaned, I felt him smile against me. He pulled out one finger and slid in two. In and out they slid, rubbing me, exciting me, making me moan. I was about to beg Colby to give it to me when his shaft pressed against my hole. Evidently he was as ready as me.

"Fuck, Cristian… bello… baby. I love you so goddamn much," Colby moaned as he teased my hole with his prick. His large head pressed against me with just a slight amount of pressure. Colby firmly gripped my hips, and I knew he was in total control—exactly what I wanted. I tried to push back to get him in me, but the hold on my hips stopped that from happening.

"Not yet," he whispered. He applied more pressure, and the head slipped past my tight ring. I gasped, and before I could catch a breath, Colby slid the rest of his length deep into me. Buried to the root, he pushed me against the wall so we were both standing straight up. It was an odd angle to be fucked, but it felt amazing. His cock was hitting parts of me that didn't get hit very often. He turned my face and kissed me, hard. Our tongues fought for control—control I didn't want but had to pretend I did.

He thrust into me, and I lost the ability to think about anything other than the dick penetrating me.

"Fuck me, fuck me, fuck me," I moaned again and again. It was my mantra as the man I loved pounded me. Over the years I'd had lots of rough sex. Rough, hard, and sweaty sex with men of all shapes and sizes. It was essentially the same act, but with Colby it was totally different. He was fucking me, but he was also making love to me. He loved me, and he told me that with every thrust and every grunt and every kiss. And I loved him. So fucking much it scared me. I'd never felt real love before him. I wasn't taught that love was something to be cherished. When I was with Colby, whether it was sex or just watching television, I felt the real, true kind of love.

At Colby's upstroke inside me, I quickly lost control, and ropes of come shot from my shaft, coating the wall.

"Oh hell yeah," Colby said as he slammed into me. I could feel him coming deep inside me, and his body went from tense to almost boneless. He slipped from me, spun me around, and kissed me softly on the lips.

"I love you, Cristian."

"I love you too, big guy."

"You already said that this month." He chuckled. That was one of the new rules I'd made since Colby and I got together. Rule number fifteen. It replaced an older rule, but I'd long forgotten what that rule was.

"This was a freebie," I said. "Since you fucked me so well, I thought you deserved it."

"If fucking you means I get to hear those words more often, I'll fuck you whenever and wherever you want."

"You already do," I reminded him.

"Let's shower. You got me all sweaty." Rule number four was no shared showers, but that was before Colby. Ignoring that rule was now one of my favorite things to do. Showering with

Colby, whether it led to sex or not, was one of my favorite activities. That rule wasn't the one I enjoyed breaking the most—that would be rule number two: no kissing. Kissing Colby was always the highlight of my day.

"So what were you doing in the neighborhood?" Colby asked when we were in the shower and sharing the spray of hot water.

"Clayton Shaw was attacked today," I answered.

"His brother doesn't live far from here," Colby said.

"I know. That's where I was."

"His brother is the suspect?" This was one of those sticky issues with Colby and me. I wanted to talk about my day with my boyfriend, but I was a cop and he was a lawyer. Information about cases was supposed to be confidential, but sometimes things hit home, and I needed to talk about it.

He must've been reading my thoughts, because he looked at me and smiled. "Cone of silence?" That was his way of assuring me that what I told him was as sacred as if he was a priest and we were in a confessional.

"Not the brother, the nephew," I said.

"You think Clayton's nephew attacked him?"

"Clayton seduced him and broke his heart," I replied.

"Shaw slept with his own nephew?" Colby asked, shocked.

"Stepnephew," I corrected.

"That's still wrong," Colby said. "So very wrong."

I hugged Colby. "I don't want to talk about it anymore," I said. I grabbed a razor and began my almost daily routine of removing my body hair. I was a diligent manscaper; I shaved my face, head, pubes, and genitals. I didn't shave my chest or legs, but what was there was so blond, it was almost invisible.

We finished showering and climbed into bed. I was suddenly exhausted, and the feel of Colby's arms around me helped me to let go for the day.

Chapter 2

COLBY DROPPED me off at work the next morning, and I walked in not looking forward to what could happen. I was afraid the evidence was going to point to Austin Shaw, and I wasn't looking forward to having to arrest him.

I had only been at my desk a few minutes when Lex showed up with a cup of coffee. Not a cup of the thick sludge they called coffee made at the station, but a cup of the nectar of the gods made at that heavenly place called Starbucks.

She handed me the cup, and I brought it to my nose and inhaled the incredible scent.

"What kind is it?" She gave me the look that said that was the stupidest question I'd ever asked. She knew what my favorite drink was—espresso macchiato. I carefully sipped the coffee, loving the burn on my tongue.

Lex's desk phone rang, and she answered it.

"Be right there," she said and hung up. "Cherry says she has the info we need."

I groaned inwardly, afraid the evidence was going to point right at the heartbroken teenager.

Cherry was sitting at her computer and barely acknowledged our presence.

"There are two different types of blood at the scene," she said without looking up from the screen. "One is Shaw's, so I assume the other is the perp's."

"That doesn't help us much without a suspect to compare it to," I said.

"I understand that, Detective Flesh," she said sarcastically. "But I also found a perfect fingerprint on the cane, and it wasn't Shaw's."

"Was there a match on the fingerprint database?" Lex asked.

Cherry shook her head.

"Fuck, if there isn't a match, then why the hell did you bring us down here?" I asked.

Lex gave me that *you're being rude* look.

"Well, it wasn't for your sterling company, Detective Flesh," Cherry said.

"I'm sorry, Cherry," Lex said in her best mother voice. "Tell us what you have."

"Based on a hunch, I decided to check the youth offender database. And I found a match. His name is Casey Thompson, and he's been brought in several times."

"For what?" I asked. But I knew the answer before I even asked the question.

"Hustling," Cherry said, confirming my suspicion.

"How many times has he been arrested?" I asked.

"Three times."

"Thanks, Cherry," Lex said. We turned to leave, but I thought of another question.

"What hunch were you following?"

"I'd heard that Shaw likes young trade," she said.

Right then, I knew the trail we were going down would most likely lead me straight into my past.

Lex and I returned to our desks and sat quietly for a few minutes.

"So what's the plan?" Lex asked.

"First we tell Austin Shaw that he didn't attack Clayton."

"And our perp?"

"It'd be next to impossible to find him during the day. He's probably homeless, so he could be anywhere he can get some sleep—parks, empty buildings, shelters, alleyways. But tonight there are a few places he'll be."

"You think he's going to be hustling? Shouldn't he be trying to get out of town?"

"How's he gonna leave without any money?"

She nodded in agreement. "You seem to know a lot about hustling," she said quietly.

"Let's go see Austin," I said, ignoring her statement.

"WHAT ARE you doing here?" Sarah Shaw asked when she opened the door.

"Relax, Mrs. Shaw," Lex said. "We have a suspect, and it's not Austin."

She sighed in obvious relief. "You didn't have to come all the way here to tell us that."

"I'd like to speak to Austin," I said.

"Why?"

"Austin's going through a hard time, Mrs. Shaw. I know what he's feeling. I just want him to know he's not alone."

Sarah thought about what I said before she opened the door and let us in. Lex followed her into the kitchen, and I went upstairs to Austin's bedroom. I knocked and heard Austin tell me to come in.

He was sitting in the same spot on the bed he had been the night before and was wearing the same clothes.

"How are you doing, Austin?"

He shrugged.

"You didn't attack your unc—Clayton. We found prints on the cane used to attack him."

Austin peered at me, and I expected to see relief in his eyes, but that's not what I saw. I saw sadness and anger, so much anger.

"It's better this way, Austin," I said. "If you had been the one to attack him, it wouldn't have changed anything. It wouldn't have made you feel any better. I know what you're feeling. You hate Clayton, but you also love him. You want to hit him, or maybe hug him. You need to make him pay for hurting you, but you also crave his love."

Tears dripped down Austin's cheeks. I wanted to hold him and tell him everything was going to be okay.

"It's not going to be easy, but you can't let this get you down. Don't let what that sick fuck did to you ruin your life. Pick yourself up, get dressed, and live your life. Find a nice boy or lots of nice boys. Be careful, but don't hold your heart back because you're afraid it'll get broken again. Because it will get broken again, maybe more than once, but someday you'll find that perfect person who makes you feel complete for the first time in your life."

Austin wiped the tears off his face and nodded at me. I gave him my card. "If you ever need anything, even someone to talk to, give me a call."

He took the card and nodded again. I was halfway out of the room when he spoke. "Thanks," he said.

I went downstairs and nodded at Lex that we could go. The sound of a shower started upstairs. Sarah gave me an odd look.

"He's barely left his room for weeks," she said. "His father had to order him to shower. He hasn't done anything on his own for a while. Everything's been a fight. What did you say to him?"

"That's between us men," I said with a slight smile. "Let's just say I know what he's going through."

Sarah launched herself into my arms and hugged me tight. "Thank you," she said. "Thank you so much."

SEVERAL HOURS later, Colby called my cell to invite me for lunch. We met at the Asian Garden on Virginia Street. As soon as Colby entered the restaurant, I could tell something was wrong.

"What's up, big guy?"

"Reuben Meade changed his mind. He signed with O'Mara."

Reuben Meade was a hotshot lawyer—a former New York City defense attorney. He had recently moved to Nevada and was courted by just about all the law firms in Reno, including McMillan, McPhee—the firm where Colby worked.

Colby's boss, Constance McPhee, had known Meade for years and had the upper hand in the negotiations. She had offered Meade the highest salary and best benefit package. The deal had been almost finalized.

"What happened?"

"Me," Colby said as he took a drink of the beer I had ordered him. "There was an impromptu lunch with everybody. A predeal celebration. He was okay when he first met me, but we were talking, and I mentioned you. He recognized your name."

"What did he say?"

"He asked if you were the gay cop involved in the Pryor mess. I said yes, and he flipped out. He called you names, and I got pissed and said you were my boyfriend. He strode straight up to Constance and said he couldn't work with a faggot. She was furious."

Colby and I had met when I was facing a murder charge. The case involved a televangelist and a dirty cop. Thankfully, I'd been cleared and had fallen in love with Colby in the process.

"She had a right to be furious at the guy. He's a narrow-minded homophobic asshole."

"She was furious at me."

"At you? Why the hell was she mad at you?"

"Because of how I talked to Meade. She said she might've been able to get Meade to change his mind if I hadn't lost my temper with him."

Colby had been in the closet when we first got together. It was a sticky point for us, but he chose to come out, and at first everything was good. Since then several clients had left the firm, several potential clients refused to hire the firm, and now Meade.

"That sucks, Colby," I said. I did feel bad because in a way the problems he was having were my fault. I had been sure his coming out at work wouldn't cause any problems, and I was wrong.

"It's not your fault," he replied. "Let's talk about something else."

"I have to go out for a little while tonight," I said.

"What're you doing?"

"We got a suspect in the Shaw attack. A hustler. I think I know where he'll be tonight."

"You going to handle that okay?" he asked.

"Sure. Why wouldn't I?"

"It could bring up some memories of when you hustled."

I instantly bristled. I had mentioned to Colby one time that I'd done some hustling when I was younger. I hadn't given him any details and wasn't sure if I ever would.

"I'll be fine," I mumbled.

"You coming to my place afterward?"

I shook my head. "It might be late. I'll just go home."

"I don't care how late it is."

"Nah. I'll just go home and crash."

THERE WERE several spots in Reno where hustlers hung out at night. Truck stops were good for some quick action, but the money wasn't much, and you ended up squatting on your knees in alleyways or on bathroom floors. The best tricks were those who wanted to take you to a motel for several hours. Sometimes you got to sleep in a nice bed for the entire night. The places to meet those guys were the bars, casinos, and motels.

Lex and I pulled Casey's mug shot and showed it around. I had more than one offer from men of varying ages, but I didn't see Casey anywhere.

"We're not going to find him tonight," I told Lex after checking out the last of the area's truck stops.

"I agree. I'm going to head home," she said. "You coming?"

"I'll leave in a minute. I gotta use the bathroom. See you tomorrow."

I walked to the bathroom and noticed a young man standing outside the door. We made eye contact and I nodded. I stepped into the bathroom, stepped up to a urinal, unzipped, pulled out my prick, and started pissing.

I heard the door open, and someone stepped up to the urinal next to me. It was the young man who had been standing outside the bathroom. He glanced at me, smiled, then shifted his eyes to my cock. No doubt he was a hustler.

"Want a blowjob?" he asked me.

I wasn't at all tempted to take him up on the offer, but I was tempted to slap him across the head and tell him he was an idiot for selling his body for cash.

"How much?"

"Twenty bucks," he answered after a slight hesitation. Two things told me he was new at this. The first was the low amount he was charging—an attractive young man like him could easily charge three times that amount. The second thing was the hesitation when he answered.

"Meet me outside," I said. He smiled and left. I finished relieving myself and exited the restroom. He was leaning against the wall, almost in the shadows. I stepped up to him, and he grabbed me. I pushed him away, and he gave me a frown.

"Where you from, boy?"

"I'm not a boy," he snapped. "I'm eighteen."

"You're eighteen?" I snorted. "I don't think so."

"Listen, man, I can be whatever age you want me to be."

"I want to know where you're from before we do anything," I replied.

"Lovelock," he said. Lovelock was a small town just an hour and a half from Reno.

"What're you doing here? Parents kicked you out because you're gay?"

"No," he answered. "It's just me and my dad. And he was cool when I told him."

"So why are you here?"

"I can't find no gay guys there," he said. "So I ran away and came here."

"But you don't have a job?" I asked.

"I'm too young for anyone to hire me." He realized what he'd said and tried to change the story.

"You don't have to lie to me," I said. "Why don't you call your dad and go home?"

"I don't want to make my dad feel bad. I don't want him to know I had to hustle to make money."

"Do you believe he'll think less of you?" He shrugged as a response. "What's your name?"

"Ronnie Julian Raymond," he replied after a few moments. "Everyone calls me RJ."

"Don't move," I said as I took a few steps away. I pulled out my cell phone and made a few phone calls. I stepped back and pulled out my wallet.

"You gonna let me suck your dick now?" he asked. "If you want to fuck me, you can."

"No, I ain't gonna touch you. You're going home."

"What?"

"Trust me on this. You don't want to get into this lifestyle. You're going to get hurt."

"I can take care of myself," he snapped.

"One-on-one I'm sure you can. But what happens when a guy takes you to his motel and three or four of his muscle-bound friends show up? Then they force you to suck their pricks, and they fuck you so hard, you bleed for weeks afterward."

Tears formed in his eyes.

"You have a place to go," I said. "Lots of kids don't. You have choices, and you need to make the right one."

"Even if I did want to go home, I don't have any money. I don't want to call my dad to come and get me."

"It's all taken care of." He gave me a questioning look. "There's a cab on the way," I continued. "He's going to take you to the Downtowner Motor Lodge on Stevenson Street. There's a room reserved for you. There's a Greyhound leaving for Lovelock in the morning, and there'll be a ticket waiting for you when you get to the bus station."

"You paid for it already?" he asked.

I nodded. "Everything's taken care of. All you have to do is walk from the motel to the bus station in the morning."

"What do I tell my dad?"

"You don't have to tell him anything. But if you want to, I'm sure he'll understand. You'll meet guys your age who are more than willing to mess around. And when you're eighteen, you'll find plenty of men to have fun with. You don't have to live this way."

"Why are you doing this?" he asked me.

"Because I can," I said. "So, RJ, do I need to babysit you tonight to make sure you get on this bus?"

He shook his head. "No, I'll go home. Thank you, sir."

"If you don't leave, and I ever see you hustling again, I *will* arrest you."

"You're a cop?" he asked. I nodded and pulled out a business card.

"Call me if you ever need help."

"Detective Cristian Flesh," the kid read off my business card before he stuffed it into his pocket. "Thank you, Detective Flesh."

"Call me Cristian," I said as I handed him fifty bucks. "Get something to eat when you get to the motel."

The young man suddenly pulled me into an embrace as he thanked me again and again. I pushed him away and saw the cab pull up.

"Here's your ride," I said. "You better get on that goddamn bus in the morning. Do you understand?"

"Yes, sir," he said. "I mean, Cristian. Thank you. Thank you so much." He climbed into the cab and rolled down the window. I gave the cabbie enough cash to get him to the motel with extra left over for a good tip.

"Thank you, Cristian," RJ said again. "I don't know how I'll ever repay you."

"You don't have to repay me. Just have a good life."

The cab pulled away, and I watched it until it was out of sight. I ambled slowly to my car and went home. I was emotionally exhausted. Colby had been right—memories of my hustling days had flooded my brain.

Feeling cheap and dirty, like I was the lowest form of life on the planet, I stripped down and climbed into bed. I was tired but couldn't sleep. A memory had possessed my mind. I had been hustling for a few weeks when a tall, hairy white guy approached me and asked for a blowjob. We went into an alley. I took the money and proceeded to suck him off. Immediately afterward, the guy grabbed my hair and pulled me to my feet. He slapped me across the face and called me a whore. The slap became a punch, and he threw me against the wall. He kicked me and punched me until I couldn't feel a thing. And that wasn't even the worst thing that ever happened to me.

I heard the front door open, then click shut. I knew who it was. I knew how Colby moved when he didn't want to wake me up. With his big body, the floor always creaked under his weight.

Colby didn't say a word as he stripped and climbed into bed. He lay on top of me and kissed me. Kissed me with such passion that the bad memory slipped from my mind. All I could think about was this magnificent man. I reached between us and stroked our cocks, then grabbed the lube from the nightstand. After squeezing some onto my fingers and on our dicks, I stroked us both for a few minutes as he continued to torture me by nibbling on my neck, my ears, and my nipples.

I reached between us to coat my hole. Colby knew what I wanted—and it wasn't rough, rock-my-world sex. I wanted the type of sex only Colby could give me. Slow and gentle lovemaking. I didn't know how he knew my moods so well, but I was fucking grateful he did. I wondered how my life would be different if I had met Colby sooner. But I think I wouldn't have known what I had. When I met him, I was ready for something different. I didn't know it before then, and I could've lost him.

Life in the future without Colby in it was what scared me the most. I couldn't go back to that lonely, horrible place. And that made me wonder why I still pushed him away so much. I wondered why I was afraid to tell him about my past. The easy excuse would be that he wouldn't think of me the same once he knew. But that wasn't true. I didn't understand why Colby loved me, but he did. And nothing could change how he felt about me.

My mind was brought back into the present as Colby entered me. With the head in, he stopped and leaned down to kiss me, his tongue sliding into my mouth. With our lips still connected, he slid in a bit farther, then pulled back. Forward and backward, back and forth, three inches in, two inches out, four inches in, three inches out. It was a slow dance of excitement and adoration.

When his entire length was buried in me, he remained still and looked down at me. I met his gaze, reached up, and ran my hands through his dark, wiry hair. With our eyes still connected, he pulled almost all the way out, then slowly slid his shaft back into my hole. I felt full and complete with Colby in me. Without him I felt like I was missing something. Only when I was with him was I whole.

He slowly and maddeningly made love to me, touching me everywhere with his lips and fingers. The wave began slowly and built until it was ready to crash through me. I pulled Colby into a kiss as I came, my seed coating our stomachs. His orgasm came seconds later with our lips and tongues still connected. He collapsed on me and started to roll off, but I held him there. I loved his big body on top of mine, and that's how we both fell asleep.

Chapter 3

I WOKE up early, but Colby was still asleep. I snuggled up against him and breathed in his manly scent. I was under the crook of his arm with my head on his chest. I ran my fingers up and down his stomach, tracing his muscles and stopping to play with his nipples.

Colby stirred and slowly woke up. He pulled me tight against him and kissed my head. "Good morning, bello."

"Morning, big guy."

"You doing okay?" he asked.

"Better than okay," I replied. "Last night was excellent. Thanks for coming over."

"I suspected you were going to need me, despite you saying you wanted to be alone."

"I love you, Colby," I said.

"Wow," he said, laughing. "You're saying the words again?"

"Keep it up, smartass," I said, "and I'll stop saying it altogether." Colby quickly moved and sat on top of me.

"I don't think so. We have a deal." He grabbed me on both sides of my torso, and there was little I could do to fight back. He knew where to tickle me to make me lose control. He didn't dig hard with his fingers, and he never did it for very long. He stopped tormenting me, leaned down, and kissed me for a moment before climbing off and standing.

"Come on, love," he said. "Let's clean up."

In the shower, Colby took the soap and slowly washed my entire body. Even as he touched my length, my balls, and my ass, it wasn't sexual—it was sensual. When he washed my bald head, he made the same comment he always did. "I wish you had hair so I could wash it, baby." I didn't know why I kept my head smooth, but I had been doing it for so long I couldn't imagine growing it out. I wasn't opposed to having hair, but I always thought the shaved scalp went along with the shaved body.

"I want a nice quiet night at home tonight," I said. "Does that work for you?"

"Of course," he answered. "My place or yours?"

"Yours," I said.

"I'll arrange it."

LEX AND I spent most of the day looking for Casey. We went to parks and empty buildings, to bars and clubs, and every other place I could think of. A few young men knew Casey but had no idea where he was.

At 3:00 p.m. Lex got a call on her cell. "Shaw's awake. Let's go," she said. We went to Renown and headed to his room.

Shaw was talking to someone when we first stepped in. I recognized the man, but I'm sure he didn't recognize me. Of course, I wasn't naked and on my knees.

"Clayton Shaw," Lex said. "I'm Detective Luther, and this is Detective Flesh. We need to talk to you about your attack."

Shaw waved us in. "This is my friend, Carl Graham." Graham, a local politician, was short and stocky. He was also extremely hairy, with a full mustache and beard. Graham stood and shook our hands. When I touched him, I had a sudden flashback to being on my knees in front of Graham and a few other older men. Shaking his hand made my skin crawl, and I let go quickly. I turned my attention to Lex and Shaw.

"We lifted a fingerprint from your cane, Mr. Shaw," Lex said. "We found a match—a young man named Casey Thompson."

"I don't know anyone by that name," Shaw murmured.

Lex handed him Casey's mug shot. The look on his face told us Shaw recognized the person in the photo.

"Yes, that's the man who attacked me."

"Can you tell us what he was doing in your house?" I asked.

"I don't remember," Shaw said.

I knew he was lying. The way his eyes avoided mine and the way he shifted uncomfortably told me he was being untruthful.

"Are you sure?" Lex asked.

"I don't think you should be questioning him right now," Graham said. "You should wait until he's feeling better."

"I disagree," I snapped. "We do things on our schedule, not his."

Lex put her hand on my shoulder. "Actually, we can wait," she said. "Some extra time might help Mr. Shaw get his memory back."

I didn't like the idea of leaving, but I knew arguing with Shaw wouldn't do us any good either.

"We'll talk soon, Mr. Shaw," I said. "I hope your memory is intact by then."

Lex and I stepped out of the room. "He's lying, Lex," I said.

"Of course he is," she said. "We'll figure it out."

AFTER A fruitless day of searching for Casey, I went home to Colby's place. When I opened the door, the sounds of classical music filled the house. The lights were low, and there was candlelight coming from the dining room.

"Hello?" I called out.

"Come in, baby," Colby answered from the kitchen.

I strolled into the dining room and saw the table had been decorated with candles and flowers. A bottle of Chianti sat with half-filled glasses ready to go.

"What's this?"

"A small, romantic dinner," he answered. "Sit down."

I sat and took a sip of the Chianti. Colby came out with two plates and set one in front of me. I laughed when I saw what the main course was—pizza. Colby smiled.

"I thought pizza was a good idea because it's the first meal we ate together."

I laughed at the memory. I had been released from jail, thanks to Colby, then spent the day cleaning my apartment after it had been trashed by my fellow police officers looking for evidence. Colby and I had shared a pizza as we sorted through my gay porn DVDs.

Colby took a drink of the Chianti and smiled at me.

"This is awesome," I said.

"You doing okay?" he asked. Once again, it was like he could sense that my inner demons had become riled up. I needed to talk, and I figured the best way was to just speak.

"I ran away from home when I was fifteen," I said. "How I ended up in Reno is another story, but when I got here, I had nothing. No place to live, no money. Hustling was easy money—at first. A couple of blowjobs and I had enough money to buy a meal."

"Couldn't you find a shelter?"

I snorted. "I went to one. Two guys forced me to suck their cocks and didn't pay me. The shelters were more dangerous than living on the street."

"Damn, bello. I'm so sorry."

I continued without responding to Colby. "Because of my blond hair and blue eyes, I was a valuable commodity. One night, a few months after I turned sixteen, I was hustling when a limo pulled up, and I got in. It took me to a penthouse suite, and my life changed after that."

"How did it change?" Colby reached out and touched my hand, but I pulled away.

"I became… his."

"Who was he? What did you become?"

"He was an older, wealthy man. I became his boy, his lover, his everything," I answered. "I guess he was my sugar daddy."

"That's sick," Colby huffed. "Taking advantage of a minor."

"What's worse for a kid—living on the streets and being used for sex, or having sex with a man who fed and clothed him?"

"Well, neither one is morally right." Colby ran a hand through his hair.

"I went from living on the streets, begging for food, and selling my body to stay alive, to living in a penthouse suite with food in my stomach and expensive clothes on my back. I was still selling my body, but I was living better. I was going to school, even though I didn't have to. And for a long time, everything was pretty good. Then things changed."

"What changed?"

What *hadn't* changed? I had been hurt by people I loved before, but I hadn't thought it would happen again. I had allowed myself to get comfortable, and that meant pain. I'd sworn right then I would *never* get hurt again, and that meant not permitting myself to love. I decided I didn't want to share any more about my past—I couldn't share anything else. Colby must've sensed my change in mood.

"It's okay. You don't have to tell me anything you don't want to."

"I can't, not right now. But I needed you to know a little of what this case is making me remember."

"I understand," he said, and I thanked God he did.

Chapter 4

AROUND 10:00 a.m. the next day, I was sitting at my desk when my cell phone rang. My caller ID read Gabe. Gabe Vargas was a good friend who had helped me out quite a bit last year and ended up in the hospital twice for it. Despite that, he was still one of my best friends.

"Flesh," I answered.

"Hey, Cristian. You busy right now?"

"Not really. What's up?"

"I need to see you. It's pretty important."

"Okay, where do you want to meet?"

"Sparks Marina Lake," he answered. "Don't bring Lex."

SPARKS MARINA Lake was a freshwater lake fed from an underground aquifer. It was surrounded by a jogging path and picnic tables. I enjoyed jogging around the lake, and it was also where Gabe and I had first met.

I saw Gabe sitting at a picnic table when I arrived.

"Cristian," he said, smiling. "How's it going?"

"Good, kid. You?" He hugged me, and I returned the embrace.

"You changed your mind about a threesome with me, you, and that hunky black boyfriend of yours?"

Gabe was joking—well, half joking. Gabe and I had slept together only one time, and it had been pretty hot. He was bisexual and had a sweet girlfriend and son at home. Violet accepted Gabe's bisexuality, and they made their relationship work.

"Sorry, Gabe," I said. "Colby's not interested."

"Dammit." Gabe laughed.

"What can I do for you?" I asked.

"I told you I've been doing some volunteer work at the Gay Youth Outreach Program."

GYOP was sponsored by the University of Nevada, Reno for young gay men and women. It was open for everyone—not just college students.

"I been talking to a kid for a couple months," Gabe continued. "He's a hustler. I've tried to make him see he has other choices, but he hasn't quit."

Gabe stopped and eyed me, but I didn't speak. He had something to tell me, and I didn't want to say anything that might stop him.

"He came to see me the other day," Gabe said. "He was in a bad place. Scared shitless. He was terrified, Flesh. So I got him a place to stay, and he calmed down enough to tell me."

I thought I knew where Gabe was going, but I waited for him to continue.

"His name is Casey Thompson," he said, confirming my suspicion.

"The hustler who attacked Clayton Shaw," I said

Gabe nodded. "He admitted that he attacked Shaw. But he says he knows a lot of shit that could get him killed."

"Like what?"

"He won't tell me, Flesh. But I believe him. That's why I came to you. I know you have to arrest him, but take it easy on him. Let him tell you what he knows."

"No problem, kid. You can trust me."

"I know," he said. "That's why I came to you."

"Where's he at?" I asked. Gabe raised his hand and waved, and Casey stepped out from behind Gabe's car. He was wearing a hoodie with the top pulled over his face. He shuffled up to me and lowered the hood. He looked pretty much like his mug shot—brown eyes, dark brown hair. But he had a black eye and other bruises on his face.

"Jesus Christ," I murmured.

"You should see his stomach," Gabe said.

"Come on, sport," I said and started toward my car. Casey appeared hesitant.

"You can trust him," Gabe said.

Casey glanced at both of us, then turned and followed me.

When we arrived at the station, I had Casey cover his face with the hood so no one would recognize him. As I escorted him to an interrogation room, I looked at Lex and nodded for her to follow me.

I put Casey in the room, read him his rights, and stepped out.

"What's going on, Cris?" Lex asked.

"That's Casey Thompson in there," I answered. "He's friends with Gabe. Apparently Casey has information he thinks is valuable to us."

"I guess we'll find out, won't we?" she said. "You want me to join you?"

"No, I think he's more likely to talk with just me in there. You tell Chief Brunson what's going on." I stepped back into the interrogation room. Casey was visibly scared.

"Listen, sport, you don't have to be afraid of me."

"Don't take it personally," Casey said. "You're a cop. I've been around long enough not to trust any cop. But I guess if Gabe says I can trust you, then you ain't all bad."

I smiled. "I understand you got something you want to say."

"I know some shit," he said. "Shit that could get me killed. Shit that could ruin a lot of people."

"Like well-known men who like to hire young guys?" I asked.

"That's just the tip of the iceberg," he snorted. "There's a whole lot more to it. And I ain't telling you all I know until I know what you're gonna do 'bout it."

"You got to give me something."

He glanced at me for a moment, like he was assessing me. "The boys these rich, older men hire," he said, "they aren't randomly selected off the streets."

"You guys work for the same pimp?"

He snorted. "I guess you could call him a pimp."

"Clarify it for me," I said.

"It's more like a… whorehouse, but the johns don't come to us. We go to them."

"Like call girls," I said.

He nodded. "But not all of us are eighteen yet. I'll be eighteen in just a few days, but I've been doing this for a couple years now."

"How big is this group?"

"At least twenty," he answered. "But guys come and go all the time."

"Where do they go when they leave?"

He shrugged. "Dunno. I always figured it was like a *Logan's Run* thing. But thirty isn't the magic age, like in that movie."

I was impressed he knew about a film made years before he was born.

"Is eighteen the magic age?" I asked.

"Not necessarily," he replied. "As long as we can still pass for young, we're still valuable. The guys who hire us are all about the appearance. I don't know what happens when the boss decides you're no longer valuable."

"Who is the boss?" I asked.

"No." He shook his head. "I ain't telling you nothing else until I know what's in it for me."

"I'll be back," I said and left the room. At the same time, Lex and Brunson stepped out of the adjacent room, where they had watched through a two-way mirror.

"What're we gonna do for him, Chief?" I asked.

"We aren't going to do anything," Brunson answered. "I'm calling the FBI. This is a federal matter."

"What makes it that?" I demanded.

"Thompson described an illegal prostitution ring using underage boys. That makes it the FBI's jurisdiction."

"I don't think we need to do that," I said.

"But I do," Brunson said. "And that's all that matters. Put him in a private holding cell. Book him under a fake name so no one else knows he's been arrested. Let's keep this between us until we hear from the government."

I thought about arguing, but I knew it would be useless. I returned to the room.

"We're calling the FBI," I said. "The Feds handle things like prostitution rings."

"Fuck," he said, running a hand through his short black hair. "I should've just taken off. I only came to you because Gabe said I could trust you. Now I'm gonna be handed off to some government agent."

"I'll stick as close to you as possible," I said. "I'll make sure everything gets handled the way it should be. I promise."

"We'll see. Lots of people have broken promises to me."

I wasn't offended by his mistrust. Trust didn't come easily to street kids, but I was going to earn his faith and keep it.

I told him about the chief's instructions to book him under a false name so no one knew he had been arrested. I told him he had to change into jail clothes—a fresh pair of boxers and an orange jumpsuit. When I got back with the clothes, Casey had stripped down to his boxers. There were bruises all over his chest and welts and cuts on his back.

Casey saw me checking out his bruises. "They pay more to beat on me," he said. "But they do a lot more than that too. Real nasty stuff."

He pulled his boxers down, and I turned around.

"You didn't have to look away."

"You're still a minor, sport. And even if you weren't, I got a boyfriend."

"I heard about your boyfriend—big guy, right? Okay, I'm dressed." I faced him as he buttoned up the jumpsuit. "I thought you guys had an open relationship."

"We do," I replied. "But that doesn't mean I play around with every guy I see."

He laughed.

"We'll get all this sorted out," I said before I led Casey to a private cell and locked him in. "I'll check in on you later."

When I returned to my desk, Lex told me Shaw was ready to talk.

"THE YOUNG man in the picture is the person who attacked me," Clayton Shaw said. Once again his friend Carl Graham was in his room.

"What was Thompson doing in your house?" I asked.

"We met at Tronix," Shaw said. Tronix was a local gay bar. "We had a few beers, and I brought him home."

"Thompson isn't even eighteen yet," Lex said.

Shaw got a shocked look on his face, but it wasn't good enough to fool either Lex or me.

"He was at the bar. I just assumed he was at least twenty-one," Shaw said.

"Did you pay Thompson to come to your place?" I asked.

"What?" Shaw said with mock indignity, once again with very little believability.

"Casey Thompson is a hustler," I said. "I assume that's why he came with you to your place."

"Most definitely not. I would never resort to an illegal act to have sex."

Lex and I gave each other a look and rolled our eyes.

"In any case, can you tell us what happened?" Lex said.

"The young man and I were in my bathtub," he said. "We were… having sex when he grabbed my cane and hit me. I begged him to stop, but he wouldn't."

"Was there any reason for him to attack you?" I asked.

"None at all," Shaw answered. "He just went… crazy."

"Were you involved in anything kinky?" I asked.

"What do you mean, Detective?" Graham asked.

"Kinky. Like bondage or whips and chains."

"Most certainly not!" Shaw exclaimed. "I do not partake in such depravity."

I wondered if he thought he could convince us by using such big words.

"Did Thompson take anything from your place, Mr. Shaw?" Lex asked.

"I don't know," he replied. "I've been in the hospital since the attack. I haven't been able to do an inventory of personal belongings."

"When do you think you'll be released?" I asked.

"His doctor said he should be able to go home tomorrow," Graham said. He acted like such a gentleman, but I knew him differently. Graham enjoyed slapping and pulling hair during his sexual encounters. He was especially turned on by the sight of blood. He had bloodied my nose on more than one occasion.

"Okay, Mr. Shaw. Please call us when you get home so you can let us know if anything is missing."

"I am most certain the depraved young man stole some of my valuables. I'm sure that was his plan from the very beginning. May I ask what has occurred in the search for my attacker?"

"We're still looking for him, Mr. Shit… I mean Shaw," I said. "We'll get to the truth of this matter. I can assure you of that."

GABE WAS waiting for me at my desk when Lex and I returned to the station.

"What's going on with Casey?" he asked.

I put a finger to my lips, telling him to be quiet. I led him into an interrogation room where I filled him in on what had happened.

"Can I see him?" Gabe asked.

I took him to the jail cell. Casey stood and dashed toward us. Gabe was already grasping the bars, and I noticed Casey's hand encircle his.

"How are you doing, Casey?" Gabe asked.

"Not bad, considering," he answered. "Any news on the Feds?"

"Not yet. I'll let you know as soon as I do."

"Thanks, Cristian," Gabe said.

"I'll be back in a few minutes," I said and left them alone, wondering about the intimate contact between them as well as the adoring looks in their eyes.

I strode to Brunson's door and knocked.

"Come in," he called.

I opened the door and stepped in. "Any word on the Feds?"

"They're sending someone," he answered. "An agent will be here Monday."

"That means Casey has to stay in jail over the weekend," I said. "I'm going to leave instructions with the weekend shift to allow Gabe to visit Casey whenever he wants to."

"No problem."

"I just hope the Feds don't run all over this kid," I said.

He looked me in the eye. "I think we can get enough cooperation to ensure that doesn't happen."

"Thanks, Chief," I said and left his office.

Gabe was coming out of the back room at the same time. I followed him outside.

"Nothing's going to happen until Monday, but I left instructions to let you visit Casey whenever you want."

"Thanks."

"What's up with you and Casey?" I asked.

Smiling and glancing at me, he said, "I got no idea what you're talking about."

"Don't bullshit me, kid. I saw something in your eyes. I hope you ain't having sex with him. He is a minor, after all."

"Relax, Dad," Gabe said, laughing. "I admit I'm attracted to him. He feels the same. We've talked a lot, and we've gone through a lot of the same shit. But I told him I wasn't gonna do nothin' sexual with him until he was eighteen. Which, thankfully, is very soon."

"What about you and Violet?" I asked.

"Things ain't perfect between us. I don't think it will ever be. I ain't giving up yet, and I'm not saying I'm leaving her for Casey. I just know that I'm drawn to him and want to test the waters. I'm not planning a wedding to Casey or anything, Flesh. Just want to see how the sex is."

"Just be careful," I said.

"I will. Oh, I almost forgot. Violet wants you and Colby to come over for dinner on Saturday night."

"I'll check with the big guy, but I'm sure we'll be there."

GABE AND Violet lived in a second-story apartment in a large complex. It wasn't in the best part of Reno, but it wasn't in the worst part either. The two-bedroom residence was decorated with used furniture that didn't match, but it felt like a home.

I knocked with Colby at my side. I laughed at the sound of little feet running on the other side. The door flew open, and Victor, Gabe and Violet's four-year-old son, flew into my arms.

"Kisstun," he yelled as he wrapped his arms around my neck.

"How you doing, little man?" I asked.

"I happy to see you," he blurted out.

"I'm happy to see you too," I said as Colby and I entered the apartment.

Violet stepped out of the small kitchen. "Victor, leave Cristian alone." She was short and petite, with dark hair that reached to the middle of her back.

"He's fine," I said. I liked Victor as much as he liked me—probably more.

Violet kissed me and Colby on our cheeks. "How're you doin'?"

"Very good," Colby replied. "Thank you so much for inviting us over."

"I made carne asada," she said. "My mama's recipe."

Gabe stepped out of the bedroom. "Hey, guys," he said.

"Dinner smells great, Vi." Gabe gave Violet a peck on the cheek, and she beamed.

"It'll be ready in about ten minutes," she said.

"Smoove," Victor said as he rubbed my head.

"*Mejo*," Gabe said. "We practiced that word, didn't we?"

"Yes, Daddy." Victor rolled his eyes. "Ssssmmmoooooothe."

He accentuated the *th*, and spit flew from his mouth. We all laughed.

"Good job, little man," I said.

A few minutes later, Violet called out that dinner was ready.

The carne asada was excellent—far better than anything I'd ever had at any Mexican restaurant.

After dinner Victor dragged me to his room and showed me his toys and comic books and video games. He even convinced me to play a game of Candy Land. I had planned on spending the evening with adults, but spending it with Victor was far more enjoyable.

"THEY'RE HAVING trouble," Colby said as we drove home.

"Who is?"

"Gabe and Violet."

"I didn't see it," I replied.

"Trust me, bello. I felt a lot of tension between them."

"They love each other, though."

"I never said they didn't. There can still be tension even if they do."

"I wonder if it has to do with Casey."

"It would be understandable for Violet to be upset if Gabe had feelings for Casey."

"She's dealt with Gabe being bi. She knows he sleeps with guys. They even do threesomes on a regular basis."

"You've said it yourself—there's a difference between sex and emotions. She can handle Gabe sleeping with other people if emotions *aren't* involved. It's totally different once feelings develop."

Chapter 5

WHEN I entered the station Monday morning, there was someone sitting at my desk—his feet propped up as he leaned back in my chair.

"Who the hell are you?" I asked as I shoved his feet off my desk.

He stood up. "You must be Detective Cristian Flesh."

"Yeah," I replied. "This is my desk you've made yourself so comfortable on."

"My apologies, Detective Flesh. I got here earlier today after about two hours sleep."

"And I'm supposed to care?"

"Wow, are you always this rude, or is it just me?"

"No," I replied. "I'm always this rude. You still haven't answered my question. Who are you?"

"Special Agent Drew Bradley with the Federal Bureau of Investigation," he said and stuck out his hand. "I'm from the Sacramento office."

I ignored the hand and he withdrew it. "The Fed sent to take over my case."

"It was your case. Now it's my case," he said.

"Look, G-man, I told this kid I was going to help him. I just want to make sure he doesn't get run over."

"Well, Detective Flesh, we can stand here and have a pissing contest about whose case it is or isn't, or we can agree to work together. I have no intention of causing any harm to Mr. Thompson."

I had to admire anyone who didn't cower in the face of my attitude but still gave me some respect. I looked at him for the first time. He had brown hair and dark-green eyes and was around five foot nine. He wore the typical FBI suit and tie, so I couldn't see what type of body he had, but he had a strong jaw with a hint of stubble.

"Okay, Agent Bradley," I said. "We'll see how this works. What's the plan?"

"First, I have to hear what Mr. Thompson has to tell me. Then I will communicate with my superiors and see what they want to do. I've already spoken to Chief Brunson, and he has given you permission to join me in the interrogation room when I speak to Mr. Thompson."

"Thank you," I said begrudgingly.

"Manners? How extraordinary. You're welcome, Detective."

I brought Casey to the interrogation room and introduced him to Agent Bradley.

"I understand you have made allegations that there is a substantial prostitution ring in the vicinity."

Casey shot me a questioning look. "I didn't understand all those big words," he said.

I smiled. "He wants to know about the hustling group in town."

"Fuck, why didn't he just say that?"

"Sorry." Bradley blushed.

I could tell he was a well-educated young man, and I wanted to be able to hold it against him, but he didn't come off as spoiled.

"You know about the Fresh Slate Ranch?" Casey asked.

I nodded but turned to Bradley to explain it to him.

"The Slate family has had a cattle ranch in the area for generations," I said. "Harlan Slate owns it right now. He got the ranch when his parents died several years ago. He's turned it into a sort of halfway house for homeless gay young men. In exchange for room and board, he puts the young men to work on the ranch."

That was the official story on Harlan Slate. Before he inherited the ranch, Slate's life had been a subject on all the rumormongers' lips. His fifteen-year marriage to his high school sweetheart had fallen apart when she found him in bed with someone else—a man. She blasted his infidelities to everyone she knew, and Slate's life was put on public display. His son, Quentin, who was fourteen at the time, ended up the real victim as the battle between his parents tore him apart.

"Seems like a good thing," Bradley said.

Casey grunted like he had swallowed something bitter. "It is a good idea. That's why I accepted a bed there with my best friend, Jed. We had both been hustling and were tired of getting the shit beat out of us. At first it was pretty cool. Harlan was decent, and we were both willing to work our asses off and happy not to be selling them anymore."

"Were the circumstances of your living arrangements altered?" Bradley asked.

Casey gave him a bewildered look.

"You're talking to a homeless kid who had to turn tricks to stay alive, Agent Bradley," I said. "These ten-dollar words aren't going to get you anywhere."

"My apologies," he said. "Force of habit." He turned to Casey. "Did things change at the Slate Ranch?"

"Yeah," Casey answered. "Jed and I had been there a couple weeks when Harlan talked to us. He said the ranch was low on money and had some bills to pay. He asked us for a favor."

"What was the favor?" I asked, even though I knew the answer.

"He asked if Jed and I could turn a few tricks. He said it would be just enough money to get out of the hole. Harlan said we could say no, but if we did, the ranch was likely to go under."

"He guilt-tripped you into doing it," I said.

Casey shrugged nonchalantly. "Jed and I talked about it. We figured it wasn't a big deal. We'd been doing it before, and we didn't want to see the ranch have any problems. It was about more than just us, you know? It was about those other kids too. I figured I could sell my ass a couple times, and it would mean that someone else didn't have to."

Casey's eyes were downcast, like he was ashamed and didn't want to look us in the eyes. I glanced at Bradley and saw the sadness and disgust in his eyes.

"Casey," I said, "you don't have anything to be ashamed of. What you did was noble."

"Being a whore was noble?" Casey scoffed.

"Yes," Bradley spoke up. "Very noble. You weren't thinking of yourself. You were thinking of others."

My respect for Agent Bradley jumped a few more notches.

"Please, Casey, go on," Bradley said.

"Harlan said he didn't expect us to go on the streets to hustle. He said he had connections and knew people who liked young men. He insisted that we could never say anything about who was hiring us because it would ruin their lives."

"Who was it?" Bradley asked.

"My first client was Clayton Shaw," Casey replied. "Jed's was Carl Graham."

Agent Bradley cocked an eyebrow.

"They're both local men with lots of money. Shaw owns a casino. Graham is a Washoe County Commissioner."

"Are they both gay?" Bradley asked.

I nodded. "Shaw is out, but Graham isn't. Everyone knows he's queer, but he likes to pretend otherwise."

"How would they be affected if what Casey told us becomes public news?"

"Being with men wouldn't hurt their reputation, but hiring hustlers, especially underage hustlers, would definitely cause damage. Even more so if it resulted in criminal charges."

Bradley turned back to Casey. "I assume these illegal and immoral dalliances occurred on more than one occasion?"

Casey rolled his eyes. "What did he say?"

Bradley and I both laughed.

"He wants to know if you tricked with Shaw more than once."

"Hell yeah, it never ended," Casey answered. "Jed and I both did it a couple times and thought that was going to be it. Harlan said the money helped out, but new bills popped up. He asked if we could keep on doing it, just for a month or so. And we agreed. We ended up tricking several times a week, with different men. Shaw seemed to like me, even though he smelled like Bengay. It disgusted me to do what I did."

"What did you do with Shaw?" Bradley asked.

"You want details?"

"No," the agent replied. "Fellatio? Sodomy? Anilingus?"

"What the hell are those things?" Casey laughed.

"I'm sorry," Bradley said. "Fellatio is oral sex. Sodomy is anal sex."

He was blushing a deep shade of purple, so I decided to help him out.

"Did you suck his dick?" I asked. Casey nodded. "Did he suck yours?"

"Yeah."

"Did he fuck you? Did you fuck him?"

"He did me. I never did him."

"What about rimming?"

This time it was Bradley's turn to be confused. "What's rimming?" he asked.

"Ass licking," I replied.

"Ohh, anilingus," he said.

I turned back to Casey.

"He rimmed me," Casey replied.

"Anything else?" Bradley asked.

Casey nodded, but he was staring at the table again.

"We're not gonna judge you, sport," I said. "But we need to know."

"He liked to hit me," Casey said in a voice so low I almost didn't hear him.

"He hit you?" Bradley asked. "During your sexual encounters?"

Casey looked Bradley in the eyes. "Yeah! He liked to pull my hair when he fucked me. Or slap me across the face or use his cane on my back while he screwed my ass. He loved to squeeze my balls so hard they hurt so I couldn't come when he fucked me. If I came and he hadn't given me permission, he would cut me with a knife and make me bleed. Is that fucking enough for you?"

Casey buried his face in his hands, and I knew he was crying. Bradley and I were both speechless for a moment.

"Yeah, umm, yes," Bradley said. "That's enough. I have enough to speak to my superior and see what he has to say."

What the agent did next surprised me. He reached across the table and gently touched Casey's head. "It'll be okay, Casey."

Bradley stood up and left the room. I stayed there with Casey without saying a word.

"I feel so dirty," Casey said, his face still buried in his hands. "No matter what I do, I feel his body pressed against mine. I can smell him all the time—sweaty and smelly and so fucking nasty."

"Listen, sport," I said, "you can't let this take over your life. You're not the dirty one. Shaw is the dirty one. Him and all the men like him. The men who like to fuck young boys. The men who like to humiliate and degrade boys who are just trying to survive. I know what you're going through."

He regarded me with angry eyes. “How can you know? You can’t know what it feels like unless you’ve been through it yourself.”

“I have been through it, sport. I sold myself on the streets and sold myself to rich and powerful men with sick desires. I eventually decided I had to help myself because no one else was going to help me. I didn’t have anyone to turn to, but you do. You have me and Gabe and Agent Bradley. Do not let this ruin your life.”

Casey wiped the tears away from his eyes. “I couldn’t take any more,” he whispered. “He was whacking me with his cane, and something in me just snapped. I grabbed the cane and hit him. I couldn’t stop. I didn’t want to. Then I saw all the blood in the water and on the floor. I dropped the cane and ran without knowing where I was going and didn’t stop ’til my legs felt like they were gonna fall off.”

“I understand, trust me. I do understand.”

Bradley stuck his head through the door. “Detective Flesh, may I speak with you privately?”

I stepped out of the room and followed Bradley to my desk. Lex was at her desk and looked like she had been filled in.

“I talked to my superior,” Bradley said. “First of all, I’d like to say that I do not agree with his decision, but I have no choice but to do what I’m ordered.”

“We can’t just throw this kid to the wolves,” I said. “If you Feds don’t want to do something about it, then I will.”

“Calm down, Detective Flesh,” Bradley said. “I have no intention of letting any harm come to that kid. Not after what I just heard. Even if I have to go off the grid to do this, I will make sure the ranch comes down.”

“You know what, Agent Bradley?” I said. “I believe you. I like you, and I don’t like very many people.” I offered my hand, and he took it.

"I appreciate your vote of confidence, Detective. I'm going to do whatever I can officially, and if I have to do something unofficially, then so be it."

Lex stood up. "If you have Cris's approval, then you have mine too."

"Thank you, Detective Luther."

"Please call me Lex," she said.

"Lex Luther?" he asked.

"Yes, I know, it's an eye-roll-worthy name. But so is Cristian's, and that's what makes us a good team."

Bradley laughed. "My name is Drew. Even after two years as an agent, I still don't feel comfortable being called Special Agent."

"So, Drew," I said, "what exactly did your boss say?"

"He wants a local conviction of Shaw before we move forward with a case regarding the Slate Ranch."

"He wants us to prosecute Shaw first?" Lex asked.

"That means Casey will have to testify twice—once against Shaw and again in the federal case."

Drew nodded. "I agree that it doesn't make sense. My boss thinks our case will be stronger with a conviction. He's hoping Shaw will agree to a deal and give us information regarding the ranch."

"This sucks for Casey," I said. "What's going to happen to him? Does he have to worry about being arrested on assault charges?"

"I've already arranged for immunity based on his testimony and to put him in witness protection. We have a local safe house, and I'll be there to protect him. I'm going to stay in town to help. My superiors will help your district attorney with the case and put it on the fast track."

"You're giving up your personal life to stay here?" I asked.

Drew laughed. "Don't have a personal life right now," he said. "I was engaged but not anymore. So I'm more than ready to stay here for a while."

"What's the first step, Drew?" Lex asked.

"I need to talk to the DA. Tell him the plan and get started on the case against Shaw. I'll have him watch the videotape of Casey, and we'll decide what charges to nail Shaw with."

Lex's cell rang, and she stepped to the side.

"I appreciate what you're doing for Casey," I told Drew.

"I've never dealt with anything like this before," he said. "I've seen depravity in several forms, but this… this reaches a new height of evil. I know a lot of people equate homosexuality to pedophilia. I may not know anything about what two guys do with each other in bed, but I know being gay doesn't make you a child molester."

"Right," I said. "And if you ever need to know anything about what goes on between two men, feel free to ask."

"You… you're gay?" He looked shocked.

"Yup," I answered.

"You don't look the type," he said.

"You mean because I don't talk funny or wear dresses or something like that?"

Drew laughed. "I admit I have the image of a stereotypical homosexual in my mind. I just don't know any."

"First of all, gay people come in all different types. Some of the most masculine men like to take it up the ass. Second, I'm sure you do know someone who's gay. They just don't flaunt it. What is the FBI's stance on gays?"

"The FBI doesn't discriminate based on sexual orientation. However, it's not exactly encouraged. It's kind of like the military's former Don't Ask, Don't Tell law. Honestly, I haven't given it much thought."

"Most straight guys don't," I said.

Lex stepped back to us. "That was Clayton Shaw. He says there are several things missing from his house. He wants us to come by and check it out."

"Let's go," I said.

"I'll go and talk to the DA."

CARL GRAHAM was waiting for us at the door when we arrived at Clayton's house. A memory struck me before I could push it back into the dark places of my brain. I was bent over a table, my hands strapped down. Graham was behind me with an extra-large dildo, ramming me with no mercy as he clawed my back hard enough to break skin.

I jammed the thought where it belonged, but I wondered if Graham had done the same thing to Casey's friend Jed. I wanted to grab Graham and choke the life out of him. I wanted to make sure he never did anything to hurt anyone again.

"Clayton has identified several missing items," Graham said. "He's in the bedroom. Please, follow me."

We walked into the master bedroom, and I immediately noticed that something was different from when I had been there the night of the attack. Something was out of place, but I couldn't put my finger on it.

"He took some valuable jewelry," Shaw said. I could tell he was lying, but by that point I was pretty sure Shaw couldn't tell the truth if his life depended on it. I remembered a line from my favorite television judge—Judge Marilyn Milian on *People's Court*. "I wouldn't believe you if your tongue came notarized." That's how I felt about Shaw.

"I had a jewelry case hidden in the armoire," Shaw said. "He found it and grabbed some diamond earrings, a pearl necklace, and an emerald ring. They belonged to my mother."

I looked at the armoire and realized that was the difference. The armoire hadn't been open when I first came through.

"We'll need a detailed list of the jewelry and their values, Mr. Shaw," Lex said. "Anything else?"

"Yes," Shaw answered. "Follow me."

We went down the stairs and into the living room. "I had a painting by Allan D'Arcangelo. His paintings are very valuable right now. The one I had cost me a hundred grand. And it's gone. That young punk took it."

Again, I knew he was lying, even if I hadn't seen the painting when I was there before. Shaw claimed that in addition to the jewelry and painting, Casey had also stolen something from the bathroom.

"My Rolex was on the bathroom sink, and it's gone. I also had three Hummel figurines sitting on my bathroom sink," Shaw said. "They're valued at more than a thousand dollars each."

"I assume you have receipts that prove you purchased the items," I said.

"Of course," Shaw said.

"We'll get back to you," Lex said.

In the car on the way back to the station, Lex asked, "Did you believe anything he said?"

"Not a single word," I said, chuckling.

"Me either. If we can get proof he was lying, we can add obstruction of justice to the charges."

WHEN WE arrived back at the station, Drew was still talking to DA Richard Cahill. Following a hunch, I got on the computer and pulled up the file on Shaw's attack. I flipped through the crime scene photos until I saw what I wanted. In the corner of one picture, I could see the bathroom sink. I enlarged that section and saw a watch and three Hummel figurines.

"Look at this, Lex," I said. She smiled when she saw the pictures.

"We got him," she said.

Drew appeared a few minutes later, and he didn't look very happy. He sat on the edge of my desk.

"Cahill doesn't think we have a very strong case," Drew said. "He's agreed to move forward with arresting Shaw, but he isn't convinced he has enough for a conviction."

"We have Casey's testimony," I said. "What else does Cahill want?"

"He says it will be Casey's word against Shaw's. He doesn't think a jury will take the word of a homeless kid over that of a respected and loved local man."

"I doubt anyone could listen to Casey's words and not believe him," I said.

"I'm with you," Drew replied. "But Cahill wants a stronger case. So I say we get him one."

"What do we need?" Lex asked.

"We need more evidence. More witnesses. Paper trails," Drew answered.

"This isn't going to be easy," I said.

"We don't have a choice," Lex said.

I saw Gabe walk into the station, and I waved him over.

"Gabe, this is Special Agent Drew Bradley. Drew, this is Gabe Vargas, Casey's friend."

Gabe and Drew shook hands. I could see Gabe trying to assess Drew as Drew did the same thing. We filled Gabe in on what was happening.

"I'll talk to Casey and see if he can give us any leads," Gabe said. "Can I go see him now?"

"Yeah," I said and led him back to the jail cell. Drew followed us back. He told Casey that we needed more proof against Shaw.

"How did he pay?" Drew asked Casey.

"I never got any of the money, except occasional tips. I assumed Harlan and his customers had an arrangement."

"I'll take a look at Harlan's accounts," I said.

"Do you know of anyone else at the ranch who went to see Shaw?" Drew asked.

"As far as I know, Jed and I were the only ones Harlan was tricking out. That's what he told us, anyway."

I doubted that was true. I was sure Harlan Slate was guilt-tripping every boy he could to peddle their asses.

"What about kids not on the ranch?" Gabe asked. "Maybe someone still on the streets."

"There was this kid named Toby," Casey said. "We looked enough alike, we joked we could be brothers. He always talked about a wealthy guy who hired him and liked to do weird things. One time I saw marks on his back. He wouldn't tell me how he got them or who the guy was, but I would swear they were cane marks. He could've been seeing Shaw."

"We need to find him," I said.

"I haven't seen him for a while," Casey said. "Not since I went to live on the ranch."

"See, Casey, I told you everything was going to be okay," Gabe said as he put his hands on the bars. Once again, Casey put his own hand on Gabe's.

"You guys need to say your good-byes," Drew said.

"Good-byes?" Gabe said. "Why?"

"I'm taking Casey to a safe house," Drew answered. "You won't be able to see him for a while."

"Then forget it," Casey said. "I'll take my chances on the street. I'd rather be on the run with Gabe's help than in custody without his help."

"That is simply not allowed," Drew said. "Only official law enforcement can know his location."

“Fuck you,” Casey said. “You want my testimony, then Gabe gets to visit me.”

“It is not allowed,” Drew repeated.

“Listen, Drew,” I said, “if it means anything at all, I trust Gabe with my life. He’s saved me and helped me out more than once. I can assure you, allowing Gabe to know the location of the safe house would not jeopardize Casey’s safety.”

Drew eyed me for a minute, and I could tell he was considering changing his mind.

“Very well,” he said after a few moments. “I will allow you to visit Casey, Mr. Vargas.”

“Gee, that’s awful kind of you, Mr. Bradley,” Gabe snapped.

“That’s Special Agent Bradley to you.”

“Whoa, guys,” I said as I stepped between them. “Let’s not get into a macho contest. We’re all on the same side here.” They both backed off.

“Can you help Jed?” Casey asked. “He’s still living at the ranch. He might be able to do something.”

“I can’t endanger his life by asking him to look around,” Drew said. “I’ll see if I can get a deal for him as well.”

BY THE time I got home, I was exhausted—both physically and emotionally. My brain was full of memories I had thought were forever gone. I wanted Colby to help push the memories away. He was sitting on the couch when I got to his place.

I strode straight to him, pushed his legs apart, and got on my knees. I buried my face in his crotch and breathed in his scent.

“Well, hello there, baby,” Colby said as he rubbed my head. He wore a pair of shorts, but I realized he was going commando when I ran a hand over his crotch. I stroked his cock as the blood flowed through it, then tugged up a leg of his shorts so his shaft could peek out. Leaning down, I licked the tip, enjoying the taste of his sweet precome. I swallowed the plump, round pink head of his dick and swirled my tongue around it.

"Damn, Cristian," he moaned. "Feels so good." I grabbed his shorts, and he lifted his hips so I could slip them off. His cock slapped his belly, but I wrapped my hands around it and gave it a few quick and tight strokes. I licked up and down his length, paying extra attention to the thick ridge of his crown. I wrapped my lips around it and quickly swallowed it to the root.

"Holy shit," Colby grunted. I sucked him hard, and he arched upward.

I pulled back so I could speak. "Fuck my mouth, Colby." I took the entire shaft again and slid up and down as my tongue caressed it all. Colby lifted his hips, pushing deeper.

"Yeah, man," I said as I jacked him. "I'm your bitch. Slap me. Make it hurt."

"What?" Colby asked.

"I said, slap me, hit me. I'm your bitch—make me pay for being a whore."

"What the hell, Cristian? I'm not going to do that. I'm not going to slap you. And you're not my whore. You're my lover, my boyfriend—not my bitch." He pushed me back, but I didn't let go of his shaft.

"Goddammit, Colby," I said. "I want you to slap me and make me hurt. Fucking ass, just do it."

Colby grabbed my face and bent my head so I was looking up, but I couldn't meet his gaze.

"What the hell is going on? We don't do that—I won't do that."

"Fucking son of a bitch," I said as I stood up. "You're worthless to me unless you give me what I want."

He stood up, and we were face-to-face.

"I don't know what's going on in your head, Cristian," Colby said. "But I'm not going to treat you like a whore. Because you're not a whore."

"The fuck I ain't," I said as I took a few steps backward. "Once a whore, always a whore."

Colby closed the distance between us. "No, bello. You're not a whore. You're a beautiful man. A loving and kind man."

"Shut the hell up." I pushed him away, but he stepped back up to me. "I just want to be fucked and treated like a slut. I like it rough and you know that."

"There's a difference between rough play and me hurting you."

"You're talking out your ass," I snapped.

"Quit being a dick, Cristian."

"It's who I am," I said.

"No, it's one of your goddamn defense mechanisms."

"Fuck, I hate it when you get all psychoanalyst on me. What I want is for you to go psycho anal on me."

"What happened today?" Colby asked.

"Nothing happened. Just forget about it. I'm taking a shower, and I'm not breaking rule number four."

I washed alone with nothing but my thoughts. I usually enjoyed using Colby's huge shower, but it felt too big now. Too big and too empty. I had learned to love breaking rule number four with Colby. Sometimes it was sex in the shower, but even when it wasn't, it was still sweet and sensual. Afterward, I walked into the bedroom and saw Colby in bed. He was facing away from me, and I suddenly felt horrible for the things I had said to him.

I climbed into bed but just lay there. I could hear Colby breathing and knew he wasn't asleep. I knew what I wanted to say, but it took me a while to get my mouth to move.

"I was seventeen. The guy was a friend of my… mentor. I had done him a few times before that, nothing more than blowjobs. I was sucking him when he slapped me. He slapped me so hard my face stung. I was shocked because it came out of nowhere. He got pissed because I had stopped sucking his dick."

I felt the bed shift and knew Colby had rolled over so he was facing me. I didn't see him because all I could see was myself and this man.

"He grabbed a fistful of my hair and pulled me to my feet. With one hand still yanking my hair, he punched me in the nose." I heard Colby gasp, but I didn't stop. "My nose was bleeding, gushing actually. He pushed me back to my knees and forced his cock down my throat. He enjoyed the sight of my blood. Both hands were grabbing my hair as he shoved his dick down my throat. It hurt, it hurt so fucking much, but he didn't stop 'til he came. Then he shoved me to the floor and kicked me in the gut. He called me a bitch, then left me there to bleed."

I felt Colby wrap his body around mine, and like that, the memory was gone. All I could feel were his muscles, his head resting against mine, his hand running up and down my chest.

"I'm not that guy, Cristian. You're not that same young man either. You're different now. You have to know that."

I knew he was right. My brain knew he was right, but it felt different in my heart and my soul. I wasn't sure if I could ever not be that same dirty whore. I touched Colby's arm, tracing my finger from the top of his shoulder, down his large bicep, and to his hand. He grabbed my hand and squeezed tight.

"I'm sorry, big guy."

"It's already forgotten." He pulled my face toward his and kissed me gently on the lips. "I love you, Cristian. Always will."

Sleep took over moments later.

"I HAVE proof he lied about items being missing from his place," I said.

"Why would he do that?" District Attorney Richard Cahill asked.

I was in a meeting with Cahill, Drew, Lex, and Brunson. Cahill was still balking at the idea of arresting Shaw.

"I don't know what the problem is, Richard," Brunson said. "We have proof of obstruction of justice. And we have Thompson's testimony that Shaw hired him for sex."

"Do you really think the testimony of a homeless kid is going to stand up against Shaw's?"

"What about the proof we have that Shaw lied about items being stolen from his place?" I asked.

"That doesn't prove he had sex with a boy. We need other witnesses, other young men Shaw hired for sex, other people who know what Shaw did."

"We'll get more evidence," Drew said. "Shaw is likely to get suspicious and could try to run. We need to get him arrested so we can ensure he doesn't leave town."

"I'll take what you have to a judge," Cahill said. "But if the judge doesn't sign off, then you'll need more evidence."

An hour later Lex and I had an arrest warrant, and we were knocking on Shaw's door.

When he answered, he seemed shocked to see us.

"What can I do for you, detectives?"

"It's what we can do for you, Mr. Shaw," I said. "We can advise you of your rights."

"What the hell?"

"You're under arrest for solicitation, statutory sexual seduction, and obstruction of justice."

Lex read Shaw his rights, but he didn't say another word. His expression was one of confidence—smug and arrogant self-confidence.

We arrived at the station and escorted the handcuffed Shaw in front of everyone and straight to an interrogation room. "You got anything to say, Shaw?" I asked.

He smirked at me. "I'm not worried about a thing. I have an *excellent* lawyer. He's going to crush you. And I am not saying another word until he gets here."

"He better have a damn good lawyer," Drew said when he and I stepped out of the interrogation room. "Any idea who that might be?"

I shook my head. "It's hard to say who he's got on retainer. There are plenty of sharks in this town who'll take his dirty money."

Twenty minutes later I saw Colby walk into the station. I met him halfway across the room.

"Hey, big guy," I said. He smiled and gave me a peck on the cheek.

"We need to talk, Cristian," he said.

"Wait, I want you to meet someone." I led him to my desk, and Drew stood up.

"Special Agent Drew Bradley, this is Colby Maddox. Colby, this is Drew, the G-man helping me with the case."

Colby and Drew shook hands.

"What are you doing here?" Drew asked Colby. "Come to take Cristian out for lunch?"

"I'm afraid not," he answered. "I'm here for business."

"You have a client who got arrested?" I asked.

Colby nodded but didn't say a word. I got a sick feeling in the pit of my stomach. "Who's your client?"

"Clayton Shaw," Colby answered.

"What the fuck, Colby? How can you represent that piece of scum?" I demanded. Shaw's earlier smugness made sense now. He knew my lover was his lawyer, and he was hoping to cause trouble in either my personal life or my professional life—or both.

"It's my job, Cristian," Colby said. "Clayton is one of the clients who joined McMillan, McPhee when I came out. He liked the idea of having a gay lawyer."

"This is an obvious conflict of interest," Drew said. "Boyfriends on either side of the court."

"My boss already thought of that," Colby said. "The conflict would only hurt our client, and if he's willing to allow me to be his lawyer, then there won't be a complaint."

"I disagree," Drew said. "The conflict could hurt our case as well. Cristian's testimony might be suspect because of his relationship with you."

"I'm sure Cristian can present a fair and balanced, unbiased case, regardless of me being there. We can separate our personal life from our business life."

I wasn't sure Colby was right, but I wasn't going to argue with him. I asked Lex to take Colby to the interrogation room.

"We need to delay his arraignment as long as possible," I said. "Colby will have him out in no time."

"We have a good case for no bail," Drew said.

"Which judge did we get?"

"Barrett."

"Trust me," I said. "If Colby goes in front of a judge today, he'll have Shaw out an hour later." Barrett had been the judge in my case, and Colby got him to go from no bail to letting me be released OR—on my own recognizance.

"I'll make a phone call and see what I can do," Drew said. A few minutes later, Drew returned. "Judge Barrett had a family emergency and will be gone all day. That's the best I could do."

"At least Shaw will spend a night in jail," I said.

"I'm getting Casey out of here and to the safe house before you book Shaw," Drew stated.

"Am I allowed to know the location of the safe house?"

Drew nodded. "I figured you and I would need to spend time together talking to Casey, so you and Lex can have the location, but I don't want anyone else to know."

"Except Gabe," I reminded him.

"I still do not like the idea of Vargas knowing the location."

"You gave them your word, Drew."

"That and your trust in him is the only reason I'm doing it. Is there something going on between those two?" he asked.

"Nothing but a strong connection," I replied. "But that connection is most likely going to become something more. I can tell you right now they're going to want to fuck. So you have to make up your mind about that sort of thing."

"I don't have a problem with two guys doing… whatever," he said with a slight blush. "But they'll have to deal with me being there if they make that decision."

"You like to watch?" I teased.

Drew's slight blush turned to a bright purple. "That's not what I meant. I'll be in the other room."

"Whatever kinks your hose, Special Agent," I said, laughing.

"I'm going to get Casey. I'll give you a call later."

Ten minutes later, Colby stepped out of the interrogation room and to my desk.

"Judge Barrett is gone for the day," he said. "I don't suppose you had anything to do with that?"

"I heard Barrett had a family emergency. How could I have something to do with that?"

"It's only delaying the inevitable, Detective. I'll have my client released tomorrow."

"Good luck, Counselor."

"I want my client in isolation—in his own cell and away from the other inmates."

"I can get him his own cell, but the isolation cell is already being used. Your client will just have to deal with some noisy neighbors for the night. It'll get him used to what it's like in prison."

“We’ll see about that.” Colby glared at me for a moment, then turned and left.

I slammed my fist down on my desk. I knew I was supposed to be able to draw a line between my work life and my personal life. The trouble was that the case seemed to be melding the two lives together. The case was bringing up many memories, and I didn’t see how I could separate the two. Colby representing Shaw felt like a betrayal—a major betrayal. It felt like he was defending all the men who had taken advantage of the young man I had once been. I didn’t know how I could deal with it and didn’t think I could.

An hour later, my cell phone rang, and I recognized the number as Drew’s.

“Yeah,” I answered.

“I got Casey set up in the safe house. Why don’t you come over, and we can plan our next move, 201 Quail Street in Sparks.”

I hung up and told Lex where I was going. She was busy with some reports, so she told me to go without her.

I pulled up in front of the safe house. It was rather nondescript—just like the rest of the houses in the area. It was painted a dingy gray and had a lawn that was more rock and dirt than grass. I went to the front door and knocked. Drew opened the door, and I almost didn’t recognize him. Instead of the suit he had worn every day since I met him, he wore a pair of blue jeans that hugged his legs and an equally tight tank top. For the first time, I could see his muscular chest and arms.

“Wow,” I said. “Special Agent, you sure do look different. I like this look better than the office-man attire.”

“We’re supposed to blend in with the neighborhood,” he said, blushing slightly. “So I’m just Drew Bradley, and he’s my younger brother, if anyone asks.”

I almost said that if I were a single man, I would be all over him. The fact that he didn’t play for my team wouldn’t have stopped me from at least trying.

"Casey's getting dressed," Drew said. "I got him some new clothes."

Drew and I took a seat at a small table in a tiny kitchen. Casey came out a few minutes later wearing a plain black T-shirt and jean shorts.

"Damn, I feel better than I have in a while," Casey said.

"Come sit," Drew said. "We need your help."

Casey sat down and looked at us.

"Can you give us names of any other boys who might've been hired by Shaw?" Drew asked.

"The only ones I know for sure are Jed and Toby."

"Do you know Toby's last name?" I asked. Casey shook his head. "What about Jed? Will he help us?"

"If he gets the same protection I'm getting," Casey answered. "Otherwise he's risking his life."

"Have you talked to your superior about getting protection for Jed?" I asked Drew. Gabe had told me Jed Harper was Casey's best friend—and occasional lover.

"He rejected the request," he said in a low voice. "He says they can't afford the cost of more protection with such a shaky case."

"The case is shaky because we don't have enough witnesses," I said. "If we had Jed's testimony, the case would be stronger."

"I agree with you, Cristian. Things could change if we get a statement from someone other than a homeless kid."

"Like who?" Casey asked.

"Maybe someone who was there with Shaw when these encounters took place," Drew replied.

"The only times we weren't alone was when Graham was there. He's as bad as Shaw."

"That's the truth," I mumbled. Drew and Casey gave me odd looks. "What about Harlan Slate?"

"Why would he flip?" Drew wondered. "We have less evidence on him than we do on Shaw. If he jumps to our side, who knows what would happen to him? He's got everything to lose and nothing to gain."

"Me and Lex will go talk to Slate and the boys at the ranch and see what we can come up with," I said. "There's got to be someone who's involved on the sidelines. Someone who handles the accounts or a middleman between Harlan and his clients."

"I'll see what I can find out," Drew said.

"What can I do?" Casey asked.

"Nothing," Drew and I said in unison.

"You have to just sit tight," Drew said. "We've got satellite TV, plenty of movies, and some video games."

"I can't leave?" Casey asked.

"Most definitely not," Drew replied. "We don't want anyone to find out where you are."

"Can I call Gabe and let him know where I am?"

"I'll call him and give him the address," Drew said. "I'll have to instruct him on the rules and regulations."

"Fuck, you're stiff," Casey said. He left the table, plopped down on the couch, and turned on the television.

"Have fun," I told Drew as I left.

AT THE station, Lex had finished her reports and was looking for information on the hustler named Toby.

"Six months ago a family from Carson City reported their son Toby missing—Toby Sherman. I'm getting a picture right now."

An image appeared on the screen. Sixteen with long, curly dark hair. I sent an e-mail to Drew with the photo attached, with instructions to ask Casey if that was the Toby he knew. A reply came a minute later: *Casey confirms.*

"I'm going to Carson to talk to the Shermans and see what they can tell me about their son. You want to come with me?" Lex asked.

"No, you handle the sweet-talking. I'm gonna book Shaw and make him as comfortable as possible. Let me know what you find out."

Fingerprinting Shaw and giving him his pretty orange jumpsuit was one of the most fun things I had ever done. He complained and whined the entire time, and I loved it.

Lex returned several hours later, and we sat at our desks to talk.

"Myra Sherman is a single mother—five kids. Toby's the second oldest. He has one older brother, one younger brother, and two younger sisters. Ms. Sherman has her hands full with two jobs and all the kids," Lex said.

"Did Toby fall through the cracks?" I asked.

"Seven months ago Toby started bringing money home to help with the family. He told his mother he had a part-time job, but she got suspicious with the amount of cash he was coming home with."

"He was hustling?"

"At first she thought he was selling drugs, but he promised her he wasn't. Eventually one of the younger kids told her that Toby was always gone at night while she worked. She followed him one night and figured out what he was doing."

"Did she throw him out?"

"No," Lex said. "She told Toby that he had to quit. She begged him to stop degrading himself, but he said he was doing what he had to for the family."

"But he didn't stop, did he?"

"Nope. Mrs. Sherman said she did everything she could think of, including following him and scaring off his johns. Then one day Toby was gone. He left a note and said he was gonna save all his money and send it to the family. She hasn't seen him since."

"So he's still on the streets," I said. "We need to find him."

"I say we head out to the ranch, ask Slate about Toby, and casually mention the illegal prostitution. Maybe if we pretend like we don't believe it, then he won't get too spooked."

"Goddamn, you're smart," I said.

"That's why we work so well together. I'm the brains, and you're the brawn."

"Yeah," I said, smiling. "I'm just a brainless hunk. I've got the looks, and you've got the wisdom."

"Are you calling me old and ugly?" Lex asked.

"No, just older than me and not as good-looking."

She punched my shoulder. "You're an asshole."

"Yes, I am," I said. "That's why you love me."

"Whatever you say." She grabbed her coat. "Let's go, young man."

"Right behind you, ma'am."

She turned around and stepped up to me. She was trying to hide a smile and pretending to be pissed, but I knew her well enough and could tell she was teasing.

"You call me ma'am again, and I will rip your fucking balls off."

I nodded, and she turned and exited the station.

A YOUNG man answered the door, and we introduced ourselves.

"Can we ask you a few questions?" Lex asked.

"Sure." He shrugged and led us into the living room.

Lex showed him a picture of Toby. "Have you seen this young man?"

He shook his head.

"We believe he's been prostituting himself," Lex said. "Do you know anything about that?"

"Why the hell would I know anything about that?" he asked defensively.

“Lots of kids end up on the streets with no choice but to sell themselves for money. There’s no shame in it,” I said.

By the look on the young man’s face, I could tell he was ashamed of what he’d done on the streets.

“I suppose *some* kids have to do that,” he said. He wasn’t ready to admit he had been one of those kids.

“How long have you been on the ranch?” Lex asked.

“I just got here a couple days ago.”

“What is it like living here?” I asked.

“Fucking awesome,” he answered. “I get a warm bed and food, and the work here ain’t that bad.”

I figured he hadn’t been on the ranch long enough for Slate to recruit him for his hustling operation.

“Can I help you?” a man in his midthirties asked as he stepped into the living room. I recognized Harlan Slate from the pictures I had seen. He was tall and thin and wore brown cargo pants, a blue plaid shirt, cowboy boots, and a cowboy hat.

I stood and shook Slate’s hand. “I’m Detective Flesh, and this is my partner, Detective Luther. Do you have a few minutes?”

“Certainly,” he replied. “Let’s go to my office.” He led us to a small room that was sparsely furnished. He had a cheap desk and not much else—not even a computer.

“We’re looking for a young man named Toby Sherman,” Lex said. “We’re hoping that he may have come to your ranch.” She handed Slate Toby’s picture. He studied it for a minute, then handed it back.

“I’m afraid I’ve never seen him.”

I couldn’t tell if he was lying about knowing Toby, but I could tell he was nervous and was hiding something. Beads of sweat had formed on his forehead, and he was tapping his fingers on the desk.

“We’re here on another matter,” Lex said. “It’s merely a formality. I’m sure the claims are totally false.”

"What claims?" Slate asked.

"We arrested a young man on assault charges the other day. His name is Casey Thompson. Do you know him?"

"Yes, he was living on the ranch until just a few days ago."

"Thompson is claiming that you forced him into prostitution in order to make money for the ranch," I said.

"What the hell?" Slate exclaimed. "That's outrageous. You can't seriously think I would ever do something like that." The classic line from *Hamlet* popped into my head—*the lady doth protest too much.*

"Calm down, Mr. Slate," Lex assured him. "This is merely a formality so we can tell our chief that we spoke to you, and you assured us that no such thing happened. You deny the accusations, correct?"

"Yes, of course I deny the accusations. I'm here to help these young men, not force them into doing anything illegal."

"I'm sure this will all go away soon, Mr. Slate," I said. "We do need to speak to all the boys living here."

"Of course," Slate answered. "I have eighteen boys living here right now. Most of them are out and about doing chores. Feel free to walk around the ranch and talk to whoever you want."

"Thank you," Lex said as we both stood. Slate stayed in his office while Lex and I went outside. Lex spoke to the boy who had answered the door, while I headed toward the barn, where I saw a couple more boys.

I spoke to two young men who didn't recognize Toby. They had been on the ranch for several months. When I asked them if Slate had talked them into hustling again, they denied it, but my instincts told me they were lying. One of them had a haunted look in his eyes that convinced me he hated what he was doing. I tried to get them to tell me the truth, but they refused to say a word.

I spoke to several boys—all of whom denied they had anything to do with hustling. It seemed as if word about the questions Lex and I were asking got around the ranch fairly quickly, because the next boys I ran into refused to say a word. I didn't give up and kept walking around.

Strolling to the barn, I saw a young man throwing hay bales from the top of a stack to a small trailer hooked to a four-wheeler. He wore blue jeans, no shirt, and a white cowboy hat. He was skinny, with black hair that reached down to his shoulders.

"Excuse me," I called out. "Can I talk to you?"

He stopped and studied me. "Gimme a minute," he said. "Need four more bales." He tossed the remaining bales, then climbed down the stack and came up to me. When he was close, I could see his ribs because he was so thin. He had brown eyes with large bags underneath. He looked tired and sad. He had a large belt buckle that looked like some kind of rodeo award.

"What's up, man?" he said and hitched his thumbs in the top of his pants.

"I'm Detective Cristian Flesh," I said.

"You're a cop?" he asked, and I nodded. "I don't like cops."

"I don't blame you," I said. "I don't like most cops either. I barely like myself." My little joke got him to grin the slightest bit.

"What you looking for?" he asked me.

"Information," I replied. "I'm looking for a missing young man." I handed him the picture.

"That's Toby," he said.

"You know him? Do you have any idea where he might be?"

"Why you looking for him?"

"His family wants him to come home."

"You're lying," he said matter-of-factly.

"No, I'm not," I said.

"Well, you ain't telling me the whole truth. You're hiding something."

"You're pretty smart, cowboy," I said, smiling. He grinned but didn't say anything else. "We believe Toby can help us with a larger case."

"I ain't seen Toby since I came here," he said. "He used to crash at the old King's Inn Casino."

The King's Inn Casino had closed down years ago and had never been reopened.

"Thanks, cowboy," I said.

"My name's Jed."

"Jed?" I recognized the name.

"Yeah, Jed Harper."

"Casey's best friend?" I asked quietly. He gave me a look of shock and relief.

"You know Casey? Do you know where he is? Is he okay? I miss him so fucking much."

I touched Jed on the arm, and we went around the stack so no one could overhear us.

"Casey is being protected," I whispered. "He's going to testify against Shaw. That's why I'm looking for Toby."

"I can be a witness too," Jed said. "I'll testify about Shaw and Carl Graham."

"We need as much evidence against Shaw as possible, but we can't offer you protection," I said. "I don't want you to get hurt."

"Did Casey tell you what's going on here?"

"Yeah, he told us about Slate."

"Case and I thought it was just us Slate was using. But we were wrong. I know of a couple other kids for sure, but I think everyone is. Slate makes us all think it's just a couple."

"Can't you leave?" I asked.

"I'd be back on the street and doing the same thing I'm doing now—selling my ass. I'd be sleeping in cardboard boxes instead of the bed I'm in now."

"But that's not what the ranch is supposed to be about," I said.

"Yeah, I know," he replied.

"If I get enough evidence against Shaw and Slate, I can make sure it stops happening. None of the other boys here want to admit to anything."

"Slate's been threatening them. He said he'll kill them if they say anything to the cops. He says he has connections to make sure their deaths would be very painful."

"Do you think you can get any of them to change their minds?"

"Maybe. I'll try," Jed said with his eyes aimed at the floor. "It sucks, 'cause I thought I could stop selling my ass. But it's still better than it was before. I could deal with it better when I had Case in my bed with me. He helped me forget the shit we had to do. Will you please tell him I miss him? Is there any way I can see him?"

"I don't think it'll be possible for you to see him," I said. "But I will pass on the message."

"Thanks, man," he said.

I reached into my pocket and pulled out a business card. I scribbled a phone number on the back and handed it to him. "That's got my number at the station, my cell, and my home number. If you think of anything that can help us, will you give me a call?"

"You want me to dig into shit around here? Paperwork or something?"

"No, Jed, I do not want you risking getting in trouble. I don't know what Slate would do if he found out. But I'm looking for names of people who deal with the money or anyone else connected to Slate and his clients."

"Got it," he answered. "Don't forget to pass on the message to Case."

"I won't forget, Jed," I promised. I didn't make promises I didn't plan on keeping.

I said good-bye to Jed and met up with Lex.

"You ready?" I asked, and she nodded.

In the car, Lex asked me if I found out anything.

"I talked to Jed Harper, Casey's friend," I said. "He said Toby used to hang out at the King's Inn Casino. He also told me that several other boys on the ranch are selling themselves at Slate's request."

"I got the same impression," Lex said. "No one would admit anything, but I'm sure Slate is using them all."

"We need to find the money," I said. "I wonder what Slate is doing with it. He's not living high on the hog. The ranch is pretty much bare bones."

"YOU GOING to call Colby and tell him you're working late?" Lex asked. I had decided to pay a visit to the King's Inn Casino after dark in hopes of either finding Toby or someone who could tell me where he might be.

"No," I answered. "I don't have to report in."

"You might not have to," she said. "But most people in a relationship do that sort of thing."

"I'm not most people."

"Yeah, I know. But—"

"Quit butting into my personal life, Lex," I snapped.

"There's the dickhead I'm used to dealing with," Lex sneered.

"Go home, Lex. Go back to your happy home with your handsome hubby and wonderful kids and don't worry about this fag's life."

"Fuck, Cristian, you can be such an ass. You and Colby fighting?"

"No," I murmured.

"Then what's the problem?"

"He's fucking defending Shaw!"

"Your professional life doesn't have to interfere with your home life, Cris."

"There's too much overlap in this case, Lex. The line between the case and my personal life is pretty fucking blurry. If he was defending someone we arrested for murder, I could deal with that. But he's defending a slimy pedophile who likes to beat on young boys. How can anyone defend scum like that? How can Colby do that to me?"

"He's not doing it to you, Cris."

"Well, it fucking feels like it."

Lex sat and stared at me for a moment. She stood and strode over to me, leaned down, and kissed me on my forehead. "Good night, Cris. Good luck tonight."

"Good night, Lex."

MOST OF the doors into the King's Inn Casino were blocked off, but I knew from personal experience that there is always a way into a place. I found a broken window with crates underneath to serve as stairs. I pulled myself into the window and moved down the hallway into the area where the casino had once been. Ropes and sheets separated spaces—creating makeshift private rooms. Sleeping bags, both occupied and unoccupied, covered the floor, as did tents and cardboard boxes.

Men and women, boys and girls, all ages and races occupied the room. Some slept, and some talked, and some just sat in silence. A few watched me, but no one approached me first. Some turned away when I tried to talk to them.

Finally, a young man who sat in the corner reading a book came up to me.

"You're a cop." It wasn't a question.

"Yeah," I said.

"If you came here to bust us, you made a big mistake," the kid said. "You're outnumbered here, and you're not the only one with a weapon."

"Relax," I said. "I'm not here to cause trouble. I'm looking for someone."

"You came here looking for a fuck?" he said as he reached out and stroked my arm. "I'll give you a good deal."

"Thanks, but no thanks," I said. "I'm not looking for a fuck. I'm looking for a missing kid. His mother wants him to come home." I handed him the picture of Toby Sherman.

"Toby," the young man said. "He's a good kid. I know him. He thinks he has to do this to help his family."

"His mother wants him home. She doesn't want him on the streets selling his ass."

"I tried to talk him into going home, but he won't listen."

"I might be able to change his mind," I said.

"Hopefully," the kid said. "You just missed him. He has a regular appointment. He was picked up half an hour ago."

"Do you know who his trick is?"

The kid shook his head.

"How long do these appointments normally last?"

"Anywhere from an hour to all night."

"If I give you my card, will you call me when he gets back?"

"Sure, I'll use my cell phone," the kid joked.

I pulled out my wallet and handed him a twenty. "Find a phone, please." The kid took the twenty and my card and nodded.

"What's your name?" I asked.

"You can call me Rebel," he said.

"That your real name?"

"Nah," he said, grinning. "But it's hella better than the name my momma gave me."

"I understand."

I HEADED home and climbed into bed. It seemed empty and lonely, but I just couldn't handle having Colby next to me. The phone rang ten minutes later, and I knew it was my big guy.

"Hello," I answered.

"Hey, baby, how are you?"

"Good," I answered.

"I was hoping you'd come over tonight," he said.

"Too tired," I answered.

"I can come over there."

"No, I need some space."

"Oh." I could feel the hurt in Colby's voice. "Is this about me defending Shaw?"

"I don't feel like talking, Colby." I hung up the phone before he could say another word. The phone rang again, but I ignored it. I turned off my cell and unplugged the house phone, pulled the covers over me, and closed my eyes.

Sleep didn't come easily.

Chapter 6

COLBY WAS at the station early in the morning. "We're going to talk tonight," he told me.

"We'll see," I said. "I might not feel like it."

"We are going to talk tonight." He ambled to the interrogation room where Shaw was waiting.

Drew showed up a few minutes later. He was once again in his secret agent suit and tie.

"How's Casey doing?" I asked.

"Going stir crazy," he answered.

"Gabe been over yet?" I asked.

"He's there right now. I called in another agent to stay there while I took care of things here at the station. I'm not sure what Gabe and Casey are doing at the moment."

"I'm sure I know," I said, smiling.

"You think they would engage in sexual activity with a stranger in the house?"

"Would they fuck? Hell, yeah, they would."

"But how—"

"How? You want to know *how* they're going to fuck?"

"No!" Drew snapped. "No, I don't want to hear about anyone's sex life. I meant how could they do that with a total stranger in the other room? *Why* would they do it?"

"You do know what today is, right?" I asked him.

"No, I don't."

"Casey's eighteenth birthday. Gabe was waiting to do anything with Casey until he was eighteen. So I'm sure they're… celebrating."

"I figured it was going to happen sooner or later," Drew said, nodding. "I remember at that age I craved sexual activity all the time. So I made sure they had the necessary… supplies."

"Condoms?" I asked.

He nodded. "And lube."

"You're all right, G-man," I said.

Colby came out of the interrogation room. "We have an arraignment in twenty minutes."

"We'll be there with bells on, Counselor," I said. Colby didn't say a word; he just turned around and returned to the interrogation room.

"Trouble in paradise?" Drew asked.

"Never said it was paradise," I said. "Fags fight just like you breeders do."

"What's our game plan at the arraignment?" Drew asked me.

"We know Shaw's going to plead innocent. The best we can do is hope for no bail."

"What's the chance of that happening?"

"Pretty slim," I admitted.

"YOUR HONOR, we request no bail for Mr. Shaw," Cahill said.

"On what grounds?" Judge Barrett asked.

"On the grounds that Mr. Shaw is an extremely high flight risk. He has the money and the connections to quietly leave the state and the country."

Colby stood up. "Your Honor, my client is a well-respected businessman in the community. These charges are absolutely ridiculous, and he has every intention of staying in town to clear his name. He is innocent and plans to prove that to everyone. The prosecution's case is very weak and—"

"We're not here to discuss the merits of the case, Counselor," Judge Barrett interrupted.

"My apologies, Judge Barrett. My client has no intention of fleeing. He is more than willing to hand over his passport to the authorities. He is also more than willing to do whatever the court requests to ensure he attends all legal proceedings."

"The state vehemently opposes bail of any kind, Your Honor. We believe there is nothing that could stop Mr. Shaw from fleeing if he chose to do so."

"Mr. Shaw has a sterling reputation," Colby said. "Absolutely spotless. He has no criminal record whatsoever."

"Sit down, Mr. Maddox," Judge Barrett said. "I'm ready to make a ruling. I am going to set bail in the amount of $250,000."

"Your Honor," Cahill objected as he stood up. "That's a drop in the bucket for Mr. Shaw."

"Sit down, Mr. Cahill," Judge Barrett said. "I've made my decision. In addition to the bail, I am ordering Mr. Shaw to turn over his passport. I am also ordering him to wear an ankle monitor—at his cost. He will be restricted to his personal property, except for court appearances. Does everyone understand?"

The lawyers nodded.

"Excellent," the judge said as he banged his gavel and left the bench.

Cahill turned to Drew and me. "Sorry, guys," he said. "I did my best. But I'm afraid this might just be the beginning of a downward slide. If you want a conviction, you better get more evidence."

"We'll get it," I said.

Twenty minutes later, Shaw had made bail and was returning home with an officer to install the ankle monitor equipment.

My cell rang, but I didn't recognize the number. "Detective Flesh," I answered.

"Hey, this is Rebel, from last night?"

"Is Toby back?" I asked.

"Yeah, he's back," Rebel said quietly. "But he won't be going home."

"I'll talk to him."

"That's what I'm trying to tell you. You can't talk to him."

"Just tell me where he is, Rebel."

"He's outside the casino. But you can't talk to him because he's dead."

"Fuck! Don't go anywhere. I'll be there as soon as I can." I hung up the phone and turned to Lex and Drew. "Let's go."

On the way to the casino, I called for an ambulance.

Rebel and several other young men and women stood outside the King's Inn Casino. Lex, Drew, and I walked up to Rebel, and the crowd parted. They were all staring at a body on the ground. His face was bruised and bloody, but I could tell it was Toby Sherman. He was naked, and blood covered practically his entire body. He had cuts and bruises and what looked like burns.

"Fuck," I said as I knelt down and felt for a pulse, though I knew there wouldn't be one.

"Did you see anything?" I asked Rebel.

He nodded. "I was just coming out of the casino when I saw a black minivan drive by slowly. The side door opened up, and they threw Toby out. They dumped him just like he was trash." Rebel was near tears.

"Did you see the plates on the minivan?" Drew asked.

"No plates," Rebel answered. "The windows were tinted, and I didn't see anyone inside."

Sirens could be heard in the distance, and the crowd slowly dissipated until only Rebel remained.

"He was a good kid," Rebel murmured. "He was just trying to help his family. This fucking sucks!"

"Yeah, it does," I agreed.

The ambulance arrived and removed Toby's body.

"I want to make the bastards pay," Rebel said. "I fucking hate them."

"I'm gonna get them. I'll make them pay."

Rebel looked me square in the eyes. "I hope you do." He turned and left.

Drew came up to me. "We need to tell Casey," he said. I nodded.

DREW AND I went into the safe house and saw that Casey's bedroom door was closed. I looked at Drew and gave him a little smile.

Drew knocked on the door. "Casey, Gabe, you guys in there?" I heard giggles before Casey replied.

"Yeah, we're here," he said.

"Get dressed and come out here," Drew said.

"Yes, sir" was Gabe's response.

It took Gabe and Casey five minutes to come out of the room. Casey was wearing a pair of shorts and a T-shirt, but Gabe had on only a pair of blue jeans. Gabe had been toning his body up since the last time I saw him shirtless.

"Happy birthday, Casey," I said.

"Thanks, man. Gabe gave me an awesome present," he said, smiling.

Gabe and Casey sat on the couch side by side.

"I got some bad news for you," Drew said.

"Fuck," Casey murmured.

"Toby's dead. He was murdered sometime last night and his body dumped in front of the King's Inn Casino."

"Goddammit," Casey said, and I saw tears form in his eyes. Gabe wrapped his arm around Casey and drew him close.

"We're pretty sure it's connected to this case," I said. "Lex and I were at the Slate Ranch yesterday. We claimed we were looking for Toby."

"Slate probably called someone, and they flipped out because they were afraid Toby would help you guys with the case," Drew said.

"I learned he had regular appointments with someone who picked him up at the casino," I said. "I'm going to try to find out who the client was. Shaw was still in jail, so it wasn't him."

"Probably Graham," Casey said.

"When you were at the ranch, did you see Jed?" Casey asked.

"Yeah," I answered. "He sent a message. He says he misses you."

Casey smiled. "I miss him so much. Is there any way I can see him?"

"Absolutely not," Drew said. "We have to keep the location of the safe house as secret as we can. I can't let anyone else know where you are."

Casey tried to argue, but Drew shut him down.

"We'll figure something else out," I said. "We can build a case without Toby's testimony."

THE REST of the day was a mess of paperwork and useless phone calls. I headed home after six and was emotionally and physically tired.

I was standing in the kitchen, slapping together a sandwich with ham, turkey, and cheddar, when I heard the door open. I knew it was Colby, but I didn't say a word. I shuffled into the living room and sat in my recliner. Colby came out of the bedroom, went to the couch, and sat down. He stared at me while I ignored him.

"Cristian, will you please tell me what's wrong?"

I finally looked at him. "You can't tell me that you don't know what's wrong. Fuck, Colby, don't be a dumbass."

"Why are you being such a dick?"

"It's my natural state," I said. "Being a dick or sucking a dick. That's my life."

"Shut the hell up," Colby snapped. "There's a hell of a lot more to you than sex and being an asshat."

"If you know me so well, then you should fucking know why I'm upset."

"You're upset because I'm defending Clayton Shaw."

"Duh! Such a smart fellow you are."

"Can we discuss this like men instead of third graders?"

"Fine," I said, standing up and walking over to him. I leaned over slightly and put my finger in his face. "Yeah, it pisses me off that you're defending scum of the earth like Shaw."

"I've defended scum before. Are you upset because this is your case?"

"No, not just because it's my case. It's because it's Shaw. I hate him, and I hate men like him." I strolled over to the window and looked outside. Out of the corner of my eye, I saw Colby stand and walk toward me. He put a hand on my shoulder, but I shook it off.

"Just tell me what's going on in your head so we can deal with it," Colby said.

I wanted to act childish and rude and push him away, but I suddenly couldn't do it anymore.

"Shaw's best friend is Carl Graham," I said.

Colby stepped up so he was right behind me, but he didn't touch me.

"He's a client of ours too," he said.

I took a deep breath. "Doesn't surprise me. Graham is…." I wanted to say it, but I was afraid to say it. Like spitting out the words would make it real. But it was real—or had been real. Whatever you want to call memories. Not physically real but just as capable of inflicting harm. Maybe the pain caused by the memories was even stronger than when it happened the first time. When it happened in real life it only hurt for a short time, but with memories the pain was inflicted again and again and again. I felt that hurt every time the memories surfaced.

I stepped back just enough so my body would connect to Colby's. He put a hand on my shoulder, and when I didn't shake it off, he put his other hand on my other shoulder. I leaned my head back so our cheeks rubbed.

"Graham is the man who…. He's the man who bloodied my nose. The one I told you about the other night. And that wasn't the only time. He loved to make me bleed. I hated him. I *still* hate him. And he's friends with Shaw. He and Shaw are two of a kind. And if you're defending Shaw, then it feels like—"

"It feels like I'm defending Graham," Colby finished my thought. I nodded slightly. "Oh fuck, baby, I'm sorry."

"Me too," I said softly. Colby turned me around and cupped my face in his hands. We locked eyes and stayed like that for what seemed like forever. Then he kissed me gently on the lips. I wrapped my arms around him and buried my face in his neck.

"Let's go to bed, bello," he said.

I turned around, and we strode hand in hand to the bedroom. Colby slowly removed my clothes, then pushed me down on the bed. After stripping, he lay on top of me and kissed me on the lips, the neck, and the nipples. Using his tongue, he trailed down my chest, then buried his face in my crotch. He took my dick in his hand and slowly swallowed it. Blood flowed into my shaft so quickly my head spun. He sucked up and down on my cock as his hands ran up my chest and gently rubbed my nipples.

Images of every blowjob I had given or received in my lifetime flowed through my mind. The good ones *and* the bad ones. The ones with men whose names I knew and the ones with men whose names I didn't. Men I liked and the men I despised. And what occurred to me as Colby slowly brought me to orgasm with his warm mouth and sweet, so fucking sweet, tongue, was that Colby wasn't any of those other men. He was the man I loved—the man who loved me. He didn't use me for sex; he made love to me. We shared sex together. We pleasured each other. Nothing was forced, no unwanted pain.

The orgasm ripped through me, and I threaded my fingers in his hair as he swallowed me and drank my seed. He kept me in his mouth with his tongue swirling around until I was soft and the head of my prick got so ticklish that I couldn't stand it anymore.

He crawled up and kissed me on the lips. I grabbed the back of Colby's head and pulled him in for a deeper kiss. My tongue forced its way past his lips, and we shared my come.

"Cristian," he moaned. "I love you so fucking much."

"Ditto," I said, laughing.

"I'll make it right," he whispered in my ear. "I don't know how, but I'll make it right."

Chapter 7

COLBY WASN'T in bed when I woke up. At first I thought he was gone, but then I smelled coffee. I shuffled into the kitchen, still naked. Colby was fixing a bowl of cereal—Shredded Wheat. The only clothes he had on were a pair of boxers. I came up behind him, wrapped my arms around him, and kissed his neck. He leaned back against me.

"Good morning, bello."

"Morning, big guy."

"How are you doing?"

"Better than last night," I replied.

He handed me the bowl of cereal and made his own. We sat on opposite sides of the island in the kitchen.

"So what are you going to do?" I asked.

"I haven't decided yet."

I HAD just sat down at my desk when my cell rang. It was Drew.

He was speaking before I even had a chance to say a word. "Do you know where they are?"

"Who?"

"Casey and Gabe," he replied.

"What do you mean? Aren't you with Casey?"

"Gabe spent the night. When I woke up, they were gone. They snuck out."

"Fuck!"

"Exactly! Do you think they ran?"

"No," I said. "I don't think so. I'll see what I can find out."

Just a few minutes after I hung up with Drew, my cell rang again. It was Gabe.

"Kid, where the fuck are you? Is Casey with you?"

"Chill out, Cristian."

"No, I will not chill out. Where are you?"

"Look, Casey wanted to see Jed, and we know Agent Bradley didn't want him at the safe house."

"Where are you?" I repeated.

"We're camping," he finally answered. "We're in a private spot. Don't worry, we're safe."

"Tell me where you are," I ordered.

"No," Gabe said.

"Listen to me, kid. You're risking your life and Casey's."

"I know what I'm doing. I can take care of all of us. We're staying another night. Bye, Cristian."

"Gabe, stop." I slammed my phone down on the desk when I realized he'd hung up. I tried to call him back, but it went straight to voice mail.

I called Drew back. "Gabe called me. He's with Casey and Jed Harper."

"Where are they?"

"He won't tell me. All he said was that they were camping, and they were going to stay another night."

"Dammit," he cursed. "What are we going to do?"

"Gabe's a smart kid, and he knows how to take care of himself. If he says he'll be back, then he'll be back. So just sit tight."

"I'm not very good at doing that," Drew said.

"Let's keep this between you and me," I said. "It's best if no one else knows about this trip. We'll act like everything is normal."

"Agreed."

A FEW hours later, my cell rang again, and I saw it was Colby.

"Hey," I said.

"You busy right now?"

"Not at the moment. What's up?"

"Can you meet me at Starbucks?"

"Yeah, see you there."

Colby was sitting at a table with coffees for the both of us when I got there. I could tell something was up. I sat down, reached across the table, and gently touched his hand.

"What's wrong, big guy?"

He cocked an eyebrow.

"I know you as well as you know me."

He was silent for a moment. "I talked to Constance today," he said. "I told her I couldn't represent Clayton. I said I was afraid I wouldn't be able to handle his defense with you on the other side of the court."

"What did she say?"

"She agreed to take me off the case, but she was livid. She told me I had better learn how to separate my personal life from my business life, especially if I'm going to be dating a cop. She also told me that it had better not happen again."

"Thank you for doing that," I said.

"It was the right thing to do. Not just for us but for me as well. I don't like defending men like him. I never have."

"You don't have to," I pointed out. "You have enough money to start your own practice or even join me on this side of the law."

"I've thought of joining the district attorney's office," he said. "And I've thought of opening my own practice. I just always thought it would be better to make a name for myself first."

"You'll figure it out," I said. "You always do."

BACK AT the station, Lex and I discussed the case.

"None of the boys at Fresh Slate will admit to hustling before or after coming to the ranch. They all deny knowing Shaw. We can't find any other young men Shaw may have hired. I've talked to dozens of people on the street and even went to the tent city. No leads there. I say we concentrate on following a different lead."

"What do you suggest?"

"We can look for the money trail and try to nail Shaw that way."

"That's more your thing than mine, Lex. I'll let you tackle that project."

"How magnanimous of you, Cris."

"Of course. What should I be doing while you're following the money?"

"Start talking to Shaw's friends and business partners. See if any of them knows anything."

"Even if they do know anything, do you think they'll say so?"

"Probably not, but it doesn't hurt to try. Start with Graham," she suggested.

"Graham isn't going to flip on his best friend!" I exclaimed.

"If anybody can find Graham's weak spot, it's you."

I WAS sure it was a pointless effort, but I called Graham, and he reluctantly agreed to meet with me at a restaurant called the Greek Café. He arrived before I did and sat at a secluded table in the corner. He shook my hand when I arrived, and another image of me servicing him flashed through my head.

"I don't know what you think I can do for you, Detective Flesh."

"I just want to ask you a few questions about your friend, Clayton Shaw."

"Ask away," he said.

"Were you aware that Shaw was hiring underage hustlers?"

Graham chuckled. "Is that the best you can do? I know Clayton *very* well, and he doesn't need to hire male prostitutes in order to have sex. He has lots of admirers more than willing to sleep with him."

"Mr. Graham, we both know how Shaw gets his rocks off. You and he have the same tastes."

"How would you know what kind of tastes I have?"

"Trust me, Graham, I know."

He scrutinized me, and I saw the recognition in his eyes. "I remember you now. You had a full head of soft blond hair back then. But your name wasn't Cristian, was it?"

"No," I replied softly.

"You were Vincent's boy, weren't you?"

I nodded. "I know you like underage men, *and* I know what you like to do with those young men. You and Shaw are two of a kind."

"Well, you can *know* something, but that doesn't mean you can prove it."

"I will put your buddy away," I said. "And I'll do whatever it takes to make sure you go down as well."

"Good luck," he said with a grin.

I MET with several friends and business partners of Shaw's. If anyone knew that Shaw hired male prostitutes, they wouldn't admit it. There was one more person I could talk to. I knew from the very beginning of this case that it was going to lead me to this man. A man I hadn't seen or talked to for almost ten years. At one point he had been the most important man in my life. Then everything changed. I'd loved him, and I thought he loved me. It all happened so fast, like the flip of a light switch. I went from thinking I would be with him forever to knowing I was just something else he owned. Nothing more than a piece of property, as easy to replace as a worn-out sofa.

Vincent Fox was both a very lucky and a very smart man. He was barely eighteen when he'd won the California lottery—almost two million. He invested the money and bought a small company. He made the company huge, then sold it. By the time he was thirty, his fortune had grown to fifty million. He was the spokesman for several charitable organizations, and his reputation and name brought in a lot of money.

Vincent was fifty-five when I first met him; I was sixteen. It was his limo that pulled in front of me one night as I stood on the streets peddling my ass. The limo took me to a fabulous penthouse suite with a huge bed and silk sheets, a bathtub big enough for five, and a tall older man with silver hair.

Vincent was gentle and sweet with me that first night—and for so many nights after. He touched me all over before we got to the main event. I was so happy to be able to sleep in a bed for the night. And in the morning, when Vincent said he didn't want me to leave, I was thrilled.

I became his boy. My body was his when and where he wanted it, and in exchange I got a place to live, clothes on my back, and money to spend. At first it was all so wonderful—a dream come true. Vincent was a good-looking man for his age. He kept in shape and was always meticulously clean, and he loved me to fuck him.

In public I was his assistant, and I called him sir and Mr. Fox. In private, I called him lots of other names, and he called me many names. I always fucked him—always. It was never the other way around.

My mind snapped back into the present when I laid eyes on the house that had been my home for many years. It was a home I'd thought I would never leave. He lived in Incline Village in a nine-million-dollar home overlooking Lake Tahoe. A curving stone path ran through the trees and led to the front door.

I strolled slowly up the path and rang the bell. A young man wearing nothing but a pair of jogging shorts answered the door. He had short black hair and was several inches shorter than me. I knew right away he was Vincent's lover, and I told myself to find out his age at some point.

"Is Mr. Fox available?"

I could tell the guy was itching to go for a jog, and my appearance was messing with his plans.

"Vinnie," he called out. "Someone's here to see you."

Vincent stepped out of his office and sauntered toward me. He hadn't changed much. He had gained a few pounds, but he still had a full head of hair. He had shaved the goatee he'd worn when we were together. He looked incredible for a man of sixty-five.

"William," he boomed. "This is a surprise." I had been with Vincent before I legally changed my name.

"You know I don't use that name anymore," I said. "I'm Cristian Flesh now, Detective Cristian Flesh."

"You will always be my William," he said.

"I haven't been yours for a very long time, Vincent," I said. I looked at the young man. "Besides, you have a new… toy now, don't you?"

Vincent laughed but didn't deny anything. "William, this is my… assistant, Stephen. Stephen, this is William."

I shook hands with Stephen.

"Are you one of Vinnie's former assistants?" he asked.

I nodded. "A long time ago."

"I figured that," Stephen sneered. "Vinnie doesn't like older men."

I laughed at the jeer.

"Behave, Stephen." Vincent swatted him on the ass. "Go and take your run while I talk to William."

Stephen smiled at Vincent and kissed him on the cheek. He pulled away and gave me an evil look before he took off out the front door.

"I hope he doesn't think I'm here to win you back," I said. "Because that isn't what I want."

Vincent laughed. "Stephen's a jealous little bitch. He is very emotional and passionate. Those are just a few of the reasons I'm with him."

"I'm sure there are plenty of other reasons." I snorted.

"He doesn't measure up to you, William. But what he lacks in size, he makes up for in passion. He's nineteen, by the way. I can show you his license if you want me to."

"Going for older boys after all, huh?"

"Let's get right down to business, William. I assume you're not here to reminisce." He led me into a living room with hardwood floors and a stone fireplace. I sat on one side of a red leather couch, and he sat on the other.

"Do you know Clayton Shaw?"

"I'm afraid I do," he answered.

"You don't like him?" I shifted my body so I could look Vincent in the eyes.

"He's a pig." He scowled.

"You guys have similar tastes in lovers."

Vincent grimaced with genuine hurt in his eyes. "William, how can you say that?"

"You picked me off the street." I snorted. "I was a minor. Clayton sleeps with underage hustlers too."

"I gave you a home. I gave you everything you needed."

"Not everything," I said.

"You had clothes and electronics, even a car. What didn't I give you?"

"The only thing I really wanted back then—your love."

"Love is a useless emotion," Vincent scoffed. "You didn't need it. No one needs it."

"That's what I used to think," I replied. "But now I know different. I'm not here to discuss the past or to compare you and Clayton Shaw."

"He and I are very different, William," he insisted. "Yes, I appreciate young men. But I bring them into my place. Clayton uses them and discards them. He puts them back on the street."

I chose not to acknowledge his words and resisted the incredibly strong urge to tell him what a hypocrite he was. "Clayton is facing criminal charges, and I'm hoping you may be able to help me."

"What do you think I can do for you?"

"Point me in the right direction. If you dislike Clayton as much as you say, then you wouldn't mind him going down for this."

"I don't care either way what happens to Clayton, but I can't do anything that would harm my reputation."

"Of course, Vincent," I scoffed. "Always thinking of yourself. I don't know why I expected any different." I stood up and prepared to leave. He came up behind me and touched my shoulder. I shook it off and spun around. We were so close I could smell cinnamon—he always chewed Big Red.

"I hope you look on our time together with happiness, William."

"Happiness?" I sneered. "What fond memories do you think I have? The first time you lent me to your friend—the Italian? Or my visits with Carl Graham? Or the times I was forced to take care of the group of businessmen with Armani suits and vodka on their breath?"

"Those were business transactions, William. What we did together was special."

"Special? Are you fucking kidding me? Do you know how many times I wanted to kiss you or shower with you?"

"Kissing is so messy."

"So what was special, Vincent? Me fucking you—sometimes for minutes and sometimes for hours—all depending on what you wanted. And when you came I was sent back to my room—even if I hadn't come."

"It's too bad you choose to be so negative, William," he said as he shook his head.

"Thanks for nothing, Vincent," I said and marched to the door.

"William, wait," he called out, and I stopped. "There's a private computer network for Clayton and men like him. You'll never get on it. You have to have multiple references; membership is very strict. It's called Eromenos."

"Thanks, Vincent."

"You're welcome, William. Maybe someday you'll change your mind about how I treated you."

"I doubt it," I said. "Watch your back, Vincent. Past or no past, if I ever learn that you're living with someone underage, I will take you in."

"Thanks for the warning. You won't ever catch me with a minor."

I noticed the wording of his sentence. He said I would never catch him, not that he wouldn't ever be lovers with a minor again.

As I left the house, I hoped I would never have to come back. I pushed the memories away; now wasn't the time for them to return. They would haunt me again, and soon, but not yet.

I CALLED Drew and Lex and told them what I had learned. I left out the fact that my former sugar daddy had given me the information.

By the time I got back to the station, Lex had found the origin of the name Eromenos. According to Wikipedia, it was a Greek word for the younger man in a relationship with an older man. Apparently homosexual relationships between older men and young boys were so common there was a name for it: pederasty or boy love. In Athens, the older man was called erastes. He was to educate, protect, love, and provide a role model for his beloved. His beloved was called eromenos. The older man's reward was his lover's beauty, youth, and promise.

Drew said he had passed on the information about the computer network to the FBI.

"Find anything on the money trail, Lex?" I asked.

"The ranch is officially a charitable organization, so I'm checking out where the money comes from."

"Anything interesting?" I asked.

"I recognize most of the names: local families and businesses. There is one name I don't recognize—Zoe H. Fusion."

"That can't be someone's real name." I laughed.

"Probably not, but I have no idea who it is."

"Who else has given money to the ranch?"

Lex rattled off names of people and businesses. I cross-checked those names in the criminal database and made a short list of people I wanted to speak to in person.

AFTER DINNER, Colby rubbed my feet while we watched Errol Flynn in *The Charge of the Light Brigade*.

"Do you know who Vincent Fox is?" I asked.

"I've met him at a few parties," Colby answered.

"I visited him today."

He stopped and stared at me. "Why?"

"Don't quit rubbing my feet. It relaxes me."

He began again but didn't look away.

"Vincent was the man who took me off the streets when I was sixteen. He was the man I told you about."

"Vincent Fox was your sugar daddy?" Colby asked, his eyes wide.

I nodded. "I thought he might be able to help with the case."

"Did he?"

"He gave us a lead." I told Colby about Eromenos.

"Other than that, how was the visit?"

"Brought up a lot of memories. But you know what? They aren't as painful as they used to be. They're my memories and just that. They can't hurt me. Not those ones, anyway. It's part of my life, and it made me the man I am today. And all that crap led me to you."

Colby leaned forward and kissed me on the lips.

"Do you want to tell me? It's up to you."

"Fuck, big guy, I am so goddamn grateful that you've been as patient as you've been. There's still a big part of my life that I'm not ready to talk about, and I might never want to. But these other things can't hurt me anymore."

I told him about moving in with Vincent and thinking I was in love with him, and when I realized he didn't love me.

"On the day I turned seventeen, Vincent had a visitor, a big Italian guy whose name I don't remember. Vincent told me I had to have sex with the Italian. I tried to say no, and Vincent slapped me. He told me my body belonged to him, and if he wanted to loan it out, that it was his right. So I fucked the Italian. And later I had to visit Graham."

I talked about being forced to perform oral sex on a group of fat and sweaty businessmen, about being loaned to two German men for a week and how they liked me to wear nipple clamps 24-7, and about the time Vincent and a dozen men forced me to fuck them all.

"I learned to hate fucking men. Absolutely hated it. When I no longer had to do Vincent's bidding, and I could choose my own partners, I decided I would never top again."

"Rule number one," Colby whispered. I nodded.

"I realized Vincent wasn't going to keep me around forever. I figured when I didn't look young enough anymore I'd be done. So I decided I had to take control of my life."

"What did you do?"

"I had been going to school but hadn't been putting much thought into it. I buckled down and worked as hard as I could. I also hid the money he gave me."

"That was damn smart of you," he said.

"I was almost twenty when Vincent said I had a week to find my own place. That's all he said. Not a word of apology. I wasn't hurt or surprised. By then I knew what the game was. Vincent paid six months' rent for a cheap studio apartment in Reno. I hated using his money, but I figured it was better than going back on the streets. So I took the money he gave me when I left and the money I had been hiding, and I enrolled in college."

"Is that when you decided to be a cop?"

"Yeah," I replied. "I had seen the horrible and shitty things in life and wanted to be able to do something about them. I earned my criminal justice degree and got a job at the Reno Police Department."

"Cristian, you are such an amazing man."

I blushed. "No, just a man."

"My man," he said.

"You got that right," I said, smiling. "Thanks for listening."

"Any time."

"Make love to me, Colby." I pulled off my shirt. He lay on top of me and thrust his tongue into my mouth. And right there on the couch he made love to me, and I realized—for the first time in my life—that I was with someone who was never going to hurt me.

Chapter 8

I WENT straight to the safe house Thursday morning. Gabe and Casey were there, and I could hear Drew yelling at them from the street. They all gawked at me for a second when I opened the front door.

"That was so fucking irresponsible of you," Drew shouted. "I've bent over backward for you both, and this is how you repay me."

"Relax, Bradley," Gabe snapped. "Nothing bad happened."

"But it could've." I stepped in. "You guys could've been hurt. Not to mention the case against Clayton."

"Nothing happened!" Gabe said.

"Fuck, is he always this pigheaded?" Drew asked me.

"Yeah, I'm afraid so."

"I'm outta here." Gabe stood. "I need to see Violet and Victor before I go to work. See ya, Case." He leaned down and kissed Casey.

"We'll discuss this later, kid," I told him. He didn't respond as he left. Casey glared at Drew, stood, stormed into his bedroom, and slammed the door.

"Did your Feeb geeks get anything on the computer group?"

"They can't find even a mention of it anywhere. Normally they're on top of things like this. Are you sure your contact wasn't bullshitting you?"

I shook my head. "He was telling me the truth. We need to find a way into that group."

THE NEXT few weeks were spent with Drew, Lex, and I doing whatever we could to gather more evidence. I followed up with the people and businesses who contributed to the Slate Ranch and got nothing.

We tried following a different money trail. We matched up the dates of Clayton's get-togethers with Casey to withdrawals from his accounts, but we couldn't find out where the money went.

Then one Tuesday we finally got something we could use.

I was working out at the gym when I saw Austin Shaw. I almost didn't recognize him without his shirt on. He was buff and had a much more positive look on his face than he had when I first met him.

He recognized me right away and came up to me.

"Detective Flesh, how are you doing?"

"I'm good, Austin. How about you?"

"Better than I've been in a long time, thanks to you."

"I didn't do a thing."

"You gave me hope, Detective."

"But looks like you've done the hard work," I said, gesturing to his muscles.

He laughed. "Yeah, I've been getting into shape. I've also been designing a new website for my parents' business."

"You good with computers?"

"Yeah, I'm kind of a hacker. I put in Clayton's home computer system. He's got it wired to speakers and cameras throughout the house."

"Cameras?"

"Yeah, when I first asked him about it, he said it was because of all the parties he held. If anything disappeared, he wanted to be able to see who took it. But I learned the *real* reason later. A few weeks after we had sex, he told me he had recorded it so he could watch it again and again."

"Bastard," I mumbled. He nodded in agreement. "If he recorded you, then he probably recorded the other men he's slept with."

"I guess so."

"Austin, are you busy later today?"

"No," he answered.

"Will you come to the station so we can discuss something?"

"Of course," he said.

WHEN AUSTIN arrived I led him to a private room where Drew was waiting. I introduced them and told Austin about Eromenos.

"Do you think you can find a back door into Clayton's system and maybe get us a link into Eromenos?"

"I don't think I can," Austin said, and my heart sank. "I *know* I can. Hackers always build a trapdoor into any system they work on. I can get into his system, but I don't know how many firewalls he has built in for other things. It may not be easy, but I'll do my best."

"While you're snooping around in Clayton's files, you might find the videos of him with other boys. Those would definitely help with the case."

"Got it."

"What do you need?"

"A computer, my iPod, and lots of Slim Jims and Strawberry Crush."

"Slim Jims?" Drew asked.

"Yeah, you know, those greasy meat sticks."

Austin flexed his arms into a pose—trying to imitate the wrestler Randy "Macho Man" Savage. "Snap into a Slim Jim," he growled in a deep voice.

Drew and I laughed. "I'll get whatever you need," I said.

Austin spent the rest of that day and half of the next trying to get into Eromenos via Clayton's computer.

On Wednesday afternoon, Austin called me over to the desk where he was working.

"Any luck?"

"Not yet. The security is pretty tight. I'm not sure I can get there from here. Maybe if I was on Clayton's computer. But that's not why I called you over. I was looking around when I found some encrypted files. There was some tough security, but I got through it."

"What are they?" I asked.

"They're video files," he replied. "But I haven't watched them yet. I thought you should be here for that."

"Play one of them," I said. Austin double-clicked on a file, and it popped up and started playing. It was Clayton—buck-ass naked—with someone on his knees sucking him. Clayton pulled the cocksucker to his feet and slapped him so hard it spun him around. It was Casey.

"Oh my God!" Austin said and put his hand to his mouth.

"Don't watch," I told him, and he left the room. What I saw transpire between Casey and Clayton reminded me of my interactions with Carl Graham. I shut off the video, took a minute to get myself together, and went to talk to Lex.

WE WENT to Cahill with the information we had.

"How did you get this?"

"It's probably best if you don't know," I said.

"You might be right, Detective," Cahill responded. "However, I do need to know."

"Austin Shaw."

"Clayton's nephew?" Cahill asked.

"Stepnephew. The same young man he seduced and discarded. He's a computer expert and installed Clayton's home system. He left ways to get in. I was actually using him to try to find a way into Eromenos, and he stumbled across these files."

"You realize that is completely illegal, don't you?" Cahill said.

"Of course," I replied. "My official story is that a confidential informant told me Clayton liked to tape his sexual encounters."

"If it comes out that we got this information through illegal measures, then the evidence will be thrown out. Do you understand?"

I nodded.

Cahill got a warrant based on my *official* story, and an hour later we had possession of Clayton's computer. We handed it to our police tech, and he found his way to the encrypted files—with Austin's help.

Clayton had more than fifty videos of himself and Casey engaged in all kinds of sexual and violent acts. A discussion regarding payment was also caught on tape. There were also recordings of Clayton with other young men, including Toby and Jed.

"Is this enough evidence?" I asked in a meeting with Cahill. "We've got the bastard on tape screwing and beating the kid. We've got him admitting he likes underage boys and discussing payment. It's a slam-dunk case."

"Nothing is ever slam dunk," Cahill responded. "Shaw's lawyer has been pushing to get a speedy trial. I've been stalling because I don't have the evidence, but I can move forward now."

THE CASE was put on a fast track, and a trial date was set for a month away. Drew and I spent hours and hours with Casey so he would be ready to face Shaw in court and testify.

Gabe also spent a lot of time with Casey, probably more than he did with Violet.

"I know you care for him, but shouldn't you be with Violet more often?" I asked. "You remember her, don't you? Your girlfriend and the mother of your child?"

"Mind your own fucking business, Flesh," Gabe snapped. "I know what I'm doing."

I wasn't convinced, but I didn't press the issue.

Chapter 9

THE TRIAL against Clayton Shaw began early Monday morning. Shaw had waived his right to a jury trial. He opted for a bench trial, where the judge alone made the ruling.

Since I was a witness, I wasn't allowed to watch the trial. The first day I waited in a private room with Casey. Drew was in the courtroom watching the proceedings. He visited us during a break after the opening arguments.

"Cahill gave a strong opening statement," Drew said. "But Shaw's lawyer—Jermaine Drake—gave one that was just as strong, maybe even stronger."

Casey was called to testify first. He was on the stand for a couple of hours and looked emotionally worn out when he returned.

"He did well." Drew patted Casey's shoulder. "Very good."

"I had to talk about a lot of the times I had sex with Shaw," Casey said. "Drake tried to get me to say that I had lied about my age. He also claimed the money Shaw gave me was a gift and not payment for sex."

"I'm sure Casey's testimony affected the judge." Drew looked at Casey with pride. "It would take a real hardass not to be affected by what he had to say."

I WAS called to the stand first thing Tuesday. I spoke about Shaw's attack, how I'd found Casey, and what he told me. I also testified about Shaw's lies regarding items being stolen from his house. Finally I talked about the confidential informant who had given me information about Shaw taping his sexual encounters.

"Detective Flesh," Drake asked me during cross-examination, "what is the name of this confidential informant?"

"Do you know the meaning of the word confidential, Mr. Drake? If I tell you his name, then it's no longer confidential, and I will lose a valuable source of information for the Reno Police Department."

"Very well," Drake said. "Is this confidential informant in any way connected to my client in a personal way?"

It was an odd question, for sure. "No," I answered.

"Thank you, Detective Flesh. You are excused."

DRAKE STARTED his case Monday morning, after a weekend break. I heard that Shaw testified first. That was a tricky move, because a good lawyer could rattle him during cross-examination. I was sure Cahill would tear him to pieces.

I was stuck at the station, not really working on anything and not knowing what was going on at the trial. Drew hadn't wanted to leave Casey alone, and I didn't blame him.

WEDNESDAY ENDED up being the day it all fell apart. I was at the station when Brunson hollered for me to come into his office.

"Get your ass to the courthouse, Flesh. You're being recalled to the stand—by Drake."

"What the fuck is this about?"

"How the hell should I know?"

I was shocked when I got to the courthouse and saw Austin leaving with his parents. I immediately knew what had happened.

Austin looked downtrodden. He saw me and mouthed the words "I'm sorry."

When I got to the courtroom, I was rushed to the stand.

"Remember, Detective Flesh, you are still under oath," Judge Barrett reminded me.

"Yes, Your Honor," I said.

"Detective Flesh." Drake stood and approached me. "You said a confidential informant gave you a tip regarding my client's habit of videotaping his sexual encounters."

"That's correct."

"And you also said that this informant was not connected to the case or to my client."

I nodded. "Yes."

"I don't see how you can claim that Austin Shaw, my client's nephew, is not connected to him."

"He's a stepnephew, actually," I said.

"He's related to my client through marriage," Drake responded.

"Which makes it that much worse that your client seduced the young man and broke his heart!" I exclaimed.

"There was nothing illegal about the relationship between my client and Austin Shaw."

"Maybe not illegal, but certainly immoral," I said.

"Regardless of morality, Austin Shaw is a scorned lover and has been very angry with my client. Was he not a suspect in the attack?"

"For a short time," I answered.

"Why did you employ Austin Shaw?"

"I didn't employ him. He volunteered to help us."

"And why did he think he could help the authorities?"

"He installed your client's computer system and knew how it worked."

"And did he also build a back door into the system?"

"I don't know about things like that," I said.

"I'm sure you do know, Detective Flesh," he sneered. "And I think you know that Austin Shaw used that back door to hack into my client's personal and private home computer system. And he did all this without a police warrant. Isn't that correct?"

"Well, yes," I admitted. "But that doesn't change the fact that we found videos of your client involved in illegal sexual relations with a minor."

Drake ignored me and spoke to the judge.

"Your Honor, I request that the video evidence be removed as it was obtained through illegal means."

"Wait," I said.

"I object, Your Honor," Cahill finally jumped in. "Regardless of how the evidence was obtained, it was still obtained."

"Objection overruled, Mr. Cahill. Mr. Drake, your motion is approved. The video evidence is stricken."

"Your Honor," Cahill said. "May we have a short recess so I can make a decision regarding this case?"

"Granted," the judge said. "Thirty minute recess."

I followed Cahill outside the courtroom and confronted him. "What the hell was that?"

"What are you talking about, Flesh?"

"This case is falling to shit, and you didn't do a thing to stop it."

"You knew we were treading on thin ice. I told you we'd be in trouble if the truth came out."

"How the hell did Drake find out?"

"I don't know, but the damage is done, and now I have a major decision to make."

"What decision?"

"Listen, if I move forward and Shaw is acquitted, then I can't charge him again. Right now I can dismiss the case, and when—if—more evidence is found, we can charge him again."

"You're going to let him go?" I asked, astonished.

"I think it's the best choice," he said. I knew his mind was made up.

I waited outside the courtroom when the trial restarted. Fifteen minutes later, Drake and Shaw came out with smiles, and I knew what had happened. Cahill appeared, gave me a pained look, and quickly glanced away.

I called Drew, Lex, and Colby and gave them the news. Drew had the unfortunate job of telling Casey, then calling his superiors.

"WHAT THE hell happened?" Lex asked me.

"They found out about Austin," I said. "I don't know how, but they did."

"It's more than just Austin," Brunson said as he came up behind us. "The whole thing sucked ass from the get-go." The trial had been recorded digitally, and he had been sent the recording on his computer. We went into Brunson's office and watched parts of it.

Had I been in court for the entire proceeding, it would've been during Shaw's testimony and cross-examination when I first would've had a clue something was wrong. Shaw admitted to sleeping with Casey on several occasions but swore Casey had told him he was eighteen. He even claimed to have seen a driver's license. He also said he did give Casey money, but it wasn't payment for sex. He claimed the money had been gifts.

I got ready for the fireworks when Cahill began his cross-examination.

"Mr. Shaw, how can you say you thought Casey Thompson was eighteen years old? One look at him and it is obvious he isn't."

"I admit he looked young, and that's why I asked to see his license," Shaw lied. "I just assumed he looked young."

"What about the video that shows you discussing his age?"

"We were role-playing."

"And what about where you and he discuss $100 for oral sex?"

"Same thing."

I was sure Cahill was going to continue the line of questioning, but he didn't. And that was my first clue that something was wrong.

"What can you tell me about the violent aspect of the sexual encounters?" Cahill asked.

"Casey liked it," Shaw said. "I didn't care for it myself, but he asked, begged me to do it to him."

"He asked to be hit and whipped?"

"Yes," Shaw answered.

Again, Cahill dropped the line of questioning and moved on to something else.

"You are also charged with obstruction of justice, Mr. Shaw. You claimed several items were stolen by Casey Thompson. However, we have proof that those items were not missing immediately after the attack."

"I don't know what happened between the time I was brutally attacked and the time I came home. For all I know, the police took those items. I just know what was missing when I returned."

"I object, Your Honor," Cahill said. "Mr. Shaw should not be insinuating that the police took anything from his house."

"Objection sustained," Judge Barrett ruled.

"My apologies," Shaw said. "I don't know who took the items. I had assumed Casey did."

"Thank you, Mr. Shaw. You're excused," Cahill said.

"That was pathetic," I said. "What the hell did Cahill do?"

"I don't know, Flesh," Brunson said. "But if you want to send Shaw away, you better get some goddamn excellent evidence—and get it through legal channels."

"WHAT DID your bosses say?" I asked Drew at the safe house.

"If we want to make a case, we have to do it fast, Cristian," Drew said. "I'm only authorized to stay for another month."

"A month? And what happens if we don't find anything in that time period?"

"I go back to Sacramento," he replied.

"And Casey?"

"He's on his own, I'm afraid."

"Fuck!"

"So we better work our asses off and find the evidence to get charges brought against Shaw again."

Chapter 10

EARLY THURSDAY morning I woke from a deep sleep to the sound of my cell phone ringing.

"Flesh," I answered groggily.

"Detective, this is Officer Simpson."

"What's up?"

"There's been a shooting—well, two, actually. One wounded, one DOA. The guy who got wounded, he's a friend of yours."

"Fuck," I said as I sat up, now wide awake. "Who is it?"

"The FBI agent—Bradley."

"Drew? Who's the DOA?"

"A young man," Simpson replied.

"Goddammit," I said. "I'll be there."

"Wait. Don't you need the address?"

"No," I said as I hung up.

"What's going on?" Colby asked.

"Drew's been shot, and Casey's dead," I said.

"Oh no, baby. I'm sorry," he said as he pulled on a pair of sweatpants.

"You don't have to come with me," I said.

"I want to."

I didn't argue with him, because I knew it was pointless and because I actually wanted him there.

Black and whites, with lights flashing, had surrounded the house. I had called Lex, and she arrived a few minutes after Colby and I did.

Drew was sitting in an ambulance and called me over.

"He wouldn't leave until you got here," the EMT said.

"He's dead, Cristian," Drew said as tears welled in his eyes. "I fucked up. It's my fault. I just went for a quick jog around the block. I wasn't paying attention and didn't even see the car until it was too late. It was one quick shot, and I was down."

"He was hit in the leg," the EMT said.

"The shooter must not have wanted to kill you," I said.

"But I couldn't get to Casey in time," Drew sobbed.

"Don't worry about it," I said. "We'll get the bastards who did this. Get him to the hospital," I told the EMT and watched the ambulance leave. It was necessary for me to enter the house, but I didn't want to.

Lex came over. "You don't have to go in there, Cris."

"Yeah, I do." I strode past her with Colby at my side.

Casey was in bed, and for a minute it looked just like he was sleeping. But as I stepped closer, I saw the blood and the hole in his head. He hadn't seen his killer—hadn't even been awake for it. Thank God for small favors. At least he didn't feel any pain.

I turned into Colby's arms, and he hugged me. I barely managed to hold back the tears.

"Come on, babe," Colby whispered. "Let's go home."

"No," I said. "I have to tell Gabe. He's gonna be so upset. I have to be there for him."

Colby and I drove home. I dropped him off and went to see Gabe. Violet was still half-asleep when she answered the door.

"Cristian," she murmured. "What's wrong?"

"I need to see Gabe," I said quietly.

"Shit," she said. "It ain't good news, is it?"

I shook my head.

"He's in bed."

"Go wake him and have him come here."

A minute later, Gabe came out wearing only a pair of boxer shorts.

"Flesh? What're you doing here so fuckin' early?"

"I got some bad news for you."

"What is it?"

"Sit down," I said.

"No, I ain't sitting down. Just tell me. Did something happen to Victor?"

"I'm sorry, kid. It's Casey."

"What happened?"

"There's no easy way to say this. Casey's dead."

"What the fuck are you talking about? He can't be dead. Bradley's protecting him."

"Drew was out for a jog, and they shot him. Then Casey was shot in the head. He was still asleep. He didn't feel a thing."

"Is that supposed to make me feel better? There wasn't any pain? Well, it fucking doesn't, you goddamn asshole."

"I'm sorry, Gabe." I reached out and gripped his arm, but he shook it off.

"I need to see him," he said.

I grabbed him and pulled him close.

"Let me go, you bastard."

He fought against me, but I didn't let him go. Finally he relaxed in my arms and buried his face in my shoulder.

I sat down on the couch and took Gabe with me. I could feel his tears on my shoulder. Violet was standing and watching us with a mixture of emotions on her face.

"It's not fair," Gabe murmured. "He was so young. His life was just beginning. Our lives together were just beginning. I think I loved him, Cristian. I think I loved him."

His statement was loud enough for Violet to hear, and now I could tell exactly what she was feeling—anger and the pain of a broken heart.

FRIDAY MORNING I visited Drew at Renown. He wasn't permanently injured from the bullet wound. His emotional health was far worse than his physical health.

"I really fucked up, Cristian," he said.

"Don't blame yourself, Drew. They would've gotten to him one way or another. I'm glad they didn't kill you too."

"Protecting him was my job. Maybe I could've stopped them before they got to him. Maybe he'd still be alive."

"You can play all sorts of scenarios out in your head, but what's done is done. We can only move on. We'll find the bastards who did this."

"You'll have to do it without my help," he said.

"They're sending another agent?" I said. "That's bullshit."

"They're not sending another agent," he said. "My boss said we're done. We don't have the finances to work a case where the only witness is dead."

"They're not going to try to find out who shot you?"

"They're cutting their losses," he said. "As soon as I'm released, I'm going back to Sacramento. But I'm going to keep working on the Eromenos angle, even if I have to on my free time."

"It's been an honor working with you," I said.

"Same here," he replied.

WE HELD a private ceremony for Casey on Saturday morning. Only a handful of people attended: me, Colby, Lex, Brunson, Gabe, Violet, and Jed, who had managed to sneak away from the ranch for the day.

Gabe and Jed spent the funeral holding each other, much to Violet's sadness. I wondered if she and Gabe could make it work. I certainly hoped so.

Toward the end of the ceremony, Drew showed up. Gabe saw him and pulled away from Jed.

"What the fuck are you doing here?" he demanded. "You don't have the right. It's your fault Casey's dead."

I grabbed Gabe and pulled him back. "Gabe, you can't blame Drew. He did his best."

"His best wasn't enough, not by a fucking long shot," Gabe screamed. "I don't want him here. Me and Jed both loved Casey the most, and we can choose who's here. And we don't want him here, do we, Jed?"

Jed shook his head. "No, we don't."

"I'm sorry," Drew murmured. "Very sorry."

"Get the fuck out of here," Gabe said. "I hope I never see your goddamn face again." Drew turned and left.

"Gabe," I said. "Drew was just paying his respects. He feels bad for what happened."

"He should feel bad," Gabe said. "He doesn't have the right to come and try to make himself feel better. I hope he rots in hell."

THE DAY after the funeral, Gabe visited me at my place.

"How you doing, kid?"

"Shitty," he said.

"It'll get better," I offered.

"I doubt it, but I'm not here to throw a pity party for myself. I wanted to tell you I'm gonna be gone for a week or more."

"Where you going?"

"Up into the mountains. Commune with nature or whatever."

"You and Jed?"

"No, he's still at the ranch. I've tried to get him to leave, but he swears it's better than nothing. I'm afraid he's going to end up like Casey."

"You guys gonna have a relationship?" I asked.

He shook his head. "I like Jed, but it was Casey I fell for."

"What about Violet?"

"I guess I love her," he said.

"You guess?"

"Well, I've always loved her, and I probably always will. But what I felt for Casey was so much more. It was passion and sex and friendship and desire. I thought about him all the time—I still do. I wanted to make him happy. I just don't feel those things for Violet, and I'm having trouble pretending I do."

"So what does this mean for the relationship?"

He shrugged. "We'll see when I get back. I'm just gonna go camp and figure things out as I go. I'll be back when I'm ready."

"Be careful, and make your way to a phone and call me every so often so I know you're still alive."

"You got it. Keep an eye on Violet and Victor, would ya?"

"Of course, kid." My nickname for him really didn't fit anymore. He didn't act or even look like the kid I had met such a short time ago.

We hugged good-bye, and I hoped he was going to be all right.

Chapter 11

I WORKED hard to find Casey's killer, though I was sure it was either Shaw or someone Shaw had hired. But there just wasn't much evidence to be found. The bullets came out of a nine-millimeter pistol and had odd marks on them, but that was all I could find. There were no unusual fingerprints at the scene, and no one in the neighborhood had seen the driver. Drew had memorized the license plate of the car the shooter was driving, but it was found in flames in downtown Reno. Whatever evidence the car may have contained was burned to ashes.

Brunson told Lex and me that we could work on the case when we weren't busy with other cases. But we were almost immediately involved in another case.

More than two weeks went by without my seeing Gabe and only talking to him once. He told me he was doing well but needed more time. He promised he was going to be okay.

Three weeks to the day that the case against Shaw fell apart, I had some free time, so I headed out to the Fresh Slate Ranch under the pretense of investigating Toby Sherman's murder. I wanted to see how Jed was doing, and I hadn't given up on exposing Slate's actions.

Slate was surprised to see me and led me to his office. I once again wondered about the lack of a computer there.

"I thought you already talked to my boys about this Toby kid," Slate said.

"I did," I replied. "But I'm hoping one of them may have remembered something that could lead me to his killer."

"I doubt that," Slate said, "but feel free to ask around."

I left the office and walked into the kitchen and was shocked at who I saw—Gabe.

"Gabe, what the hell are you doing here?"

He put his fingers to his lips to quiet me down and motioned for me to follow him outside. He had shaved his facial hair and cut his hair and was dressed more like the typical gangbanger.

"Slate thinks my name is Miguel Santos," he said when we were outside.

"Why the fuck does he think that?"

"Because that's what I told him," Gabe answered. "He also thinks I'm seventeen." With the changes in his looks, it was easy to see how Slate would believe him.

"What the hell are you doing?"

"I'm going to find proof that Shaw likes young men," he said. "I'm going to expose what Slate is doing to these boys, and I'm going to find out who killed Casey."

"This is dangerous, Gabe. You could end up getting yourself hurt."

"I can take care of myself," he said. "I have to do this—for Casey. Jed probably won't be here much longer because he's almost nineteen. He's helping me."

"Look, kid," I said softly. "I understand why you're doing this, but you have to be careful."

"Flesh, I said I can take care of myself."

"It's not just that," I responded. "We fucked up the first case because we got the evidence the wrong way. We have to do this right. You tell me what you find out, and I'll follow through."

"You got it," Gabe said. "Thanks, Cristian."

I pulled him into a hug.

"Tell Violet and Victor I love them and I'm okay."

"I will."

"HE'S WHAT?" Brunson roared. "Get him the fuck out of there." The chief wasn't very happy about Gabe being on the ranch.

"Listen, Chief," Lex said, "I agree it's a dangerous idea, but you know as well as I do that Gabe Vargas is a smart kid. He helped us with Cristian's problems last year."

"I'm just asking for him to be listed as an official confidential informant so any evidence he finds can be used in court."

Brunson was quiet for a minute. "It's your job to make sure he doesn't get his stupid ass killed," he said.

"Does that mean you're allowing it?" I asked.

Brunson shook his head. "This might be the worst idea ever, but yes, I'll have him listed as a CI. Now get out of here."

Lex and I left his office and sat at our desks.

"I guess we just have to wait for Gabe to find something," Lex said.

"I'm not good at being patient," I said.

"No way!" she mocked. "I didn't know that."

"Smartass."

THAT AFTERNOON I had two surprise visitors. The first was Austin Shaw.

"I wanted to apologize about what happened," he said.

"Austin, you got nothing to apologize for."

"I could've lied on the stand and denied everything," he said.

"No, you should not have done that. You told the truth. You did the right thing."

"Is Clayton going to be arrested again?"

"We're trying to find more evidence," I replied. "I haven't given up."

"I want to help," he said.

"I appreciate the offer, but you need to get over this and get on with your life. Forget the asshole ever existed."

"I wish I could," Austin said softly. "I don't want him to hurt anyone else."

"I'll call you if I need your help," I said as Austin stood. We were saying good-bye when I saw Rebel walking toward me.

"Detective," Rebel said, "I was hoping to see you." He noticed Austin and shot him a small smile. "Am I interrupting you?"

"No, it's fine," I said. "Rebel, this is Austin Shaw."

"Rebel? What kind of name is that?" Austin asked.

"A cool one," Rebel retorted. "Shaw? You related to that asshat who should be in jail? I read about all that in the paper."

"He's my stepfather's brother," Austin said. "And I agree with you—he should be in jail."

"Austin tried to help me with the case," I told Rebel.

Rebel gave Austin a look of respect—and attraction.

"Anything else on Toby's murder?" Rebel asked me.

"Who's Toby?" Austin asked.

"A friend of mine. I think your uncle killed him."

"He's not my uncle," Austin snapped. "Did Clayton kill him?" he asked me.

"I think the cases are connected," I answered.

"Maybe we should get together sometime and see what we can come up with." Rebel crossed his arms and eyeballed Austin.

He shrugged and glanced away. "Sure. Would you like to grab some lunch?"

Rebel smirked and winked at me. "Let's go."

They spoke and walked out without saying good-bye to me. I chuckled at the obvious attraction between the two and wished I had been able to be carefree when I was their age.

COLBY MADE lasagna for dinner, with burned garlic bread on the side. I pretended the burned bread didn't taste like charcoal.

"I had lunch with Kai Yung today," Colby said after swallowing down a bite of the lasagna. Yung was a deputy district attorney and an excellent lawyer. "I have a client who is charged with embezzlement. He admits he did it and wants to make a deal. Kai said he'd do what he could. He also told me some interesting things about Cahill."

"Like what?" I set down my glass of red wine.

"Kai said Cahill has been acting odd for the last few months."

"Odd? How?"

"Kai said it was hard to describe. He said Cahill has always been calm and easygoing, but lately he's been tense and snappy."

"He did seem different during the Shaw trial," I replied.

"Oh yeah. He mentioned that too. Kai was originally assigned that case. Cahill was dealing with two other large cases and had said anything that came up would be Kai's job. Kai was all set to run with the Shaw case when Cahill announced he was taking it after all."

"And that's unusual?" I asked.

"Very much so," Colby said.

Chapter 12

WHEN I got to work Monday morning, a cup of coffee was on my desk, and Lex sat at her computer.

"Good morning, Lex," I said.

"Morning, Cris."

"What are you doing?"

"Looking at the Slate Ranch financials."

"Those were dead ends," I replied.

"I know. I just have a hunch there's something I'm missing. I kept coming back to this Zoe H. Fusion person."

"Any idea how to follow the trail and find out who it is?"

"Nope, and our techies are too busy with other shit to bother them," she replied.

"I'll call Austin," I said. "He wants to help."

"You know anything he finds won't be admissible in court," she reminded me.

"Of course I know that," I said. "I just need the trail."

I called Austin and gave him the name. He was more than happy to be able to help.

Austin called me back less than three hours later.

"Next time give me a harder challenge." He chuckled.

"You got it already?" I asked, stunned.

"It was easy," he said. "The trail wasn't covered that much. There are no other bills. It's a shell for a larger business."

"Get to the point," I said.

"When I traced it back to the real owner, it made sense. Zoe H. Fusion is an anagram."

"What's an anagram?" I asked.

"Letters from several words scrambled to make other words. Zoe H. Fusion is an anagram for House of Zion. As in Anthony Zion."

Zion was a local businessman and the largest criminal in the area. He had dealings with just about every criminal activity near us. He dealt in drugs, gambling, prostitution, and more. We had tried several times to take him down but had never gotten close.

"Zion is giving money to the ranch?" I asked.

"Yes," Austin answered. "Why would he do that?"

"I don't know, but I'm going to find out."

A FEW hours later, my cell rang, but I didn't recognize the number.

"Flesh," I answered.

"It's Gabe," he said quietly. "I don't have long. I got two things to tell you."

"Go for it," I said.

"Slate was in his office today, and the door wasn't shut all the way. I peeked and saw him on a computer."

"I didn't see a computer when I was there," I said.

"I know. It's in a hidden compartment in the wall. I guess he doesn't want anyone to know where he keeps all the details of his business transactions. I'm gonna try to see if I can get to it."

"Be careful, kid," I warned.

"Yeah, I know. I followed Slate to town the other day. He met a guy at the Marina Park. I tried to hear what they were saying, but I couldn't hear much. I could tell they were talking about money so I think he's Slate's accountant."

"Did you catch a name?" I asked.

"No, but I took a picture with my cell phone. I'm gonna send it to you in a minute. I gotta go."

He hung up before I could say good-bye. A minute later a picture came through on my cell phone. I told Lex what Gabe had said as I hooked my phone to the computer, transferred the pic over, and enlarged it.

The accountant was short and fat with stringy dark hair and thin eyeglasses. I didn't recognize him but ran him through the database. I wasn't expecting a hit, but I was pleasantly surprised.

"His name is Loren D'Amico," I said. "He's only been in town for a couple years, and he is currently facing charges of embezzlement. He worked for a few local businesses and allegedly stole money from his clients." The case rang a bell in my head, and I looked up the name of his attorney. "Hell. His lawyer is Colby," I said.

"Is this going to be another conflict?" Lex asked.

"I don't think so," I answered. "We might be able to help each other out."

I called Kai and was in his office a few minutes later.

"Tell me about this embezzlement case against Loren D'Amico," I said.

He gave me an odd look but didn't question it. "He's admitted to embezzling about fifty grand from a few local businesses."

"Did he say why he did it?" I asked.

"Purely altruistic reasons, actually," Kai replied. "His boyfriend was sick and needed surgery to save his life. They didn't have health insurance, so Loren stole the money to pay for the surgery. The boyfriend made it. He's agreed to pay the money back, and I'm trying to convince the businesses to take it easy on him."

"I see."

"Why are you asking about him?"

"I've been trying to find proof that the boys at the Fresh Slate Ranch are being sold to men like Clayton Shaw. I have reason to believe that Loren has been handling the money for Slate. He could be an invaluable witness."

"You do know who Loren's lawyer is, don't you?"

I nodded. "You think Colby will go for some kind of deal?"

"I think so. Let me think about this, Detective. I'll get back to you."

"Thanks, Kai." I was about to leave when I thought of something else to ask. "Colby told me you said Cahill has been acting odd."

He eyed me for a minute. "Is this between you and me, Detective?"

"Of course." I nodded.

"In the last six months, Richard has changed dramatically. He's always tense and jumpy. He's lost weight, and he's not on his game. He's been losing cases he shouldn't be losing."

"Like the Shaw case?"

"Exactly."

I left Kai's office and stepped into Cahill's. I didn't have a solid plan but decided to do a little fishing.

I had to cough to get Cahill's attention. He looked up at me but didn't say a word.

"You have a minute?" I asked.

"That's about all I have, Flesh. One minute."

"I just wanted you to know I haven't given up on the Shaw case."

He stared at me with an unreadable look. "I think it's a waste of time, but you do what you want."

"I just want to be sure that you'll prosecute if I find enough evidence."

"The case had better be damn strong," he said curtly. "And none of this shit with using illegally obtained evidence."

"Oh, I'm doing everything by the book." A ringing noise came from Cahill's pocket. He reached in and pulled out an iPhone. I recognized it as one of the phones Cahill had purchased for himself and all the deputy DAs. There had been a little stink about the use of public funds for the phones, but Cahill had insisted it was needed.

He spoke on the phone for a minute. "I'm sorry, Detective. I need to go."

"Where you going?" I asked.

He gave me a dirty look. "Business meeting," he said, and I could tell he was lying. "Good-bye, Detective." He basically pushed me out of the way.

My instincts told me I should follow Cahill, so I did, discreetly. I almost lost him when I had to get in my car, but I found him after a few minutes. He drove into downtown Reno and to the Peppermill Casino. I had to wonder what kind of business meeting would take place there.

The Peppermill wasn't my favorite casino in town. Inside the lights were bright and pink and purple, and they hurt my eyes. Cahill walked through the casino to the poker room. He handed over the buy-in money, bought what looked like a few thousand in chips, and started playing. I watched from the back so he couldn't see me. Either it wasn't Cahill's lucky day or he just sucked at the game, because during the hour I watched he didn't win a hand, and his large starting stack was totally depleted.

I guessed Cahill's stressed-out attitude was due to a gambling habit he had no control over. I quietly left, unsure what I was going to do with the information.

COLBY WAS sitting at my desk and talking to Lex when I returned to the station.

"Hey, big guy," I said.

"I hear you were discussing my client with Kai," Colby said. I couldn't tell what he thought about it.

"Yeah. That's not a problem, is it?"

"Of course not." Colby broke out in a big smile. "I don't think Loren is a bad guy at all. He just made a few mistakes. A deal would help him out immensely. I appreciate what you did."

He smiled at me, and I returned the smile.

"Glad I could help," I replied.

He stood up and whispered in my ear, "I'll thank you properly tonight, baby."

I blushed and grinned from ear to ear. Lex grinned as Colby walked away.

"Why are you looking at me like that?" I asked her.

"I love seeing you happy, Cris. I wasn't sure it would ever happen."

WHEN I went to Colby's place that night, I was expecting a romantic dinner with candles and music, but instead there were Chinese takeout containers on the kitchen counter. Colby exited the bedroom wearing nothing but a pair of silk boxers.

"Damn, you're hot," I said. He smiled. "I was expecting a fancy dinner because of what I did for your client today."

"Oh, you're going to get something special for that, but it's not dinner. It comes after dinner."

"Then let's forget about dinner and get right to the treat." I grabbed him and pulled him close, putting my lips to his. My tongue parted his lips and licked the roof of his mouth. He pushed me away and kept me at arm's length.

"No," he said. "Dinner first. You're going to need your strength."

We sat at the kitchen table and ate the Chinese food. I couldn't keep my eyes off Colby's amazingly massive chest. I wanted to reach out and touch his pink and pert nipples. I wanted to bury my face in his chest and cover his torso with my tongue.

"Fuck, Colby," I said. "I can't concentrate on eating when you're sitting there half-naked. All I can think about is you and your incredible body."

He smiled at me as he stood and gathered our plates. "Go shower," he said.

"You going to join me?" I asked.

"I already showered. Make it fast, but make sure you shave. Everywhere."

I tried to argue, but he wouldn't listen. He just waved me toward the bathroom. I washed up and shaved my face, my crotch, and my ass. Colby loved my smooth skin down there.

I came out of the bathroom wearing only a towel, and Colby led me to the bed. He removed the towel and let it drop to the floor. Cupping my face in his hands, he kissed me tenderly. After running his large hands down my sides, he reached around, caressed my ass, and felt between my cheeks. "So smooth," he said and grinned.

"Just the way you like it, babe."

"I love you, Cristian Flesh," he whispered in my ear, then went lower and sucked on my lobe. I shivered as goose bumps covered my body.

"The feeling is definitely mutual, Colby Maddox." I reached into his boxers and circled my fingers around his erect shaft. I stroked it a few times, and he groaned. He grabbed my hand and removed it from his shorts.

"Not yet," he said.

He spun me around and pushed me down on the bed. I crawled forward a bit so my feet weren't hanging off the edge. A second later, Colby's large body was on top of me—minus the boxers. I loved the feel of his bare skin on mine, and I especially loved his dick nestled between my cheeks. He kissed the top of my head and licked down. His lips went all over the back my neck, and he stopped occasionally to bite and suck in areas that wouldn't be seen if he left marks. I loved it when he marked me, because I was his. I belonged to him, but not like I had belonged to Vincent. This was a mutual thing, and he belonged to me just as much.

He kissed down my spine and stopped just above my ass. He sat up, which pushed his groin hard against my ass. His hands traveled up and down my back—soft and gentle rubbing—and progressed to a harder massage. It hurt and felt good at the same time, the way he kneaded my muscles and the way he knew my body like he knew his own.

His sensuous and loving massage lasted for ten minutes. Ten long minutes in which I alternated between telling him to never stop and begging him to stop and make love to me. Finally his hands moved down to my asscheeks, and he rubbed them for a moment before he pulled them open.

I felt my lover shift backward and lean down. With my cheeks still spread, he blew a soft breath against my hole. The cold air made me shiver, and he did it again. I buried my face in a pillow and moaned softly. He kissed all around my hole. "So soft," he murmured before he placed his lips to my rim. His mouth stayed there, and I waited for what I knew was coming next—what I wanted so much to come next. And finally it did.

It was just a quick, soft thrust at first. His tongue hit my hole and quickly retreated back into his mouth. My body tensed up, waiting for it to happen again, and just as I relaxed, he did it. His tongue jabbed at my hole repeatedly, and my cock leaked precome onto the bedspread beneath me.

Colby pulled his face out of my cheeks, and I missed the intimate contact, but it was back before I had a chance to finish the thought. This time his tongue started at my taint and traveled all the way up, then back down. When he came back up, his tongue stayed on my hole, and he softly swirled it around. I lifted my hips and pushed backward, desperately begging for more. Pressing his face even harder against my cheeks, Colby's tongue did its best to push past my rim. He licked me and kissed and tongued my hole until I was moaning and groaning and practically crying.

He sat up and lay down on me again. His length once more pressed between my cheeks, and I swore—though I knew it wasn't possible—that it was bigger than it ever had been before. His entire body pushed against me, and he bit my neck.

"Colby," I murmured, barely able to say the name.

"Yes, my love," he whispered in my ear. "Tell me what you want."

"I want—" I gasped as he chewed on my neck again. "I want you… to make love to me."

"Is that what you want?"

"Yesss," I moaned as he sucked on my earlobe. "Please."

Colby reached over for the lube he had ready for us. I heard him flip open the lid, and I felt his fingers coat my ass with the liquid. One finger, then two, slipped inside me and stretched me. His fingers retreated, and I felt his large head poised outside my hole.

He lay down on me, and I could feel his hot breath on my neck. He pushed in as I lifted my hips. I gasped when the ring eased and let him in. He stayed still and allowed me to adjust. When I finally relaxed, he slid in. Slowly, inch by inch, Colby impaled me with his length. He rubbed against my prostate, and my body tingled all over. He buried himself to the root, then slowly took his cock almost all the way out. He stayed there with just the head in me for a maddeningly long time before once more sliding into me.

My body was experiencing every possible sensation. Even if I had wanted to, I wouldn't have been able to isolate any single feeling for any single body part.

"I love you," I moaned. "Forever. I'll love you forever."

"Always, my love." With a quick thrust, he pushed into me, and then he did it again. "Always," he repeated. With each push, with each plunge deep into me, he repeated the word. "Always."

The orgasm tore through me quickly, and I shot onto the bedspread. I cried out as I came. I don't know what I said, because I couldn't even hear myself. But I know my orgasm brought Colby to his own. He pushed as deep as possible, and I felt him spray inside me. He collapsed on top of me and kissed my neck again and again, and sleep quickly overtook us.

I woke about thirty minutes later and rolled onto my back. Colby was already awake, and watching me.

"Hey," I said.

"Hey back," he replied.

I stood up.

"Where you going?" he asked.

"To wash up."

"Don't do that," he said.

"Baby, I got your come in me."

"I know. Don't clean up. I want to fuck you again."

He was lying on his side, and I lay in front of him, his chest to my back, and snuggled close. I could feel his erection pressed against my hole. He lifted my leg and began to press his dick into me. I smiled and pushed back. I knew we were in agreement that this time was going to be vastly different than what we had already done that night. This was going to be rough and quick. I was still stretched out from before and didn't need—or want—any preparation. I pushed back abruptly and took all of him in one quick move. We both gasped—me at the mix of hurt and pleasure and him at the sudden warmth surrounding his length.

He grabbed my hips and slid in and out. I took hold of my own erection and stroked in rhythm with him fucking me. I was close to shooting and could tell Colby was too, though I was sure he was holding back for me.

“Let it go.”

He grasped my hips so hard I knew there were going to be bruises and slammed into me again and again. The sound of skin slapping skin was so loud I couldn’t hear anything else, not even the grunts and groans I knew were coming out of my mouth.

Colby suddenly stopped moving, and I knew he was coming inside me once again—filling me until it spilled out. When he stopped moving, I took hold of my shaft and stroked it just twice before I shot my seed into my hand.

I didn’t move until I felt Colby soften and slide out of me. “Can I go clean up now?” I asked as I wiped the sweat off my brow with my forearm.

“Sure,” he said. “But I’m joining you.” Rule number four was out the window for good as far as I was concerned.

Chapter 13

IT FELT like I had just gotten to sleep when the ringing of my cell phone woke me up. The alarm clock said 3:00 a.m. Just three hours since Colby and I'd had sex for the third time that night. I was exhausted and very happy.

"Flesh," I answered without looking at the caller ID.

"It's Gabe," he said.

"What's up, kid? Is something wrong?"

"No, but I need to tell you something. I was having trouble sleeping, so I was walking around, and I saw the light on in Slate's office. I heard him talking to someone, and when I looked, he was on the phone."

"So what?"

"I didn't understand the conversation, but it seemed like Slate was getting his ass chewed. If I didn't know better, I would guess Slate was talking to his boss."

"There's a chance Anthony Zion is in charge."

"Well, I didn't think Slate was smart enough to do all this on his own."

"I'll get the phone records as soon as I get to work," I said. "Now get to bed so Slate doesn't see you." We hung up, and I snuggled against Colby. I wasn't sure I'd be able to get back to sleep. That was my last thought before I was out again.

WE BOTH dragged ourselves out of bed when the alarm went off and ate a quiet breakfast together. I wasn't sure about Colby, but I wasn't quiet because I had nothing to say. I was quiet because I had so much to say I didn't know where to begin.

I spoke at the same time Colby did, and we laughed. "You first," he said.

"Last night was…." I searched for the right word.

"Mind-blowing."

I nodded in agreement. "I meant it when I said I wanted to be with you always."

"I know you did, bello. I meant it too."

What else needed to be said?

AT THE station I told first Lex, then Brunson about what Gabe had told me.

"My guess is the boss is probably Anthony Zion," I said. "We just need to prove it."

"Go get your warrant for the phone records and let me know what you find."

Following my instincts again, I decided not to go to Cahill for the warrant. I went to Kai instead and asked if we could keep it from Cahill. He agreed without asking why, which was good, because I couldn't have explained my reasoning.

An hour later we had gotten the call records from the phone company. I looked at the phone number for the call made from the ranch just before 3:00 a.m.

"Calls to and from this number go back for months," I said.

"I'll see if we can come up with a name for the number," Lex said. It came back as a disposable cell phone, with no way to trace it.

"Dammit," I said. "One dead end after another."

"Not a dead end," Lex corrected. "We just haven't connected everything yet."

AN HOUR or so later, Colby and Loren D'Amico sat at a table opposite Kai and me in the DA's conference room.

"Look, D'Amico," I said. "I know you've been doing the financial records for the Fresh Slate Ranch."

"I don't know what you're talking about." He clasped his hands together and refused to meet my gaze.

"Mr. D'Amico," Kai said softly. "We believe you have information that could help us in another case. If you work with us, I can make sure you do no jail time for the embezzlement charges."

"You can arrange that?" D'Amico asked.

"Yes, I can," Kai answered.

"It's a good deal," Colby said.

"If I talk, I could end up dead," D'Amico said.

"We can protect you and your boyfriend from Anthony Zion," I said.

"Zion?" D'Amico asked. "What does he have to do with this?"

I was shocked. "Isn't he the real power behind the ranch?"

D'Amico laughed. "You are so looking in the wrong direction. I'm not talking until I have a solid deal. I'll pay back the money I owe, but I don't want any jail time. I want protection for me and my boyfriend, and I want a guarantee on who will and won't learn this information. I don't trust very many people around here."

"We'll get working on that right away," Kai said.

I LEFT the conference room and immediately noticed that Cahill wasn't in his office. As I headed to my car, I called Lex and told her that it looked like Zion wasn't the boss after all.

I drove to the Peppermill and went to the poker room. I wasn't surprised to see Cahill there—losing. I watched him for a while, not knowing what I was expecting to find out. I was about to leave when I saw Cahill pull out a cell phone. It wasn't the iPhone I had seen before. I maneuvered as close as I could without him seeing me. The phone was a far cheaper model than the iPhone, and I wondered if it was a personal one. I stepped out of the room and returned to the station.

Kai called me a minute later. "I just wanted to let you know we're working out the deal with D'Amico right now. I'm sure he's going to sing before too long."

"Thanks for letting me know, Kai. Hey, I have a question for you."

"Shoot."

"Does Cahill have a different cell phone for personal calls?"

"No, we're allowed to use the iPhone for personal calls too. The county takes out a portion from our checks to pay for the bill. Why?"

"Uh, I'll explain later." I hung up. Things were falling into place for me, but I wasn't sure where the evidence was pointing.

I SPENT several hours trying—and failing—to put things together. If Zion wasn't the boss, then who was? Did Cahill's strange behavior connect to anything?

I snapped out of my thoughts when I heard Brunson yelling, "Flesh, Luther!"

"Yes, sir," she and I said in unison as we stood up.

"There's a situation at Clayton Shaw's house. Get your asses there now!"

Without another word we took off and sped to Shaw's house. Two black and whites were outside the residence with lights flashing. I recognized one of the uniformed officers—Simpson.

"What's going on, Simpson?" I asked. "Shaw been attacked again?"

"Actually, no," he replied. "Shaw's the suspect this time. The victim is a young kid. They're in the kitchen."

Lex and I stepped in and walked back to the kitchen. Shaw was wearing a silk bathrobe and sitting in a kitchen chair with his hands cuffed behind his back. A young man sitting with his head in his hands appeared to be naked underneath a policeman's jacket. He peered at me, and I realized I knew him—Rebel.

"What the hell happened here?" I demanded.

An officer named Arvin spoke. "We had an anonymous 911 call concerning screams coming from this residence. We were nearby and responded quickly. We heard someone crying for help, so we busted the doors in. The young man here," he said, gesturing toward Rebel, "was crying. He has marks around his neck and other bruises. Mr. Shaw was unconscious on the floor."

"Has either one told you what happened?"

"Mr. Shaw hasn't said a word," Arvin said. "The victim claims Shaw was choking him. He fought back and knocked Shaw out with a glass."

"Is the victim okay?" I asked.

Arvin nodded. "He's terrified, but he doesn't seem too hurt. We haven't touched anything yet, Detective, but he said Shaw mentioned a secret camera hidden in the clock." Arvin pointed to a clock on the wall. It was one of those kitschy ones shaped like a black and white cat with a bow tie. The tail moved back and forth with the time, as did the eyes. It was totally out of place in a house full of expensive pieces of furniture.

"He said he was going to kill me," Rebel murmured. "He said he had done it before and enjoyed it."

"Don't touch a thing," I ordered. "I'm going to call and get a warrant for everything in this house. Arrest Shaw for attempted murder and get him the hell out of here. I'll take the victim to the station in a bit."

"This case won't be any more successful than the last one," Shaw remarked. He tried to exude the same confidence he had shown during the prior arrest, but he wasn't successful. He had to know he was in trouble.

Arvin forced Shaw to his feet and read him his rights as he and his partner escorted him outside. I sat down beside Rebel. “How are you doing?”

“I’m okay,” he answered.

“I hope this charge sticks,” I said.

“It will,” he said with a slight smile.

“I don’t want to hear anything else until Shaw is put away. You realize you’ll have to testify and give us your real name.”

“I can do that,” he said. “I’ll do it for Toby.”

DRAKE, SHAW’S attorney, was at the station when I got there with Rebel.

“This is harassment,” he yelled at me. “You set this up, I’m sure of it. I’ll have you thrown off the force for this, Flesh.”

“I don’t think so, Drake. This time it’s going to stick. Your client’s going down.”

He scowled and stormed off.

Cahill was right behind Drake. “What the hell is this, Flesh? If this is another of your tricks, it won’t work.”

“I had nothing to do with this. Lex and I were ordered to respond to a call from Shaw’s house. Other officers were there before we got there.”

“This better be the real thing,” Cahill barked.

“I need a warrant for Shaw’s house,” I said.

“I’m not going to bother a judge at this time of the night.”

“Night? It’s barely 4:00 p.m.”

“That’s right, and all the judges are getting ready to go home for the night. It can wait until the morning.”

“What the fuck?”

“Forget it, Flesh,” he said as he stalked off.

I immediately called Kai. "Look, I hate to do this to you, but there isn't any other way. I need you to do an end run around Cahill. I need a warrant for Shaw's place, and I need it now."

"What did Cahill say?"

"He said he wasn't going to bother any judge tonight, and it could wait until the morning."

"What the hell is he thinking?"

"Will you do it?"

"Consider it done. I'll call you back in twenty minutes."

Twenty minutes later—on the dot—Kai called me. "You got your warrant. It covers everything, including the computers and any hidden cameras. Get your techie out there immediately and get the information the right way."

Lex and I returned to the Shaw house with the technician and several other uniformed officers. The techie quickly got into the computer system and found the link-ups to all the cameras around the house. He opened up the latest file, which showed Shaw and Rebel engaged in sexual acts that quickly turned into acts of violence. I could see their mouths moving, but their voices weren't loud enough to make out what they were saying. At one point, Shaw grabbed a scarf, wrapped it around Rebel's neck, and attempted to choke him. Rebel fought back, grabbed a large glass mug, and knocked Shaw out.

"We fucking got the bastard now," I said.

WE HAULED a shitload of evidence back to the station, including the scarf.

Cahill was pacing around the station, waiting for me to get there.

"How the hell did you get all this without a warrant?" he demanded.

"I did get one. You wouldn't help, so I went to Kai."

"He went behind my back! I'm going to fire his ass."

"Do it—if you can."

Cahill sputtered a few words and stormed outside. I quietly followed him and watched as he pulled out the cheap phone and dialed a number. Whoever he was calling must not have answered, because he hung up quickly. I pulled out my cell and a slip of paper with a phone number on it, the phone number for the disposable cell phone that had been making calls to, and receiving calls from, the Slate Ranch. I dialed the number and saw the disposable phone light up in Cahill's hand. I heard him say "Hello" and watched him do it at the same time. I quickly ended the call and walked back inside. I doubted he knew my number by heart, because it was programmed into the *official* phone, and he wouldn't have done so with the secret phone.

I had to make a decision, and fast. I had to tell someone. I had a suspicion things were going to happen quickly. I looked at my watch—6:00 p.m. I didn't see Lex anywhere, so I called Colby.

"What's up, babe?"

"Has D'Amico talked yet?"

"Not yet. We were going to sign the deal tomorrow."

"It can't wait that long. I need him to do it tonight. Can you get him here right away?"

"What's going on?"

"Trust me, Colby. Just get him here."

"Okay," he said and hung up.

I called Kai next. "I need to see you right now." He and I met in an interrogation room, and I told him my new suspicion—that Cahill was the boss behind the ranch.

"Why would he get involved in something like that?"

"I don't know. Possibly gambling debts. We need D'Amico to name Cahill and tell us about the ranch's financial records. That should give us enough to get a warrant for the ranch."

"I'll have my investigator pay a visit to the local bookies, see what they can dig up."

Colby showed up with D'Amico, and I led them to the room with Kai.

"Look, we don't have much time," I said.

"I'm not talking without a solid deal," D'Amico said.

I slammed my fist on the table. "We don't have time for that. Believe me when I say we have much bigger fish to fry. I'm not here to fuck you over, but we need to know what you know. You have my word. Ask your lawyer if you can trust me. He'll tell you the truth."

Colby glanced at his client. "You can trust him, Loren. I'd put my life on it."

D'Amico looked from Colby to me and nodded. "Okay, I'll talk."

"Is Cahill behind the ranch selling young men as hustlers?"

Colby's jaw dropped, and D'Amico raised an eyebrow.

"I have to say I'm surprised you figured it out."

"Holy shit!" Kai exclaimed.

D'Amico spilled his guts about the many financial transactions between Cahill, the ranch, and its patrons, including Shaw, Graham, and several others who surprised even me. D'Amico even had proof of Cahill's gambling debts.

Lex went to find Cahill and arrest him while I headed to the ranch with a large team and the warrant I needed to find the computer. We were five minutes from the ranch when Lex called me on my cell.

"Yeah," I answered.

"Cahill's arrested," she said. "But he made a phone call before I could stop him. It could've been to the ranch."

"Fuck, Slate might've been warned." I hung up and drove even faster. When I arrived, I ran toward the house hoping my order that no one other than Slate was to be arrested was obeyed.

"This is the Reno Police Department," a uniformed officer called out over the megaphone. "We are looking for Harlan Slate. No one else needs to be afraid. Just come out with your hands up, and there will be no arrests."

The young men poured out of the house, and I had to push my way through to get to the front door. I saw Jed and grabbed him.

"Where's Gabe?" I yelled.

"I don't know. He wasn't in bed when I woke up. What's going on?"

"I can't explain now, but the case finally came together." I finished pushing my way to the door and ran in.

"Gabe!" I called out. "Gabe, where are you?"

"The office, Flesh!" I recognized Gabe's voice. "The office. Hurry!" I ran to the room and saw Gabe and Slate struggling on the floor. I pulled my gun and aimed it at Slate.

"Freeze, Slate, or I will shoot your goddamn head off!"

Slate stopped moving, and Gabe crawled out from under him. I pulled out my cuffs and threw them at Gabe.

"Christ, Flesh, now's not the right time for some kinky play."

"Secure him, smartass," I said.

"Book 'em, Danno." Gabe laughed as he put the restraints on Slate. I holstered my gun, pulled Slate to his feet, and read him his rights.

"He was going to erase the hard drive," Gabe said. "I had to do whatever it took to stop him."

"You did good, kid."

"Is it over, Cristian?"

"There's a few more pieces to the puzzle," I said. "But we're going to find them. So, yeah, it's over."

There were a total of four arrests that night: Cahill, Slate, Shaw, and Graham. I stayed until all four had been processed and were in their cells. When I left the station, I was still pumped up and full of adrenaline.

Colby was sitting on the couch, wearing jeans and a button-up shirt when I got home. I didn't say a word as I moved toward him, unzipping my pants and pulling out my cock. I was hoping this was one of those times where Colby could read my moods, because I didn't feel like explaining what I wanted to do—or asking if he wanted the same thing. I knew if he didn't want it, he would tell me so, but goddamn, I was hoping we were on the same page.

He smiled when he saw me approach him with my hard dick in my hand. I stood on the couch, straddled him, and put my shaft to his lips. He opened wide, and I slid it in. The feel of his hot, slick tongue was incredible.

"Oh fuck," I moaned as I slid the rest of my cock down his throat. I grabbed a handful of hair and held him there until he gagged. Colby and I had done our fair share of rough play with each other—always with complete trust and understanding. But usually it was Colby as the aggressor. I had turned the tables on him and was going to dominate him. It felt so good to finally be letting go of so many things from my past.

With my hands on either side of his head, I slid my cock out of his mouth, then made him swallow it again. His hands were on my hips, but I was the one in control. I fucked his mouth, sometimes ramming it down his gullet, while other times it was leisurely movements in and out, letting myself revel in the feel of his tongue and lips.

The pressure in my balls was a slow build despite the rapid movements. When I knew the wave was going to crash, I grabbed his hair and fucked his mouth hard again. With one rough, final shove, I pushed my length down his throat and sprayed my seed. It felt like I was shooting forever, and Colby did his best to swallow it all.

I pulled out, and he looked up at me with a lascivious smile. Dollops of my come were on his cheek. I knelt down so we were face-to-face and licked off my seed. Colby grabbed my head and slammed my lips to his. His tongue thrust into my mouth and pushed against my tongue. I reached down, grabbed his shirt, and tore it open, causing buttons to fly everywhere.

I sucked his tongue into my mouth and felt him groan. I pulled at his hair lightly and bit his bottom lip.

"Holy shit, Cristian," he moaned.

I didn't want to talk, to explain what I was feeling or why I was feeling it. I just wanted to fuck. I silenced him by pushing my tongue into his mouth. I pulled back and looked into his eyes, hoping he saw the raw lust and desire and didn't question it.

I pulled his hair enough so he bent his head to the side and bared his neck to me. Leaning down, I sucked on his skin. I wanted to mark him all over his body, but I settled for parts where only I would see. I bit and sucked at several spots on his neck, and he let me. His hands wandered over my back and to my head. I knew what he was thinking because he said it often—*I wish you had hair*. I understood at that moment, because I loved tugging at his hair and the way it made him moan. He wanted to do the same thing to me.

I licked my way to his nipples, and when I found that soft mound of skin, I bit down for a second. My hand went to the neglected nipple and pinched it while I sucked and bit at the other one. I kissed my way to his belly button and rubbed the tent in his pants. I tore his pants open and sucked his dick to the root in one quick move.

"Oh fuck," Colby moaned as he arched his hips up. I pushed his hips back down so I could control how much of his shaft I sucked in. I licked around the ridge of the crown, then the tip—tasting his sweet precome. My tongue went up and down his shaft, and I took all of him again. He tried to arch up into my mouth, but I held him still so he couldn't.

I grabbed his pants and underwear and pulled them down with his assistance. I took them off, spread his legs, and put my face in his crotch, licking the musky skin between his dick and leg. After tonguing both sides of his upper thighs, I went lower and gently licked his tight ball sac. I took each of his balls into my mouth, one at a time, then both together. When I released them from my mouth, I traveled down, craning my neck so I could get where I wanted. I licked that awesome sweet spot between his balls and his asshole. For such a small piece of skin, it was incredibly erotic for both the giver and receiver. I sucked and bit the taint, driving myself as crazy as Colby.

I pulled Colby down so his hips came off the couch and I had easier access. I spread his cheeks and looked at his beautiful hole. I licked it gently, then with more and more passion, covering the area with my saliva. He moaned as I pressed a finger against the ring; his rim relaxed, and the digit slid in. The muscle contracted slightly as I prodded him with one finger for a few minutes before adding a second. I kissed my way up his inner thigh to his balls and dick as I nudged his prostate.

Gripping his shaft with my free hand, I gently stroked it before taking the head in my mouth. Two fingers glided out, and three went back in, slamming into him as I sucked down his entire length.

"Oh fuck, oh fuck, oh hell, goddamn," Colby muttered as I assaulted his ass and his cock at the same time. I knew he was going to come when his babbling got more unintelligible. I increased the speed of my mouth and my fingers, and he arched up. His ass squeezed my fingers, and he filled my throat with his seed. When I was sure he was done, I let him slip past my lips.

"Holy shit, bello," he moaned.

But I wasn't done yet.

I grabbed Colby's shoulders and pulled him down to the floor on top of me. I was rock hard again, and even though Colby wasn't, I still loved the feel of our cocks rubbing together. I kissed him passionately, thrusting my tongue against his. I bit his neck and nipples and other parts of his chest and stomach. There were going to be marks all over his body.

Before I knew it—before I expected it—Colby was erect again. He gyrated against me, our precome mixing to create needed lubrication.

"Fuck, Cristian," he whispered in my ear. "Fuck, no one's ever made me feel like you do. I've never been this turned on by anyone."

"Same here." I beamed, the joy spread through my entire body.

"I can't believe I'm hard again," he said.

Tugging on his cock, I said, "I'm glad you are."

"You want me to fuck you, baby?" he asked. "Is that what you want?"

"That's what I need."

"I'll get the Astroglide," he said.

"No," I said. "No lube."

"Are you sure? That's going to hurt."

"I'm positive." Dry fucking when done wrong can cause damage, but when it's done right, it can be amazingly awesome.

Colby slid down my body until he rested between my legs. He lifted my hips, allowing him access to my ass, then licked my hole, covering the area with his tongue. It was incredible, but I didn't want to wait any longer.

"Fuck me," I growled. "Now."

Colby set my hips back on the floor, took his prick in his hand, and pushed into me. I forced myself to relax, and the head popped in.

"Oh fuck! Don't move." The pain was intense, but the pleasure was stronger—a thousand times stronger. The pain only added to the enjoyment. I moved my hips so I could take more of my lover into me. I grabbed his neck and nodded for him to give me more.

With each added inch came even more pleasure. Damn, it felt good.

"Fuck me, big guy. Fuck me hard, but do not come until I tell you."

He nodded but didn't speed up.

"Pound me, goddammit," I ordered. He slammed into me so forcefully it took my breath away. "Yeah, that's it." He began a rapid fucking that made me gasp each time he reamed me. He was fucking me so hard, I thought I could feel his cock in my chest—and I loved it.

"You feel so good," Colby murmured. "So hot, so tight. So fucking tight."

"Pick me up," I said. "I want to ride you, but keep your dick in me."

He reached down, cupped my ass, and lifted me as he sat up. He got his legs out from under himself so they were straight out. My hands were on his neck, and I was trying to keep my ass pressed on him so I didn't lose the absolutely amazing feeling of his cock in me.

He leaned back, and there I was, riding him. That position—me on top—used to be one I didn't do. *Rule number five.* It was one of those bad memories of my past, though I hadn't told Colby who it was who'd forced me to get fucked in that position and hit me as I did. We didn't fuck in that position very often, but at that moment it was exactly what I wanted.

Between the force of me sitting and the power of his thrusting, it felt like his shaft was twice as long as it was. The pressure on my prostate was unbelievable, and I wanted to come so badly, it hurt to hold it back. I had to stop touching myself to make sure it didn't happen, and even then it felt like I could shoot at any second.

"Tell me when you're gonna come." I sat down on him hard. It seemed as if his entire body was in me.

"I'm so close, baby," he moaned. I sat forward a bit, reached behind me, and grabbed his cock at the base so he couldn't come.

"You fucking tease," he muttered.

“Yeah, and you love it.” I chuckled.

“Yeah, I do. I love you… so fucking much.”

“I love you too.”

I rode him for a while longer before I couldn’t hold back anymore. I grabbed my prick and stroked it. Come shot out, hitting Colby in the face, the shoulder, and the chest.

“Oh fuck yeah,” he moaned as he buried himself in me. I could feel his hot seed shooting into me.

When the adrenaline from the day left me, it wasn’t a slow halt. It was a sudden stop. My body felt heavy, and I couldn’t keep my eyes open. I rolled off Colby and fell asleep.

At some point I felt Colby carry me into the bedroom and lay me in our bed. I was deep asleep again as soon as I felt Colby curl up against me.

Chapter 14

I WENT into work Wednesday morning knowing I had a thousand things to do, but I was damned if I knew what to do first. I was hoping someone would be able to tell me, because I was still physically and emotionally weary from the previous day and night.

When I got there, Lex was at her desk and a Starbucks coffee sat on mine.

"Morning, Cris," she said, smiling.

"Hey," I replied. "I'm fucking exhausted."

"Well, get over it. We have a hell of a lot of shit to handle today."

"Agreed. I just don't know—"

"Let me guess," she interrupted. "You have no idea where to start. Don't worry, I've got it all organized. Just listen to me and don't be going off on your own. We have to be careful and make sure everything is done just right."

"Got it, boss," I replied.

"Don't be a smartass, Cris."

"But I'm so good at it." I laughed.

"Rebel is in the interrogation room," she said. "You need to get his statement. I'll handle Cahill."

"Yes, sir." I stood, saluted her, and marched to the interrogation room. I had taken Rebel's official statement about the incident the previous night. This interview was to learn more about Rebel and get any other necessary information.

Rebel was wearing new clothes and looked much cleaner than he had the previous times I'd seen him. I sat across from him at a small metal table.

"How you doing?" I asked.

He shrugged. "Not bad."

"This shouldn't take long. I just have a few basic questions."

"Go for it."

"What's your full name?" I asked.

"Buford Harrison Moskoff," he replied.

Damn, poor kid.

"My mom named me without my dad's permission. He gave me my nickname. His favorite movie was *Rebel Without a Cause*."

"How old are you, Mr. Moskoff?"

"Nineteen." He shifted and crossed his legs.

"Have you ever been arrested?"

"Yeah, a couple times."

"What were the charges?"

"Prostitution."

"How old were you the first time?"

"Sixteen. They put me in a youth home, but I ran away. The next time I was arrested I was seventeen, and I did some jail time."

"Do you have any family?"

"My mom died when I was just a few years old. My dad took off when I was seven, and I been with my uncle ever since. He kicked me out when I was sixteen."

"Why? Because you're gay?"

"Sort of. He's gay too. But he got upset because I slept with his boyfriend." He grinned.

"What did he do to the boyfriend?"

"Nothing. I actually saw them not too long ago. They were eating at a fancy restaurant here in town."

I asked a few more official questions before I shut off the tape recorder.

"This is off the record and just between the two of us. You and Austin cooked something up, didn't you?"

He nodded. "He and I talked after we met here at the station," he answered. "We both wanted to make sure Shaw didn't hurt anyone else, but we weren't sure what to do."

"Who came up with the idea?"

"Austin. He's a smart kid. His first idea was to follow Shaw the next time he tricked, but I decided it had to be me."

"Why did it have to be you?"

"I wanted to be sure we got the creep and didn't want to risk someone else's life. Austin didn't want me to have to do anything sexual with Shaw, but I said that was an important part. 'Sides, it's not like I hadn't already done shit like that."

"So what was the plan after Shaw took you home?" I asked.

"Austin followed us so he could watch from a window in the kitchen. He knew Shaw had a camera in there. I led Shaw on and got him to admit he was taping us. I told him I liked to be choked, and he seemed to get off on that."

"When I watched the video, there were spots where I could see your lips moving, but I couldn't hear what you were saying."

"I was whispering." Rebel smirked. "I told him I knew he'd killed a kid. I egged him on and got him to admit that he did murder Toby. That's when Austin called 911."

"You were taking a big chance, Rebel. He could've killed you."

He shrugged. "He didn't. 'Sides, I had to do it for Toby."

"What're you going to do now?"

"Probably keep doing the same thing I been doing. Austin says he can help me, but I don't take handouts."

"What if I found a place to help you get back on your feet, and you can earn your keep while you do it?"

"I guess that wouldn't be too bad," he said.

"Let Austin help you out for a couple days," I said. "I'll get it arranged."

SLATE WAS the most scared of all four arrested men. Despite being part of a large moneymaking operation, he had no finances, and he had no choice but to get a public defender. I laughed out loud when Lex told me who his lawyer was—Peter Giles.

Last year when I'd been arrested, before Colby became my lawyer, Giles was the PD assigned to my case. Giles was pretty much the bottom of the barrel when it came to lawyers. He had a nervous habit of stuttering and stammering with everything he said.

"Giles might be our best chance to convince Slate to work with us," Lex said.

"Let's do it," I said.

Lex and I strode into the interrogation room where Slate and Giles were waiting.

"Mr. Giles," I said, "how are you doing?"

"Umm, Detective Flesh, errr, how are you, ummm, doing?"

"Umm, I'm good," I answered, trying to hold back a smile.

"We'd like to discuss a deal for your client," Lex said.

"These are some serious, uhhh, charges, Detective," Giles said. "I, uhhh, don't think it's in my, errr, client's best, umm, interests to, umm, discuss a deal."

The look Slate gave made me think he was already questioning his lawyer's abilities.

"Look, Mr. Giles," I said. "Frankly, your client isn't the one we want. We're willing to make a very good deal."

"I, uhhh, think we have an, umm, excellent chance at, uhhh, acquittal," Giles said.

I turned to Slate. "Do you want to hear what we're willing to offer? I've already cleared it with Kai Yung."

"No, uhh, we're done here," Giles said. "We're not, errr, interested in any, umm, deal." He stood up. "Let's, uhhh, go, Mr. Slate."

"No," Slate said. "I want to hear what they have to say."

"Umm, Mr. Slate," Giles said. "I, uhhh, highly advise you not to, ummm, take any deal."

"I want to hear it," Slate said.

Giles sat down, obviously not very happy.

"It comes down to this, Slate," I said. "We want proof that Cahill was running the operation."

"What do I get in exchange?"

"Just one charge of solicitation of a minor gets you five years to life in prison." Lex leaned over and put her hands on the table. "We could hit you with twenty counts and make all the sentences run consecutively. But if you work with us, you'll only be charged with one count. I'm sure with good behavior you could get out in five years."

Slate glanced from me and Lex to Giles, then back. "I'll take the deal. Where do I sign?"

"Umm, I don't think that is, errr, a good, uhhh, idea."

He glared at Giles. "I am definitely not going to trial with you as my lawyer. No goddamn way."

We already had the agreement drawn up, so Slate signed it and began the story.

"It started a year ago. Quentin, my son, was arrested for possession. It was enough drugs to send him away for a couple years. He'd been through so much because of me, and I didn't want him to suffer anymore. Cahill said he'd lower the charges so Quentin wouldn't do any time."

"But he wanted something in exchange, right?" I asked.

He nodded. "I started the ranch with the best intentions, I promise. I wanted to help those boys. I hated the idea of getting them to sell themselves again, but I needed to do something to help my son. I'd already caused him too much pain."

"How much of the money did you take?" I asked.

"None." He looked me in the eye. "I didn't touch a penny of that dirty money for the ranch. I gave all the money to Cahill. I swear to it."

I believed him, but I knew D'Amico would be able to prove it one way or another.

"How is Anthony Zion connected to the ranch?" I asked.

"Zion?" Slate's brow furrowed. "I wouldn't have anything to do with him or his money."

"He contributes money to the ranch through a false name," I informed him.

"I promise I had no idea," Slate insisted. "If I didn't take Cahill's dirty money, then I wouldn't take Zion's either."

Slate had done the wrong thing for the best of reasons, but I was sure his testimony, and the rest of the evidence I had, would send Cahill away.

D'AMICO'S RECORDS proved that all the money Slate got from the hustling went straight to Cahill. It also appeared Slate had no idea that Anthony Zion had been funding his ranch. We couldn't prove one way or the other if Zion knew the ranch was more than what it appeared to be. Zion did donate money to worthwhile causes, and I assumed that was the case here.

Carl Graham was charged with several counts of solicitation of a minor. He refused all offers of a deal.

Cahill was equally adamant that he was innocent and insisted on a trial. His resolve stayed strong even after I uncovered evidence that he'd shot Drew and killed Casey.

Though I'd known Cahill was behind Casey's murder, I'd originally thought he had arranged for someone else to do the dirty work. I figured if he had used Slate's son to get what he wanted, then maybe he would do the same to someone else. I pulled all the cases Cahill had been working on and meticulously searched through all the files. I hit pay dirt with a case involving a young, drugged-out kid holding up a 7-Eleven. The gun used in the robbery was a nine millimeter—the same type of gun used to kill Casey.

By itself, that didn't mean much. Nine millimeters are used fairly often, but my instincts told me this was no coincidence. I went to the evidence locker, found the pistol, and looked at the chain of possession—Cahill was the last name on the list. I got permission from Brunson to check out the pistol and have it tested. Cahill must've been desperate, arrogant, or stupid, because his prints were all over the gun. The markings on the bullets we found at the scene of Casey's murder matched the inside markings of the barrel of the pistol. It was more than enough evidence to charge him with murder and the attempted murder of a federal agent.

A few days after the arrests, we got the final piece of evidence needed to nail Shaw. Toby's blood was found on the scarf Shaw had tried to choke Rebel with. Faced with the strong proof, Shaw was smart enough to accept the deal Kai offered him. Shaw would be sentenced to life in prison but saved from the death penalty.

Except for preparation for my testimony and the trials themselves, there was very little for me to do with the cases. It was in Kai's hands now. He had been appointed interim DA and would run for, and most likely win, the seat in the next election.

Chapter 15

I WAS pleasantly surprised when Colby showed up at the station around noon.

"You come to take me to lunch, big guy?"

"No," he said abruptly.

"What's wrong?"

"Do you know who both Graham and Cahill hired to represent them?" He was obviously very angry.

"Who?" I asked.

"My goddamn firm!" he exclaimed. "My colleagues are representing those twisted, disgusting perverts."

"I guess everyone is entitled to a good defense. At least it's not you."

"Fucking right, it's not me. I couldn't do it. I won't do it… ever." He paced a few steps around my desk.

"That'll always be a possibility when you work for someone else," I pointed out.

Shaking his head insistently, he replied, "Not anymore. As of right now, I don't work for anyone else."

"What?"

"I quit, baby. I fucking quit. I'm going to open my own practice, and I will defend who I want to defend."

I pulled him into a big embrace—not caring who saw us.

"It's a good day for big news," I said. "I have some of my own."

"What's yours?"

"I'm buying a ranch."

He furrowed his brow. "Excuse me?"

I grinned. “The Fresh Slate Ranch. Slate needed the money, and I wanted to be sure the place was run the right way.”

For years I had lived a rather meager life, saving most of my paycheck and spending very little. I had also learned how to invest money and as a result had enough to make a down payment on the ranch and good enough credit to finance the rest.

“Do you know how to run a ranch?”

“No,” I replied. “But I don’t need to. I have the perfect foreman right now, and if he leaves, I’ll hire a new one.”

“Who’s the foreman?”

“Jed Harper was raised on a farm. He knows what needs to be done. I’ll hire an accountant to handle the money side of things, and I figured you could help me with anything else that came up.”

“Of course I’ll help,” he said. “It’s a great idea.”

AFTER WORK Colby and I drove out to the ranch. I had already discussed the idea with Jed, but I hadn’t told anyone else. Jed gathered the boys in the living room.

“The ranch has a new owner,” Jed announced. “And there’s going to be a few changes—for the better.” Everyone watched him; he was a natural leader. “The new owner is Detective Cristian Flesh.”

Suddenly all eyes were on me. “I may be the new owner,” I said, “but let me be perfectly clear about something. This is not my ranch. It is yours. You all will do the work, and you will reap the rewards. Jed is the foreman, and if you are unable to settle disputes, you can turn to me.” I gestured to Colby. “Mr. Maddox will be part of things too. He and I are in charge, but Jed is the boss.”

“There will be strict rules.” Colby stepped forward. “No drugs, no alcohol. I understand you are all young men with strong sexual desires, but this is not going to turn into a bathhouse, with parties and orgies every night. Any underage boys will have their own rooms, and the older boys are strictly prohibited from doing anything sexual with them. Not everyone should be fucking, and I know that's a foreign concept for many of you. That's part of the new beginning we're making here."

EVERYTHING FELT so complete—except my heart. Not the romantic part of my heart, because Colby took care of that with no problem. But there was something missing, and I knew things wouldn't be complete until I took the final step. A massive decision that meant a trip out of town.

There was still so much of my life that I hadn't shared with Colby. I didn't like to think about it, let alone put it into words. But I knew I had to do something, and it was more than just sharing things with Colby. I wasn't sure I remembered everything about my childhood, and I wanted to be able to have total recall before I talked to Colby about it.

There was another reason the trip was necessary. I had seen how Clayton Shaw, Carl Graham, and Vincent Fox moved from one victim to another. I didn't know why I'd thought the man who had abused me wouldn't find another victim. I'd just assumed—or hoped—he wouldn't hurt anyone else. I'd prayed that he'd done what he did to me because he hated me and that when I left he'd return to being a normal person. Not the most logical thought, for sure.

The trip back home wasn't about me confronting him; it was about reconnecting with other people I'd cared about. And it was about finding out for sure if there were any other victims.

Having decided I had to return to the place I'd grown up—a small beach town in Oregon called Newport—I just needed to work up the courage to actually go.

Fortunately, I was good at finding reasons to put it off.

Chapter 16

GRAHAM'S TRIAL took place four months after his arrest. His lawyer presented a strong case—but not strong enough. Graham was convicted and sentenced to three terms of life in prison with the chance of parole after five years. The sentences would be consecutive, so Graham would serve at least fifteen years in prison.

Cahill's case took place four months later, eight months after his arrest. He had a table full of lawyers, but Kai was better than his former boss. Cahill was convicted of ten counts of solicitation of a minor and ten counts of child endangerment. The solicitation charges alone netted him ten sentences of life in prison with the chance of parole. Just like Graham, all sentences were consecutive. But the convictions of murder and attempted murder carried the worst sentences—ten to twenty years for the attempted murder and life without the possibility of parole for the murder. Cahill would be spending the rest of his life behind bars.

At some point after Cahill's conviction, I ran out of excuses for postponing my trip. I decided it was time. I secured several weeks of leave—not sure how much or how little of it I would use. I'd hardly told Lex anything about my plans, just that I was going to my hometown.

Colby was the last person to know. After a quiet dinner at home, I finally filled him in.

I chewed the last bite of chicken Kiev, set down my fork, and said, "I'm going out of town."

"Why? For work?" he asked without glancing up from his plate.

I shook my head. "No, it's a… personal trip."

He lifted his head and peered into my eyes. "Why do I get the feeling that I'm not going to like this?"

I shrugged. "You might not. Just please don't take anything personally."

"Fuck, now I know I'm not going to like this. Where are you going?" He leaned forward on the table and clasped his hands together.

"Newport, Oregon."

Cocking his head sideways, he watched me through half-closed eyes. "Why the hell are you going there?"

"That's where I'm from. That's where my parents and brother live."

His face lifted for a second, then darkened. "You don't want me to come, do you?" He spoke in a low voice.

I licked my lips and shook my head. "No, baby, I don't. I need to do this alone. Because I probably won't be in the best of moods while I'm there."

"Bello, I'm used to you being a dickhead." He laughed.

The sound surprised me for a second, and I cracked a smile. "Yeah, I know, and I appreciate that. But I need to go alone. I have things I must do by myself."

"Things you aren't ready to talk about yet," he said. It wasn't a question.

"Exactly. But after this trip, and after I deal with the last of my inner demons, I won't be holding anything back from you. That's the purpose of going there."

"I'm afraid you're going to get hurt. And I don't mean physically." He gazed at me with such intensity and caring that it caused an involuntary shiver.

I stood, strode to him, and put my hands on his shoulders. "I'm strong. So much stronger because of you."

"Promise me you'll call me if you need me." Colby craned his neck so we could make eye contact.

After leaning down and hugging him, I replied, "I promise."

"When are you leaving?"

"I fly out in the morning."

"Want me to take you to the airport?"

"No," I answered. "It's an early flight, and I want to say good-bye to you while you're naked in our bed."

"I love it when you say that." He laughed.

"Say what?"

"Our bed. Our place. I hope you feel like this is your place. If you don't, we can get our own place. If you're ready to get rid of your apartment. I don't want to push you."

"We'll talk about that when I get back," I said. "Right now I want to go to bed."

"Yeah, I guess you need your sleep."

"Who said anything about sleep?" I grinned as I pulled off my shirt and tossed it on the floor.

We raced to the bedroom, and Colby tore my clothes off, kissing and caressing every part of my body.

He prepared me with his tongue and his fingers. He entered me as our lips and tongues were connected. He made love to me slowly and gently, and we cried out as we came together. Afterward, he washed me up with a warm cloth and snuggled, pulling my body to his.

Chapter 17

I WOKE up early Saturday morning and packed a few things into a duffel bag. When I kissed Colby on the cheek, he smiled in his sleep. I missed him as soon as I left our house. I took a cab to the airport and ignored the questions from the cabbie. As I waited in line at the security checkpoint, I wanted to turn around, go back to Colby, and slip back into bed. But I knew I had to make this trip. So I got on the plane and flew back to the place I hadn't been since I was fifteen years old. A place I thought I would never see again and people I never thought I would want to see again.

I flew into Portland and rented a car to make the two-and-a-half-hour drive from there to Newport. I didn't go over the speed limit by even a mile. I was in no hurry to get there.

When I arrived, I drove slowly through the touristy part of the town. Newport was relatively small, with around 10,000 people. I could see the beach from the road and remembered hanging out there when I was young. Sometimes I'd spent time there with my mother and my brother, sometimes with friends, and sometimes I just hid there. Hid from the screaming and yelling and from what I knew was going to happen.

As far as I knew, my family still lived in the same house I had grown up in. I made a few turns and went into the residential area. I pulled up in front of the tan three-bedroom home I'd thought I'd never see again. I knew right away my family still lived there. My mother's car—a rundown 1976 Chevy Nova—sat in the driveway. I assumed my… dad was at work.

I got out of my rental, ambled to the front door, and knocked. When she opened the door, I was shocked. Her long, bright golden-blonde hair was now totally gray. She had always been thin, but now she looked almost anorexic, with dark bags under her eyes. She looked very tired.

"Yes," she said. "What can I do for you?"

"Mo—" I coughed to clear my throat. "Mom?"

She tilted her head and stared at me before her memory kicked in.

"William? Willy, is that you?"

"Yeah, Mom, it's me."

She threw her arms around me and squeezed. I wrapped my arms around her without even thinking about it. I breathed in and inhaled the same familiar scent. I'd never forgotten it.

"My baby boy," she said, and I could feel her tears on my neck. "My beautiful boy. I never thought I'd see you again. What are you doing here?"

"I have some business to take care of here," I replied.

She narrowed her eyes. "Personal business?"

I nodded.

"You're not going to be digging up old bones, are you?"

"I didn't come to see him. I came to see you and my brother," I said softly. "I also have to know if he has hurt anyone else like he hurt me."

"That was so many years ago, Willy. I promised you. He's a changed man."

"I need to know that for sure," I snapped. "But I also want to see you and Chucky again. I've found someone I want to spend the rest of my life with, and I'd like to reconnect with my family."

She smiled widely. "You found someone? What is she like?"

"He is wonderful," I said. "His name is Colby, and he's the best man I've ever met."

"A man? You mean you're—?"

"I'm gay, Mom. You should know that. That's why Dad kicked me out. I was only fifteen fucking years old."

"Watch your mouth, William."

"Cristian," I replied. "My name isn't William J. Singer anymore. My name is Cristian Flesh."

"Cristian?"

"Yeah, like Christopher. You remember him? Someone else whose life was ruined because of my father." I was getting angry, and my pleasant reunion with my mother was becoming decidedly unpleasant. I didn't know why I'd thought it could be anything other than ugly.

"Where is he?" I asked. "Where's Dad?"

"He's at work."

My dad had worked at AT&T for more than twenty-five years.

"Where's my brother?"

"Chucky's on a camping trip with some friends. He'll be back tonight. Please, Willy. Leave Newport. Go back where you came from. Live your life with your… boyfriend. And forget about us."

"I wish I could," I sneered. "I wish I could forget everything he did to me. But I can't."

"He's a changed man, son," she pleaded. "What he did was horrible, but it's in the past."

"That past affects my present *and* my future," I replied. "I'm sorry. I can't leave. I won't leave. I'll come back later to talk to Chucky."

"Please, Willy." She reached out and caressed my cheek. I grabbed her hand and kept it there.

"I want you and my brother in my life. Please don't shut me out because of Dad."

I DROVE to Mo's Restaurant—home of the best clam chowder I had ever had. The waitress looked familiar to me, but I couldn't place how I knew her. Her name tag said Lily, and it didn't ring any bells. She didn't seem to recognize me, so I didn't worry about it. I ate my chowder in silence and asked for the check. When she put the bill on the table, she ogled me for a second, and I met her gaze.

"Willy? It is you, isn't it?"

"Do I know you?"

"It's me," she said. "Lily Hurner. Well, you knew me when I was Delilah Bright."

"Delilah? Christopher's sister?"

"Yeah!" she exclaimed and sat down at my table. "How are you doing? What are you doing here?"

"I didn't think you or your family would ever want to see me again," I said.

She reached out and grabbed my hand. "Why would you think that?"

"What happened was my fault," I answered.

"No, it wasn't." She frowned. "Christopher killed himself. We don't blame you. We never did. I've thought about you almost every day since you left, Willy. I wished you were around so we could talk about Christopher. You were a connection to my little brother."

"He wouldn't have killed himself if it weren't for me. If we hadn't done what we did."

"Willy, stop," she insisted. "Stop blaming yourself. Christopher loved you. I'm glad he had the chance to know love. He chose to kill himself because he didn't think things would get any better."

"I don't go by Willy anymore." I wanted to change the subject from Christopher's suicide. I could still feel Christopher's love as much as I felt his loss from my life. That was still an open wound, mostly because I'd never allowed it to heal.

"William?" she asked.

"No, I had my name legally changed. Cristian Flesh."

"Cristian?"

I nodded. "My way of remembering Christopher."

There were tears in her eyes. "That's so sweet," she said. "I'm sure Mom and Dad would love to see you. Are you going to be in town for a while?"

"I'm not sure."

"Give me your cell number, and I'll give you mine." We exchanged digits, and I promised to call her before I left town.

I went back to my motel and sat in the darkness for a while. Finally I turned on the light, opened up the curtains, pulled out my cell phone, and dialed.

"It's me," I said when he answered.

"Hello, love," Colby replied. "How are you doing?"

"I was wrong, babe," I said. I didn't just want Colby to be there—I *needed* him to be there. The things I was facing were in my past, but Colby was my future. Everything I did would affect him because of our relationship. I knew he would never purposely hurt me like other people in my life. I wanted him at my side as I took the steps to putting my past behind me.

"I'll be there as soon as I can," he responded.

"You might be able to catch a late flight," I said.

"I'm checking right now," he said. "There's a flight that leaves at eight. I'll get into Portland around ten tonight. Do you want me to rent a car from there?"

"No, I'll be there," I said. "Can't wait to see you, baby."

"Ditto," he said, laughing.

"Colby," I said.

"Yeah?"

"I love you."

"I love you too."

I took a long, hot shower and tried to pick something to wear. I was on my third choice when I realized I was worried about impressing the man who'd kicked me out when I was fifteen because I was gay. I randomly picked a pair of pants and a shirt and headed out.

I pulled up to my parents' house and saw my mother's Nova in the driveway next to a truck—a bright red Denali I was sure was brand new. It had lots of chrome and tricked-out rims. The kind of truck that usually belonged to a self-conscious young kid and not a man in his sixties. I didn't hesitate as I strode to the door and knocked. My mother answered the door, and I knew she wasn't happy to see me.

"William, please," she whispered. "I'm begging you. Let this go."

"I want to see Chucky," I said.

"He's not home yet," she said. "Please go."

"Who is it, Miranda?" I recognized the mean, gravelly voice of my father—James Singer.

"Nobody important, Jimmy," my mom answered, making me wince. My dad stepped up to the door, and I knew from the look on his face that he instantly recognized me.

"Well, look who's here," he sneered. "Our faggot queer son. I didn't think I'd ever see you again. I sure as hell never wanted to see you again, gay boy."

I looked him over. He was as scary looking as ever. He had beady dark brown eyes and a full head of jet-black hair with a matching goatee. He was a few inches taller than me, and I remembered what it felt like when he had several feet on me.

"I'm not here for you. You're nothing to me," I said.

"Nothing?" he snorted. "That's bullshit. You think about me *all* the time. You don't make a move without my voice in your head."

I laughed before I could stop myself. The man was so egocentric that he actually believed what he was saying. "You want to think that, don't you? You want to have power over me."

"I *do* have power over you, boy."

"You are so fucking wrong, man. I am *not* the same little boy you could push around. Not by a long shot. I may be gay, but I'm still a better man than you, a thousand times over."

"Now listen, fag," he said, his face turning red with outrage.

"No," I said loudly. "You are listening to me. You know what you did to me when I was a kid. I don't have to say it aloud. But right now it's not about me. I came to see my mom and my brother—not you. I don't care if I ever see you again. I'd be more than happy if I didn't. But I'm also here to find out if you victimized anyone else. If you did, I will find out, and I will send you away."

"Willy," Mom said. "I swear to you, he's a changed man."

"Yeah, Willy, I'm a changed man," he sneered.

"I hope you're different," I said. "But I doubt it."

I turned away from my dad and faced my mom. "Please tell Chucky I want to see him, Mom. I want to see you again too. I'll come by when I know *he's* not here," I said with a nod toward my dad. I marched to my car and drove to Portland.

COLBY'S FLIGHT arrived right on time, and I waited anxiously to see him again. When I spotted him, I didn't even try to hold back a smile. Not worrying about the airport full of people, I went to him and pulled him into a kiss. He wrapped his arms around me, and he slid his tongue into my mouth. When he finally pulled away, he smiled at me.

"Is that a pistol in your pocket, or are you just happy to see me?" he said, laughing.

"Trust me, love, I am very happy to see you. Shall we slip into the bathroom and take care of things?"

"And risk getting arrested? I don't think that's a wise idea."

I chuckled and said, "Party pooper."

"We can wait until we get back to your hotel, can't we?"

"That's a two-and-a-half-hour drive," I said.

"I think you'll survive, love."

"SO WHAT made you decide to call me?" Colby asked when we had gotten out of Portland and were headed to Newport. He was driving, partly because I was tired and partly because I knew I was going to be even more emotionally exhausted when I said what I had to say.

"I realized that everything I was going to be doing here would affect you as much as me. I'm facing things from my past because I want to have a future with you."

"So these are the last of the things about your past that you haven't told me?"

I nodded.

"And you're going to tell me now, right?"

I nodded again. He didn't say anything, and I knew he was waiting for me to begin.

"My real name is William Singer," I said. "Well, that's the name I was born with. Everybody called me Willy. My dad was never a kind man. He drank a lot when I was very young. I remember a lot of screaming and fighting between my parents."

"Did he hit you?" He reached over and squeezed my leg.

"When I was eleven, he came into my room and talked to me about sex. He told me about how guys get boners, and… then he showed me his cock. It looked huge to me. And he jacked off. I thought it was cool because he was treating me like I was a big kid. I didn't think it was wrong, not at first, anyway."

"But it didn't stop there, did it?" Colby asked.

"No, it didn't." I told Colby how it escalated to all kinds of forced touching and sex—up to and including him penetrating me.

"He told me that if I let him do it to me, then he wouldn't get as angry at Mom or my brother."

"Fuck, that's horrible, Cristian."

"He was always in charge. He told me what to do and when to do it. And even when I did what he said, he'd slap me."

"And he made you ride him?"

When I first broke rule number five about that sexual position, I had told him that at a point in my life I had been forced to ride someone, and while I did he would slap me and call me names.

"Yeah, he's the one I told you about."

"Christ, Cristian, no wonder you're so mess—" He stopped himself, but I knew what he was going to say.

"That's why I'm so messed up?"

"I didn't mean it like that."

"It's okay," I replied. "I was messed up. Still am, just not as much. And that's thanks to you." I caressed his cheek.

"Did your mother know what he was doing to you?"

"Not while it was happening," I answered. "But I told her before I left. She didn't want to believe me, but she knew it was the truth."

"How long did the abuse last?"

"Until the day I left."

"Is that why you took off?"

"No." I chuckled. "He had pretty much beaten it into my head that getting fucked was all I was good for. I was just a piece of shit to be used. He seemed to leave my mom alone, and my brother was still real young. There's eleven years between us. I didn't want Dad to hurt him or Mom, so I took everything he gave me."

"You know that wasn't right, don't you?"

I nodded. "Yeah, now I do. At the time I thought I deserved it, at least in the beginning, until Christopher kissed me for the first time."

"Who's Christopher?"

"Christopher Bright was my best friend from first grade on. He's the first person I felt real love from. My father didn't make me gay, of course. I would've been attracted to men no matter what. His abuse affected how I looked at sex but not which gender I was attracted to."

"Of course," Colby responded. I loved it how he didn't say too much, knowing I needed to talk.

"Christopher and I spent all our time together. His dad played ball with him, took him to sporting events, and they did fun things together. Christopher's dad was everything mine wasn't—loving and caring. I didn't tell Christopher about what my dad was doing to me, but we did go through puberty together. We were almost thirteen when we went camping and shared a tent. We were doing the normal boy thing and comparing sizes when suddenly he kissed me. It was awkward and sloppy, but it was also incredible. He was afraid that it had pissed me off and tried to apologize, but I shut him up by kissing him back. We explored everything we could think of together, and it was cool. It was hands and mouths for a while, but on my fifteenth birthday I convinced him to let me fuck him, and we both loved it."

"I bet you did," Colby said.

"We were both so horny, we fucked all the time. I didn't want to get fucked because of what my dad was doing to me, but Christopher didn't care. We made each other happy, really happy. I loved him, Colby. It wasn't just puppy love. I know we were young, but I loved him so much. And I loved his family. I liked to pretend I was a foster son brought into the family. His older sister, Delilah, and his parents treated me like their own."

"Did Christopher ever know what your father was doing to you?"

Nodding, I said, "I couldn't hide the bruises from him. He was so angry when I confessed. He wanted me to tell my mom or his parents or the police. He even threatened to kill my dad. But I convinced him not to tell anyone. I loved being with Christopher so much, it almost made me forget what my dad did to me. It was so good between me and Christopher, until we got caught in bed."

"By who?"

"Christopher's older sister, Delilah," I replied. "But she didn't make a big deal out of it. She told us to make sure we were safe, and she gave us condoms."

"That was cool of her."

"Yeah, she's the best. And she didn't even tell their parents. But they found out anyway. They found the condoms in Christopher's room and made him admit he was having sex. He told them everything—that it was me he was having sex with."

"Were they angry?"

"They were upset but didn't go overboard. They sat us down and said they thought we were too young to be involved that way. Christopher told his parents that he loved me." I felt tears running down my face. "He stood up for me, Colby. He didn't care what his parents thought. He said he loved me and wasn't going to stop seeing me. They were impressed and agreed to allow us to see each other. But they couldn't approve of us having sex, even though that's like trying to close the barn door after the horse got out. We found ways to have sex no matter how hard his parents tried. But they caught us again and were upset. They decided they had to tell my parents. I begged them not to, but they insisted."

"Uh-oh," Colby murmured.

"They thought they were doing the right thing. They couldn't have known what my dad was like. Good people like the Brights don't always realize that there is such evil in the world. My parents flipped out when Mr. and Mrs. Bright told them. I think Christopher's parents realized right away what a mistake they had made. My mom broke down in tears, and my dad yelled and screamed. The Brights wanted to allow Christopher and me to see each other, but only under strict supervision. They told my dad it wasn't wrong to be gay, and he flew off the handle. He said homosexuality was evil and disgusting."

"He said that after what he did to you? He's a goddamn pedophile, and he judged you?"

"I know, pretty stupid. But I stood up to him just like Christopher did to his parents. I told my dad that I loved Christopher and wasn't going to stop seeing him. He was furious and ordered Christopher and his parents to leave. He hit me as soon as they left. He punched me, and I fell down, and he kicked me. Then he dragged me to the basement and told Mom he was gonna tan my hide. But he raped me. He said he'd do it again if I didn't stop seeing 'that other faggot.' I said he could do whatever he wanted to me, but I wasn't going to stop seeing Christopher. I was lying on the cold concrete floor bleeding, and he leaned down and whispered in my ear. He swore he would kill my mom and my brother if I didn't dump Christopher."

"Oh my God!" Colby exclaimed.

"And I did, even though it broke my heart to do it. I told Christopher I couldn't see him anymore. I was honest with him. I told him that if we stayed together, he would end up getting hurt. I refused to do that to him. He begged me not to leave him. He said we could sneak around, and my dad would never find out, but I wouldn't take the chance. I had to stop taking his calls and ignored him at school. It devastated him, and it broke my heart."

"You thought you were doing the right thing."

"It wasn't the right decision, though. And what happened next was my fault."

Colby glanced at me and waited for me to continue.

"A couple weeks later, Christopher killed himself. He killed himself because of what I did. He was home alone one night and got into his mother's medicine cabinet and found her sleeping pills. He took them all and went to bed. They were worried when he didn't wake up for school in the morning. He was already dead. I was at school when I heard the announcement. I threw up right there in class."

"I'm so sorry."

"My dad didn't even want me to go the funeral, but my mom convinced him to allow it. Afterward he told me I better not ever touch another boy again. He said I belonged to him and no one else. I didn't listen because I stopped caring. I didn't want to ever fuck or kiss a boy again. That's what I had with Christopher, and I wanted it to be special. But I did let other guys fuck me. Older boys in school, older men, even married men. And soon everybody in Newport knew I was gay. And that's what pissed my dad off. That's when he kicked me out. He said he refused to have a faggot son live in his house. So I left."

"Where did you go?"

"I went to the nearest truck stop, found a trucker, and asked for a ride to wherever he was going. The first guy was cool, didn't ask for anything. But the next one expected payment, and by then I didn't care. I was only good for sex, so I gave him what he wanted. I hitched rides from truck drivers and single men and married men driving alone, and once even a married man and his wife. I got free rides, free food, and even free clothes and cash. I eventually made it to Reno and decided it was as good a place as any to stay. And you know the rest."

"It's incredible you made it through all that as well as you did. You're such an amazing, strong man."

"And getting stronger because of you."

We were quiet for a while before I spoke again. "I saw my mom and dad today."

"How did that go?"

"My mom asked me not to be digging up the past. She swears Dad is a changed man and that he never did that to another boy."

"Do you believe her?"

"I want to," I answered. "And that's something I'm going to find out before I leave. Now, enough about that. Let's discuss something far more interesting."

"Like what?"

"Like the fact that I love the feel of your hard cock in my hand and in my mouth and in my ass. Or that you're only the second person who I actually enjoy kissing. Or that I'm getting hard just thinking about what we're going to do to each other when we get to the motel room."

"Stop, baby," he said, smiling. "You're making me hard."

"Me too," I said.

He looked at my crotch.

"How much longer 'til we get there?" he asked.

"Half an hour, going the speed limit." I smiled when he increased his speed to twenty miles over the limit.

COLBY'S HANDS were all over me, and he was biting the back of my neck as I tried to fit the hotel card into the slot. I had to slide the card a couple of times because I couldn't open it before the little green light turned red again.

We finally got inside, and Colby spun me around and mashed his lips to mine, gliding his slippery tongue into my willing mouth. I was trying to get his shirt off as he was attempting to remove mine, and we ended in a tangle of shirts and arms. We reluctantly backed up so we could get naked, and as soon as our clothes were off, we were touching and kissing and groping. The heat emanating from his body was so intense, I swore I was going to burn up. Our hard shafts bounced against each other, and Colby reached behind me and grasped my butt cheeks. He broke our kiss to slide a finger into my mouth, and I sucked on it like a cock. He pulled the finger out and replaced it with his tongue. The spit-soaked digit slipped between my cheeks and pressed against my hole. It popped in quickly, and I took a deep breath. He sucked on my tongue, then my bottom lip before licking down to my Adam's apple and the concave spot at the base of my throat. The finger pushed in deeper, then suddenly pulled out.

"God, Colby, I need you to fuck me. But I don't have lube." I hadn't been planning on any sexual encounters on this trip.

"In my bag," he whispered. "Side pocket." He dropped to his knees and licked the head of my cock, tracing the crown with his tongue. I reached over to the bag and fumbled with the side-pocket zipper before I managed to get it open. I reached blindly into the pocket, trying to concentrate on finding the lube as Colby swallowed my length. I finally found the bottle.

"Got it," I said.

Colby stood and pushed me so I fell back on the bed. "Get yourself ready," he commanded. I loved the way his voice got deeper when he told me what to do. And even though we were in the roles of dominant and submissive, it was nothing like the times my father ordered me around or the times I was dominated by the other men I had slept with. I submitted to Colby because I wanted to and because I loved him and knew he would never hurt me.

I opened the lube and squeezed some onto my fingers and onto my cock. After setting the bottle down, I slipped one hand between my legs, found the hole, and slid in. With my other hand, I grabbed my dick and slowly stroked it.

"Yeah, bello," Colby murmured as he caressed himself. "That's so hot. You fingering your hole, getting ready for my dick."

I slid three fingers into my ass with my legs in the air and gazed at Colby as he stroked himself quickly. I loved knowing he was excited by just watching me. "Babe, please fuck me," I pleaded as I shifted so my ass was on the edge of the bed.

Colby grabbed the slick and greased himself up. I pulled my fingers out and felt the head of his shaft prodding there a second later. With one hand on his cock, Colby pressed against my rim. The head popped in, and he grabbed my legs to keep them in the air. He slowly slid in, and I almost lost it when I felt his length press against my prostate. I let go of myself and concentrated on the incredible feel of him penetrating me.

"Cristian… so fucking tight. So fucking good."

"Yeah, you feel awesome in me, Colby." He slid in and out of me, slowly increasing the speed and tempo with each thrust. He battered my gland again and again. It felt like he fucked me for hours, but I knew it wasn't even close to that long.

He pounded me harder, and the force on my prostate was just too much. I grabbed my cock, and with just a few quick jerks, I came—shooting hot loads of seed onto my stomach and chest.

"Oh damn, that was hot," Colby moaned. He released one leg, picked up a bit of my come with one finger, lifted it to his mouth, and sucked the finger clean. "You taste so good." A moment later his breathing got faster, and he buried himself in me. His cock pulsed, and then his body relaxed. He pulled out and fell down on the bed. I curled up next to him.

"Thanks for coming," I said.

"What? Did you expect me to fuck you and not come?"

"I don't mean that coming," I said, laughing. "I meant coming here—to Newport. Thanks for dropping everything."

"That's what lovers are for."

"I know, but still… thank you."

"You're welcome, my love. Let's shower, because I am exhausted."

Chapter 18

I WOKE up Sunday morning, thrilled to be in Colby's arms again. With him there I knew everything was going to be all right. We stayed in bed for another hour, just touching without much talking. He ran his fingers over the beginning of growth on my scalp—it had been a week since I'd shaved my head. I caressed up and down his muscular chest. I lay on top of him, and we made out like teenagers, kissing and petting but not going beyond that. We caressed each other until we were hard and close to exploding, then backed off and let ourselves soften. Then we'd bring each other to the brink and back off again.

"Unless you want to actually come," I said, "we need to stop."

"I want to save it for later. I want to make love on the beach," he said, smiling.

"Really? Well, I happen to know a few private spots."

"I figured you would."

"But first I want to introduce you to some people," I said.

"Who?"

"The Brights." I told him about running into Delilah, who now preferred to be called Lily, at Mo's. I wanted to see the Brights again, and I wanted them to meet Colby.

"What about your family?"

"We'll get to them," I answered. "Fun stuff first, though."

I CALLED up Delilah and asked if she and her parents were free for lunch. She returned the call right away.

"Mom's making a big lunch for us," she said. "She's thrilled. They still live in the same place. Be there at noon."

"My boyfriend's in town with me. I was hoping I could bring him."

"Of course," she replied.

Colby and I stayed in bed and watched *MythBusters*. We finally crawled out and took a slow, hot shower together—washing and touching each other everywhere. Colby took his time as he washed what little hair I had, and it felt damn good.

We dried each other off, stopping often to kiss lips, nipples, fingers, and legs. Finally we dressed and headed to the Bright house—the place that had always felt like more of a home than my own.

We were ten feet from the front door when it flew open and Mrs. Bright ran into my arms. She was tall for a woman—six foot—with long red hair. She hugged me tight for a minute, and it felt great to have her arms around me.

"Willy, it's so good to see you." She cupped my face in her hands and kissed my forehead. Mr. Bright sauntered out a second later; the smile on his face was just as big as his wife's. He was a short man—five foot six or so—and had lost most of his hair.

"Willy," Mr. Bright said. "You're looking good." I extended my hand, but he knocked it away and tugged me into a hug.

When he stepped back, Mrs. Bright pushed in and hugged me again. I laughed and heard Colby do the same. I pulled back and said, "I want you guys to meet someone. Mr. and Mrs. Bright, this is Colby, my boyfriend."

"Willy, forget the Mr. and Mrs. Bright stuff," Mrs. Bright said. She hugged Colby. "I'm Penny."

"I'm Warren," Mr. Bright said as he and Colby shook hands.

She took my arm and escorted me inside. The house had a few different pieces of furniture and new pictures on the wall, but it had the same warm and inviting feel I remembered.

Before we even had a chance to sit down, the door opened and Delilah entered with a tall, dark-haired man in a business suit.

"Willy." She smiled. "You came."

"Did you think I wouldn't?" I asked.

"I wasn't sure," she replied. "Willy, this is Ian Hurner, my husband."

Ian and I shook hands.

"Delilah, Ian." I gestured to Colby. "This is my boyfriend, Colby Maddox."

Ian and Colby shook hands, but Delilah embraced him.

"Would anyone like coffee?" Mrs. Bright asked.

We all nodded.

"Thank you, Mrs. Bright," I said when she handed me the coffee.

"It's Penny," she said and slapped me on the shoulder.

"Thank you, Penny," I said.

"What have you been doing with yourself, Willy?" Warren asked.

"I'm a detective with the Reno Police Department," I answered.

"Nevada?" Delilah exclaimed. "How'd you end up there?"

"It's a long story," I said, and Colby put his hand on mine. "I changed my name years ago. I'm Cristian Flesh now."

"Cristian?" Penny put a hand over her mouth.

"Yeah," I replied. "So I'd never forget Christopher. I'm so sorry for what happened."

Penny looked into my eyes. "Son, we never blamed you. Christopher made the choice to kill himself."

"But he did it because I broke his heart," I said. It hurt just to remember his face when I'd dumped him. Those memories were burned into my brain.

"You can't blame yourself," Delilah said.

"We can't change the past," Warren said.

"Dear, you are so right," Penny said. "We will *never* forget Christopher, and of course we'll always wish he was here. But I say we focus on tomorrow and not worry about yesterday."

We had a lunch of homemade potato salad and barbecued burgers. We talked about Christopher and all the good times we'd had. I noticed Colby and Penny talking and wondered what they were discussing—pretty sure it was me.

At one point, Penny and I were alone. "He's a good man, and he loves you," she said.

"Yeah, I'm pretty lucky," I replied.

"Christopher would be happy for you," she whispered as she embraced me once again.

AFTER LUNCH with the Brights, Colby and I went to the beach, hid our shoes behind some driftwood, and strolled along the shore. We heard some whoops and hollers and saw a group of teenagers sitting on logs, drinking beer, and smoking cigarettes.

"Holy shit," Colby said when we were near the teens. "That kid. He looks just like you."

He was right. He looked like a younger version of me—just like how I remembered myself at the age of seventeen. He was tall and skinny with blue eyes and shaggy blond hair.

"I think that's my brother," I murmured.

"Are you sure?"

"Look at him," I said. "It has to be him." Motioning for Colby to stay where he was, I ambled up to the young man.

He looked up at me with a glare. "What the hell do you want?"

"Chucky?"

He stood up quickly. "How the fuck do you know my name?"

"Chucky," I repeated. "It's me, William, your brother."

"My brother? What the fuck are you talking about?"

"I'm your brother. I know you remember me."

"My brother took off years ago," he spat. "My brother left me alone to live in that… house with that man. My brother is a fucking queer. I got no desire to see my brother."

"Chucky, please," I said. "I know it's been a long time. But I want to see you. I want to talk to you."

"Well, you've seen me, and you've talked to me. So now get the hell away from me because I got nothing to say to you."

"Please," I whispered.

I saw the punch coming, but I didn't try to block it or dodge it, though I could've. I fell to the sand, and he stood over me with his fist still clenched. A brunette with big tits stood next to my brother and grabbed his arm.

"C'mon, Chuck," she said. "Let's go." He glared down at me and stormed away. When all the kids were gone, Colby came up to me.

"You okay?"

I shook my head. "No, I'm not okay. Mom was wrong. Dad didn't change. He didn't stop when I left. I wasn't the only boy he hurt."

"What do you mean?"

"He did the same thing to my brother that he did to me."

"How do you know?"

I stood up with Colby's help.

"I just know," I said. "I can see it in his eyes. I know that anger."

"What're we going to do about it?" Colby asked.

"I don't know. Chucky will never admit it. If my mom knows, she won't either."

"Why don't we find out exactly what she knows?"

We found our shoes, went back to the car, and drove to my parents' house. Dad's truck was gone, but the Nova was there. I knocked on the door, and Mom gave me a small smile when she saw me.

"Mom, this is my boyfriend, Colby Maddox."

"It's a pleasure to meet you, Mrs. Singer."

She nodded as she took his hand and invited us in.

"I ran into Chucky at the beach," I said. "He wasn't very happy to see me."

"He's having a rough time," she said. "Being a teenager is tough."

"You don't have to tell me that," I replied. "I spent my teenage years living on the streets."

Mom grimaced with sadness in her eyes but didn't say anything.

"Look, Mom, you know what Dad did to me when I was a kid."

"Do you have to bring this up again?" she asked in an exasperated voice.

"I'm so sorry that the fact that your husband raped me and beat me bothers you."

"William, please."

"But I'm not here to talk about me. I want to know about my brother."

"What about Chucky?"

"Do you know that Dad did the same thing to Chucky that he did to me?"

Gawking at me, she said, "That's a lie!"

"I don't think so," I said. "He has the same anger I had. He has the same haunted, empty look in his eyes that I remember having."

"Get the hell out of here," she said as she stood. "I will not listen to these lies."

Colby and I stood. "It's not a lie, Mother. And I will find out the truth before I leave."

Colby and I left, and we returned to the hotel in silence. I fell on the bed and fought back the tears. Colby lay next to me and pulled me close to him. I fell asleep as he ran his fingers over my hair stubble.

Colby and I went to dinner at Mo's, where Delilah waited on us. She took a short break and joined us for a few minutes. We laughed and talked, and I realized I enjoyed simple moments like this. When her break was over, she returned to the kitchen. A minute later she was back at our table, and I knew from the look on her face that something was wrong.

"Willy, something's happened."

"What is it? Did something happen to your parents?"

"No, not mine. Yours. There's a police scanner in the kitchen. Your dad's been shot."

"Dammit."

Colby and I stood, left money for the bill, and ran out of the restaurant. We drove to the hospital and immediately saw my mother in the emergency room waiting area.

"Mom, what happened?"

She turned to me and didn't hesitate before pulling me into her arms. I noticed she had the beginning of a black eye. She buried her face in my neck and cried. I held her tight, kissed her cheek, and whispered in her ear. "It'll be all right, Mom."

It took several minutes for her to calm down enough to speak.

"I'm so sorry, baby. I'm so, so sorry."

"Tell me what happened," I said.

"I confronted Jimmy when he got home. I demanded to know if he hurt Chucky. I asked if he raped him like he did you."

"Did he deny it?"

"No," she said quietly. "He punched me and admitted it. He claimed it was my fault because I couldn't satisfy him, so he had to do what he did."

"Don't blame yourself, Mom," I said. "That's his game. That's what he did to me. He said he'd hurt you and Chucky if I ever said anything about what he was doing to me."

"Oh, my baby boy." She started crying again. "I'm so sorry."

"What happened here, Mom? Did you shoot him?"

She shook her head. "It wasn't me. I wish it had been. He took off, but I followed him. We were down at the docks, and I was screaming at him. He pushed me, and I fell down. I heard a shot and saw blood on his chest. There were dozens of people behind him, where the shot came from. They scattered, and I never saw who shot him."

"But someone had to have seen the shooter," Colby said.

"Mom, where's Chucky?"

She shook her head. "I don't know. Probably with his girlfriend, Stephanie. I like her—she's good for him. Her dad is Councilman Graham Whitewater."

Mom sat down in one of the chairs, and I sat next to her. Colby sat next to me and grabbed my hand. I put my arm around my mother, and she rested her head on my shoulder. She dozed off for a while and woke with a jump.

"Shh," I whispered. "It's okay." I felt her body relax and was happy to realize that I could make her feel better.

"We have to find Chucky," she said. "He needs to know what happened." She pulled out her cell phone and dialed his number. "There's no answer."

"What about Stephanie?" I asked.

Mom found her number on her cell and dialed it.

"Stephanie? This is Mrs. Singer. Is Chucky with you?" She paused. "Do you know where he is? Listen, Stephanie, this is very important. His father's been shot. Can you find him and bring him to the hospital? Thank you, sweetie." She closed the phone.

"What did she say?" I asked.

"She hasn't seen Chucky for a couple hours, but she knows where he is. He's drinking with some of his buddies down on the beach somewhere. She's going to find him and bring him here."

Stephanie, the chesty brunette from the beach, showed up with my brother about twenty minutes later. I could tell he was still three sheets to the wind. Mom embraced him, and he hugged her back while glaring at me. Stephanie quietly left.

"What the hell are you doing here?" he asked me.

"Charles, don't be rude," Mom admonished him. "Your brother is here for me… for us."

"He ain't here for me," Chucky slurred. "He's never been here for me."

"Your father's been shot, Chucky. Now isn't the time for sibling rivalry."

Chucky didn't seem to be surprised about our father being shot.

"You guys should go home and get some sleep," I said.

"I'm not leaving," my mom said.

I'd inherited my stubborn streak from her and knew she wouldn't change her mind.

"I'm going home," Chucky said. "I'll be back in the morning."

"I'll take you home," I said. I turned to Colby. "I'll drop him off and be right back."

"He's pretty drunk," Colby said. "He shouldn't be alone."

"Stay with your baby brother, William," Mom said. "Make sure he's okay. Bring him back in the morning when he's sober."

"What about you?" I asked. "You shouldn't be alone."

"I won't be alone," she said as she grabbed Colby's arm. "I'm sure this big man here can take care of me."

"Of course I can." Colby smiled.

"Thanks, big guy," I told Colby as I pecked him on the cheek.

Chucky didn't say anything on our ride home. He could barely walk, and I had to help him into the house and to his bedroom. He flopped onto the bed and started snoring right away.

I threw the blankets over him, grabbed a trash can, and put it near his bed in case he puked.

He had an old recliner in his room, but it was covered with dirty clothes. I threw the clothes on the floor, sat, leaned back, and dozed off.

An hour or so later, Chucky screamed in his sleep. “No,” he cried out. “Please, Dad, not again. Please don’t hurt me.”

I quickly went to him and tried to calm him down. “It’s all right, baby brother. That’s never going to happen again. Dad won’t hurt you anymore.” He stopped squirming around and went back into a quiet sleep, so I returned to the recliner.

I slept for a few hours before I got out of the chair—my back ached, and it was hard to move. Chucky was now in his boxers. He must’ve gotten up in the middle of the night.

I went to the kitchen and made coffee. My brain started functioning once the caffeine got into my system. I looked around the cupboards and found pancake mix, as well as bacon in the fridge. I fried the bacon and worked on the pancakes.

“Smells good,” said a voice from behind me. I spun around and saw my brother. He was wearing a pair of sweatpants but no shirt.

“Want some?” I asked.

“’Course I do,” he said.

I gave him the first serving of pancakes, then made my own. We ate in silence for most of the meal. Chucky spoke when he finished his food.

“Thanks,” he said.

“No problem, bro. Pancakes are easy.”

“Not just for the breakfast,” he said. “Thanks for last night.”

“You were pretty drunk.”

“Yeah.” He nodded. “I’m drunk a lot of the time.”

“I understand,” I said. “It makes the pain disappear for a little bit.”

"But it's always there when I sober up."

"It'll eat you up if you don't deal with it."

He was quiet for a minute. "I had a bad dream last night, didn't I?"

I nodded.

"I don't have many memories from last night. I remember Stephanie dragging me to the hospital but not coming home. But I do remember you telling me it was going to be okay."

I shrugged. "Just doing what I could."

"You're not like him at all," he said matter-of-factly. "I was so out of it last night, you could've done whatever you wanted to me. But you didn't even take my clothes off."

"You're my brother," I said as our eyes met across the small kitchen table. "I would never do anything like that to you."

"He's our father, and look what he did."

"He's a sick man. He's a pedophile and a rapist. I'm not."

"I'm afraid I'm going to be like him," he said as his eyes went to the half-eaten pancake left on his plate.

"You're nothing like him, Chucky. I'm nothing like him. That kind of sickness isn't inherited. We're our own men."

"He hurt me so bad," Chucky said in a voice so low I could barely hear him.

I stood, strode to him, knelt down beside him, and grabbed his hand.

"I know he did, bro. I'm sorry I wasn't here to protect you. I'd never have left if I thought he would do that to you. I thought he hurt me because he hated me. I'd have let him do that forever if it meant he wouldn't have harmed you or anyone else."

He turned to me and leaned down so our foreheads pressed together. "I remember one time when Dad got pissed at Mom because she burned his steak," he said.

I recalled the incident as well. Despite being broke, Dad insisted on having a steak, while the rest of us ate macaroni and cheese. Chucky was three, Mom got distracted watching him, and the steak burned. He threw the steak across the room and dropped the macaroni and cheese on the floor. He said that if he couldn't eat, then we couldn't either.

"You took me and said we were going for a walk," Chucky said. "We went to the beach. I was so hungry, my stomach hurt, and I was crying. You bought us a burger and fries with money you had been saving."

"I was hungry too," I said.

"Yeah, but you gave me most of the burger and the fries. You only ate like three bites and just a few fries."

"Nah, I had more than that." I grinned.

"That's right. You ate the pickles, lettuce, and tomato off the burger." He chuckled. "You were a good big brother."

"I could've been better," I whispered. Chucky grabbed my face and looked me in the eyes.

"Dad would've hurt me no matter what. I'm sure of that."

I stood up and wiped the tears from my eyes. "You better get cleaned up so we can go see Mom. You reek, baby brother."

"You don't smell so good either."

Chucky showered while I cleaned up the kitchen. I had just reconnected with my mother and my brother. Those were good things, so I wondered why I felt like something bad was going to happen. Nothing good in my life ever lasted for long.

Chucky cleaned up well. He combed his hair and brushed his teeth and put on a pair of tan slacks with a white button-up shirt.

"Looking good," I teased. "Can I borrow some clothes? Mine feel gross on me."

"Help yourself," he said. I showered and looked through Chucky's closet. I found a stack of magazines—*Playboy* and *Hustler*—and in between several copies of each was an issue of

Inches, a fag mag. I put the magazines back where they were and grabbed a pair of black jeans and a gray T-shirt.

“Damn, we resemble each other,” Chucky said when I came out.

“Scary, isn’t it?”

“Not really,” he said. “There’s worse people I could look like.”

MOM AND Colby were drinking coffee when we arrived at the hospital.

“Wow, don’t my sons look good?” She hugged us at the same time.

“Any word on Dad?” Chucky asked.

“He made it out of surgery an hour or so ago,” Mom answered. “But he’s still sedated.”

“There was a cop here a little bit ago,” Colby said. “Here’s his card.”

He handed it to me, and I was a bit surprised when I read the name. “Harold Zimmerman?”

“Yeah, Hal’s a cop,” Chucky said.

“You know him?” Colby asked, and I nodded. Hal had been a jock, the all-star quarterback who dated the hot blonde cheerleader. He had also loved to fuck my ass after football games.

“Hal’s got the cutest wife,” Mom said.

I didn’t figure anyone needed to know that Hal was most likely a closet case.

“Do they have any idea who shot Dad?” I asked.

“Not yet. He said he’d stop by again later.”

MOM ENDED up with a parade of well-wishers. It was hard for me to hear all these people saying such good things about the man I knew to be a sick pedophile.

Such a good man. Honest. Sweet. I couldn't believe these people had no idea what kind of man Jimmy Singer really was. Apparently, Chucky had as hard a time as I did listening to all the bullshit about our dad. He stood up quickly and ran out of the hospital. I followed him out, and we sat down on the curb.

"Let's talk about the real James Singer," I said. "He was mean."

"He never said a nice thing to anyone," Chucky muttered.

"He's a son of a bitch."

"He'll rot in hell when he dies, and that won't be soon enough." He pounded a fist on the ground, then buried his face in his hands for a moment as I remained quiet.

"Are you gay because… because of what he did to you?" Chucky asked.

"No," I answered. "I would've been queer no matter what."

"Does what he did to me make me…?"

"No, it doesn't make you anything. Do you think you're gay?"

"I don't know. I mean, I like sex with girls. I've been fucking Stephanie for a while, and I like it. A lot."

"So why would you think you're homosexual?"

"I don't know. Sometimes it feels like I should be, so maybe what he did to me wasn't so wrong."

"Chucky." I put my arm around him. "Whether you're gay or straight, what he did to you was wrong. Totally wrong."

"I know that," he said. "I mean, logically it makes sense. But I can't quite wrap my head around it. He's our dad, and dads don't hurt their kids. They're not supposed to, ya know? So I tried to convince myself that what he was doing couldn't be wrong. I tried to tell myself that I was gay, and I looked at porn and magazines, but they didn't do anything for me."

"I guess some dads do hurt their kids. Because what he did was bad, Chucky, very bad. Don't try to blame yourself or make excuses."

"Hello there," I heard someone say.

I looked up and saw a uniformed cop—Hal. Chucky and I stood up.

"Hello, Hal," I said, and we shook hands.

"Willy Singer, how the hell are you?"

"I'm good, Hal. I'm a cop in Reno."

"That's what your boyfriend told me," he said.

"Any word on who shot our father?" Chucky asked.

"I'm trying to track down some of the witnesses," he answered. "We'll find whoever did it."

"Willy, you got a minute?" Hal asked.

"Sure," I said. "Go check on Mom," I told Chucky. He nodded and walked into the hospital.

"So, Willy," Hal said.

"Cristian," I said. "I changed my name."

He smiled, but I wasn't sure if it was genuine or not. "Okay, Cristian, between you and me, I know what your father did to you and to your brother. I was never able to get proof, but if I could've, I would've sent him away for a very long time."

"I'm willing to talk on the record, Hal, and I'm sure I can convince Chucky to do the same thing."

"There could be others," he said.

"Really?" I didn't know why that surprised me. I figured it was a power thing to hurt his own kids, but being a pedophile, he probably used us because we were convenient, and when we weren't convenient, he found other boys.

"What I'm saying is that there could be lots of people who want Jimmy Singer dead. With you, your mother, and your brother at the top of the list."

"Mom was there when it happened, and I was at Mo's with Colby."

"That's good. What about Chucky?"

"He was drinking with buddies."

“Where?”

“The beach,” I answered.

“Most likely right where the shooting took place,” Hal said. “I suggest you talk to Chucky and see who can give him an alibi.”

“Thanks. I will.”

“Hey, Willy—I mean, Cristian?”

“Yeah?”

“That stuff we did in high school? That was just boys being boys. I’m married now.”

“Don’t worry, I won’t tell anyone.”

“Thanks, buddy.”

I CONVINCED Mom to leave the hospital, and we all went out to eat. As soon as we were done, she insisted on returning to the hospital. I couldn’t figure out why she was so adamant about being near the man she now professed to despise. Old habits die hard, I guess.

Colby went with Mom to the hospital while Chucky and I took a walk on the beach.

“Has the abuse stopped?” I asked after several minutes of silence.

“The sex stuff stopped a couple years ago when I was about fifteen,” Chucky said. “But he still liked to slap me around. That’s why I tried not to be home very often.”

My gut told me that if Dad had stopped molesting Chucky, then Hal was probably right and there was another victim—or victims.

“Where were you last night?”

“Drinking under the pier.”

“The pier where Dad was shot?” He nodded. “Who was with you?”

"Three or four other guys. Stephanie's older brother. He's twenty-one, so he gets us the booze. A couple other buddies I've known for years."

"We need to talk to them," I said. "You must have an alibi. You're going to be a suspect."

He nodded. "I figured. Like I told you, I don't remember much of last night. Hopefully someone else does." He gave me everyone's names, and I wrote them all down, along with numbers if he had them.

"There was someone else. A younger kid I'd never seen before."

"Do you remember his name?"

"Carson or Carter or something like that."

"First name or last name?" I asked.

He shrugged.

"Okay, I'll get started on your friends."

We went back to the hospital, and I began making phone calls. Most of them had already talked to Hal, and none of them were any help. Carson or Carter could also have been Cooper, but no one knew if that was his first or last name.

I knew something was wrong when Hal and two other uniformed officers entered the waiting area and marched right toward Mom, Chucky, and Colby.

"What's going on, Hal?" I asked.

"I'm sorry," he said. "But I have to place Chucky under arrest."

"Why?" Mom stood and took Chucky's hand.

"A witness came forward. Glenn Copeland was drinking with Chucky and his friends. He said Chucky had a gun and was talking about killing his dad."

"He's lying," Chucky exclaimed.

"We have the gun," Hal said apologetically. "We need to fingerprint you to compare them to the prints on the gun. You're under arrest."

One of the cops slapped cuffs on Chucky and read him his rights.

"I'll meet you at the station," I said. "I'll get you a lawyer."

"He already has one." Colby stepped forward.

COLBY, CHUCKY, and I sat in a private room at the Newport Police Department, waiting for my brother's interview to begin.

"Don't you have to be licensed here in Oregon to represent me?" Chucky asked.

"McMillan, McPhee had a client who does business here. In order to do work on the case, I was licensed here."

"I'm sure I can't afford to pay your usual rate."

"Knock it off," Colby replied. "You're like family."

"Well, thank you. You too, Willy. Sorry… Cristian."

"It doesn't matter what you call me. I changed my name to escape my past. You can do the same thing. You don't have to be Chucky Singer. You can be Charles Singer, Chaz Singer, or you can get rid of the Singer name. You can be a Flesh like me. What about Chance Flesh?"

"That's a soap opera name if I ever heard one." Colby laughed.

"Thanks," Chucky said. "I appreciate the offer. I'll make a decision if I don't go to prison for trying to kill our dad."

"You won't go to prison, young man," Colby said. "We haven't heard about the fingerprints yet. If they don't match, there goes half the case."

The door opened, and Hal came in. His eyes were cast downward. "The fingerprints match."

"Dammit," I cursed.

He hung his head. "Maybe I did do it. God knows I hated him enough to do it."

"I didn't hear that," Hal said as he left.

CHUCKY HAD to spend a night in jail. Thankfully, because Newport was such a small town, the only other inmates were a couple of drunks sleeping it off in their own cells.

Dad still hadn't woken up, so I convinced Mom to go home and sleep. I didn't want her to be alone, so Colby and I agreed to keep her company. Sleeping in Chucky's room had been okay, but I hadn't walked around the rest of the house. As Mom showered, I went to my room first, then the basement. The basement had been where the worst of the abuse had taken place. That was where he had worked out the nastiest of his anger.

At the far side of the basement was an old wooden sawhorse, and that brought back an event I must've blocked out. If memories were solid, I would've been punched in the gut. I had been about thirteen but couldn't remember what I'd done to piss him off. He'd practically thrown me down the stairs, and I landed on the floor flat on my stomach. My dad had yanked me to my feet by grabbing a handful of my hair. My legs buckled under me, but with his hand in my hair, he kept me upright. He was yelling and screaming at me, but I couldn't recall the words, just the emotions. It was his usual language of fury, hatred, and abuse.

He threw me over the sawhorse and yanked my pants down to my ankles. With one hand still pulling my hair, he shoved himself into me, and I cried out in pain. Unbelievable pain. When he was done, he left me lying over the sawhorse as I bled and cried.

I turned away from the sawhorse and the recollection, and I ran up the stairs from the basement and right into Colby's arms.

"Bello, what's wrong?"

"Just old memories coming back," I said.

"Where are we going to sleep?"

"The couch is comfy," I said.

"I'm fine as long as I'm next to you." Colby sat on the couch and pushed back the recliner. I lay down on the couch and put my head in his lap. He rested a hand on my stomach, and he quickly fell asleep. Sleep didn't come as easy to me. Like ghosts, the memories flew around in the air, whispering evil words in my ears, trying to scare me. I kept telling myself they didn't have any power over me, and eventually I believed it enough to close my eyes.

Chapter 19

I WOKE up Monday morning with a strong resolve to do whatever it took to get my brother cleared of the charges. I had just gotten him back, and there was no way I was going to lose him.

My cell rang, and the caller ID said it was Colby. "Hey, babe," I answered.

"Your dad's awake," he said. "Miranda and I are at the hospital right now."

"I'll be right there."

I GREETED Mom and Colby at the hospital. "Have you seen him yet?"

"No, and I don't know if I want to," Mom said. "I don't know what I'd say to him."

"I'll go talk to him."

A nurse escorted me to his room. He was very pale, with tubes in his nose and an IV attached.

He opened his eyes halfway and managed a scowl even in his weakened state. "What the hell are you doing here?"

"Near death, and you still don't have something nice to say?"

"I got nothing to say to a fag, nice or otherwise."

"How can you judge someone else, considering the things you've done?" I asked.

"What the hell do you mean?"

"You molested and raped me—your own son. And you did the same thing to Chucky. Who the hell knows how many other boys you've hurt."

"Go to hell, boy."

"You first." I turned and left, hoping I would never have to see him again. He was just another ghost—another memory. One of those things that could no longer hurt me. He was a physical being with absolutely no physical power over me.

I strode into the waiting area and hugged first Colby, then my mother.

"He's such a bastard," I growled.

Colby ran a hand over my head. "What did he do to you?"

Shaking my head, I replied, "Nothing. He can't ever hurt me again." I turned to Mom. "You have to make your own choice. You can stay with him and try to make the marriage work. If I have anything to say about it, he's going to prison. I'll talk about what he did to me, and I'm going to convince Chucky to do the same thing. His other victims might come forward as well."

"No, baby," she said. "I'm done. I've suffered all these years because I thought I was doing the right thing. I honestly had no idea he'd do anything to Chucky—or anyone else. I thought he wouldn't hurt anyone else if I kept his rage centered on me and took the punches."

"I can get divorce papers drawn up right away," Colby said.

"Do it," my mom said with a smile.

"HOW ARE we going to prove Chucky didn't shoot our dad?" I asked Colby when we were alone for a few minutes.

"The case depends mostly on the testimony of this Copeland kid. If he's lying, we need to prove it."

"Of course he's lying," I snapped.

"Cristian, you have to face the possibility that Chucky might've done it. He doesn't remember what happened that night."

Shaking my head, I replied, "I don't think he did it. Just a gut feeling."

"I have to admit, your gut feelings are pretty good."

"Damn right. They led me to you." I leaned in and kissed him, then pulled out my cell and called Hal.

"Zimmerman," he answered.

"Hey, it's Cristian. Are you talking to Copeland again soon?"

"He and his mother are going to be here in an hour. Why?"

"Is there any way I can sit in on the interrogation?"

"I can't let you do that, but you can watch from the other room."

"Thanks, Hal."

GLENN COPELAND was a short young man with long, stringy dark hair and deep-set eyes. He wore a permanent frown on his face as Hal interviewed him, with the mother present. He said he had just turned fifteen years old.

Copeland also talked about getting drunk with Chucky and his friends. "Singer pulled out a pistol and was showing it to all of us. He was, like, 'my dad's a bastard, and I'm gonna make him pay.'"

My gut instinct told me the kid was lying and that self-preservation was the reason he wasn't telling the truth. I had no doubt Copeland had shot my father. Now I just had to find a way to prove it. Then it came to me. I picked up my cell, called Hal, and watched as he answered it.

"Yes?"

"Ask him if his family has had phone company work done in the past couple years."

"Why?"

"Trust me, Hal." I closed the cell, and he did the same.

"Mr. Copeland," Hal said. "Has your family had any work done by AT&T in the past three years?"

"What the fuck does that have to do with this?" Copeland clinched his hands into fists.

Hal leaned forward. "Just answer the question."

The teenager chewed on his bottom lip a moment, then nodded. "Yeah, a couple years ago my parents had the Internet upgraded to wireless, and someone from the phone company came and did all the installation."

I left the viewing room and called Lex.

"Cris, how's everything going?"

"There's a shit storm going on here, and I need a favor."

"What do you need?"

"I need you to get into some AT&T records from a couple years ago. A major wireless installation for a home. Copeland is the last name. I need to know who the work was done by."

"I'll get on it right away."

She called back thirty minutes later. "Just call me the master."

I chuckled. "How'd you get it so fast?"

"I called up the office in Newport, pretending to be Mrs. Copeland. I asked if they could look at their records and tell me who did the installations. I said I was going to do another upgrade and wanted to make sure the same guy came over."

"And who was it?"

"Jimmy Singer."

"I knew it!" I did a fist pump.

"Why does it matter that your father did the installation?"

I froze for a second as I took in what she had said. "How do you know he's my father?"

"Cris, I've known your real name for years. I looked into your past when we became partners. It wasn't a hard trail to find."

"I should be pissed that you investigated me, but I'm not."

"I wouldn't give a shit even if you were pissed. I'd just tell you to get over it."

That was one of the reasons I loved her.

"You dealing with the past?" she asked.

I took in a deep breath and slowly released it. "Yeah, all the skeletons are out of the closet."

"Come home soon. We miss you."

I CALLED Colby, and he told me that he and my mother were at her place, and she was taking a nap. I headed there and told Colby about Copeland's connection to my dad.

"We need to find a way to talk to him."

"Chucky's preliminary hearing is tomorrow," Colby said. "The DA will have to put Copeland on the stand to make his case."

"Do you think you can get him to tell the truth?"

"Of course I can," he said.

My cell rang, but I didn't recognize the number.

"Hello."

"Is this Chucky's brother?"

"Yes, who is this?"

"This is Stephanie, Chucky's girlfriend. My brother wants to see you. Can you meet us at Mo's in thirty minutes?"

STEPHANIE AND her brother showed up just a few minutes after me. Chucky had told me Seth was twenty-one and the guy who bought the alcohol for the kids.

"So what is it you want to tell me?" I asked after we had ordered.

He looked like he didn't want to talk, but Stephanie elbowed him.

"Cope's telling the truth," he finally said. "I went to take a piss. When I came back Chucky was holding the gun. I didn't want nothing to do with whatever he was talking about, so I hung out with some other kids nearby."

"So all you saw was Chucky holding the gun, but you didn't hear what they were talking about?"

Seth shook his head.

"Was anyone else there besides Copeland when Chucky had the gun?"

"Nope."

"Do you happen to remember what time that happened?"

"Yeah. I looked at my watch because my girlfriend was showing up at eight. It was around seven thirty."

"That was after the shooting, wasn't it?" Stephanie asked.

"Yeah," I answered. "Dad was shot around six." I glanced at Seth. "Were you with Chucky at six?"

"No. I didn't show up until six thirty. I don't know who he was hanging out with before that. Is this going to help Chucky?"

"I think so. Will you be willing to testify if it's needed?"

Seth nodded. "I'll do it if I can help Chucky. I'm embarrassed because I was so drunk that night."

I scratched my neck. "I don't think we'll need you to testify. I doubt there's going to be a trial."

20

CHUCKY'S ARRAIGNMENT took place at 9:00 a.m. My gut told me everything was going to work out.

Idris Bashir, the Lincoln County DA, called Hal to the stand first. He detailed the investigation and how it led to Chucky's arrest. Colby questioned Hal a little about Copeland's statement.

When Copeland was called to the stand, I knew there was going to be fireworks. Bashir's questions were simple and to the point. He thought he had a slam-dunk case, but he was very wrong. A few seats down from me, I recognized Copeland's mother.

"Mr. Copeland," Colby said when it was his turn to question the witness. "How long have you known Charles Singer?"

"I've known who he was for a while, but that night was the first time we actually met."

"Have you met any of his family members?"

"Objection!" Bashir stood at his table and gestured at me. "What does this have to do with the attempted murder of the victim?"

"I'll make it clear if I'm allowed to continue," Colby said.

"Objection overruled," the judge said. "You may continue, Mr. Maddox."

"Mr. Copeland," Colby said, "have you ever met any members of the Singer family, besides Charles?"

"No, I haven't." Copeland glanced away as he answered.

"Let me refresh your memory." Colby approached the stand. "Three years ago your family had some work done by an AT&T workman by the name of James Singer, the defendant's father."

"Oh, okay." Copeland shrugged. "I didn't know his name."

"But you do remember him?"

"Sure. Yeah, I guess." He fidgeted in his seat.

"And why is it that you remember James Singer when the work was done so many years ago?"

He tugged on his ear and shrugged again. "He kinda talked to me."

"He spoke to you at length, didn't he? He was in your room installing the wireless router, is that correct?"

"Yeah, he was in my room," Copeland said. "I was doing homework, and he talked to me for a while."

"Objection!" Bashir exclaimed.

"Overruled," the judge replied.

"James Singer had to get on the Internet on your computer to complete the installation, is that right?"

Copeland nodded.

"You must answer verbally, Mr. Copeland," Colby said.

"Yes, he got online on my computer."

"And he looked at the history of your computer and saw some of the sites you had visited."

"Yeah," Copeland replied.

"Did he come across anything of a homosexual nature?"

"Yes," Copeland murmured.

"I'm sorry," Colby said. "I didn't hear what you said."

"Yes, he found several gay sites. He asked me if I was queer."

"What was your answer to the question?"

"I admitted I was."

"What did he do?"

His face reddened, and he stared at his hands. "He asked if I thought he was good-looking. I said yes."

"Did he do anything else? Did he touch you or kiss you?"

Copeland wrung his hands and didn't answer.

"Did this much older man touch you?" Colby repeated, this time much louder.

"Objection!" Bashir yelled. "He is badgering my witness."

"Overruled," the judge ordered. "Answer the question, Mr. Copeland."

"Fine," Copeland snapped. "Yeah, I was twelve years old, and he kissed me. And he asked me if I wanted to see him again. Someplace more private. And I did."

"You and James Singer have been involved in a relationship for several years, haven't you?"

Bashir stepped around his table and approached the judge. "Your Honor, what is the purpose of this line of questioning?"

"I'm establishing that the witness has a reason to lie."

"You may continue, Counselor," the judge said.

I was amazed but not surprised at Colby's legal acumen.

"Do you need me to repeat the question, Mr. Copeland?"

He shook his head. "Yeah, I've been meeting Jimmy secretly since we first met."

"Did you know that it was wrong, what this older man was doing to you?" Colby asked.

"Yeah, I knew it was wrong. But someone was finally paying attention to me. I've always been the invisible boy. No friends, my parents barely acknowledge I'm there."

His mother gasped and covered her mouth.

"And Mr. Singer made you feel special, didn't he?"

"Yeah. Even when he hit me or said things that hurt my feelings, I still kept seeing him. Because he said I was special."

"Did something change?"

"Yeah, a few months ago he told me he was done with me. He said I wasn't any good for him anymore. He called me horrible names." Tears streamed down his face.

I felt bad for the kid but didn't know how else to save my brother.

"And that made you mad, didn't it?"

"At first I was just sad," Copeland answered. "I felt empty inside. But then I got pissed."

"You got angry, and you wanted to do something about it. Isn't that right?"

"Yeah."

Colby was just inches from the witness, and his eyes were locked on Copeland's.

"You got a gun and waited. And you got angrier and angrier. Then something set you off. What drove you over the edge?"

"I don't know what you're talking about."

"Something happened that made you boil over into utter hatred and rage. What was it? Did you find out that you were never special? That James Singer had several other victims?"

"Yes!" Copeland shouted. "Yes. I saw the bastard with another kid. And I knew he had used me and was hurting other boys."

"You learned he was a monster," Colby stated.

"Yeah, a monster. An evil, disgusting pervert. A waste of skin."

"A monster," Colby repeated. "A monster that needed to be slain not just because of what he did to you, but so he would never hurt anyone again."

"Yeah!"

"And you saw him on the pier fighting with his wife. You had the gun and a clear shot and you took it. You shot him in the back."

Colby was practically shouting. His and Copeland's eyes were still locked together—like the conversation was just between them and there was no one else in the room.

"Yeah, I shot the bastard. I'm sorry he's not dead, because he needs to rot in hell." Copeland blinked and looked around. He realized what he had just said. "I'm not saying anything else."

"Bailiff," the judge said. "Please take Mr. Copeland into custody." Copeland stood and allowed the bailiff to cuff him, then looked at Chucky and said, "I'm sorry."

Copeland's mother stood and called out to her son. "Don't worry, son, we'll take care of this."

"Your Honor, considering the statements made by Mr. Copeland, I believe there has not been enough evidence submitted to move forward with the charges against Charles Singer."

"I have no objection," Bashir replied.

"Of course you don't, Mr. District Attorney," the judge said. "The charges against Charles Singer are dropped."

Chucky stood up and hugged Colby, then me, then Mom.

I embraced everyone, but I kissed Colby. "Thank you, big guy."

"No problem, bello."

We celebrated Chucky's freedom with a lunch at Mo's, where we shared the good news with Delilah. She instantly called her parents, and they insisted on us joining them for dinner that night.

Penny made a cake and a huge meal of fried chicken. Tons of people were there in addition to my family and the Brights: Stephanie, Seth, and lots of Chucky's friends.

Hal showed up around seven. He congratulated Chucky and pulled me aside. "Your father's about to be arrested. Right now we have Copeland's testimony about the abuse. We'll add more charges as other victims come forward. Since he can't leave the hospital, we'll have a police guard put on him."

"What'll happen to Copeland?"

"I think he has a good shot at a temporary insanity defense," Hal said. "I don't want to see the kid do any time for what he did. He's suffered enough. I'm going to try to get him some time in a mental health facility so he can work through his issues. We could press charges against him for trying to frame Chucky, if that was something your brother wanted."

"I don't think so," I replied. "I think we all feel bad for Copeland."

"But you don't feel bad for your father?"

"I don't feel anything for him. He'll pay for what he's done. I'm not going to waste any more time on him."

"I don't suppose your boyfriend will be his lawyer, huh?"

"Did Liberace like to eat pussy?" I said. "Though I do know a public defender in Reno who would be perfect for him."

Chucky pulled me aside a few minutes later.

"I've been thinking about what you said. About my name? And I made a decision."

"Yeah?"

"Nothing against what you did, but I'm keeping the name Singer. The name has been trampled on recently, and even before now there were a lot of people who didn't respect the name. I plan on changing that. So I'm sticking around. It's time to man up and prove to everyone that there can be a good, decent Singer man."

"Good for you, Chucky," I said.

"But I do think it's time to dump that particular nickname."

I laughed, because I had always hated being called Willy. "Okay, Charles."

"Well, I don't need to go that formal. I think I'll go with Charlie."

"Good idea."

"There was one other thing I wanted to tell you," he said. "I think I love Stephanie. She stood up for me and never once thought I was guilty. I'm pretty sure she's the one for me, and I want to see where things go with her."

I patted his shoulder. "So you're not confused anymore?"

"Yep, I'm straight."

COLBY AND I left early and took a walk on the beach.

"Remember that fantasy of yours, big guy? The one about having sex on the beach?"

"Of course I remember. You said you knew a good private spot."

"Where do you think we're going?" I asked.

I led him to a section on the beach where the wall of rock had curved inward, covering the entrance so it wasn't easily seen. Colby and I climbed over, and we were alone.

I turned and kissed him, forcing my tongue past his lips.

"Damn, it feels like forever since we fucked."

"It's only been a day or two," Colby said.

"In the time that we've been together, how long have we gone between fucks?"

"Twelve hours," Colby said, laughing. "Longest half day of my life."

"Get naked, big guy."

We removed our clothes as quickly as possible, and I reached out and caressed his semierect cock until it was totally engorged. I stepped closer to him and wrapped my hand around both our shafts and stroked.

"Feels good," he whispered in my ear. After tracing my tongue around the large muscles on his chest and torso, I licked his nipples until they became stiff, then bit and sucked on them. I knelt down and licked a drop of precome from the tip of his dick. I ran my tongue up and down his length and licked his balls. His soft moans urged me on. I sucked the head of his cock into my mouth and slowly swallowed it all. With my nose buried in his pubes, I breathed in the scent of sweat and sex. I grabbed my own cock and jerked it. With his cock buried in my gullet and sliding in and out, I stroked myself harder. The orgasm came quick, and I shot onto the sand below me. I slid my mouth off him.

"Fuck me, Colby."

"You don't have to ask me twice," Colby said.

I reached into my pants, pulled out a travel pack of lube, and threw it to Colby. He smiled as he opened it and slathered it on his cock. I lay on my back in the sand, and he climbed between my legs. He put some lube onto his fingers and slid two inside me.

"I'm good, babe. I'm good," I said. "Please, I want you in me."

Colby leaned down and kissed me. He pressed his cock against my hole, and when the head popped in, it felt so fucking marvelous, so incredible that my cock was rock hard again. In one thrust, Colby was in me and part of me. As he slid in and out, his lips never left mine. We separated only long enough to catch our breath; then our lips were together again. Our tongues explored each other's mouths and pressed together as he fucked me.

My cock was trapped between our bodies, and the feel of his rippled stomach rubbing against me made me leak a pool of precome between us. The friction of his body against mine and the feel of his rock-hard shaft penetrating me again and again made me lose all control.

"Ohh, ohh, ohh hell, fucking yeah!" I screamed as the jizz pumped out of me and coated our bellies.

"Yeah, that's fucking awesome," Colby groaned as he came in me. He rolled off and lay in the sand.

"Was it as good as you hoped?" I asked.

"Better. Way better."

"I'm glad it was good for you," I said, laughing. "Because I got sand in my ass crack and my hair. And I'm sure I'm gonna have road rash up and down my back."

Colby rolled me over and laughed hysterically.

"What's so funny?"

"Your butt is all scratched up from the sand. It looks like you slid down a hill of gravel bare-assed."

“That’s what it feels like too. I don’t think this is a fantasy I want to enact again. Unless we bring a blanket.”

“That’s a deal.” He wiped the sand off my back, stood up, and helped me to stand.

“We could take a dip in the ocean to clean up,” Colby said.

I laughed. “You obviously haven’t been in this water. It’s pretty cold.”

“It can’t be that chilly,” he said.

“Go for it,” I said. “I’ll make sure no one’s around, and you can go in your underwear.”

I got dressed, and Colby slipped on just his boxer briefs. I climbed over the rock and made sure no one else was around.

“All clear,” I called out.

Colby climbed over the rock and handed me his clothes.

“Sure you don’t want to join me?”

“I’m sure,” I said, chuckling.

Colby ran right into the water and didn’t stop until he was chest deep.

“Holy shit!” he cried out. “This is fucking colder than ice.”

“I told you.” I laughed and couldn’t stop. Colby quickly came out of the water.

“Damn,” he said. “I think my dick inverted.”

“I hope not.” I laughed harder. “I do not do innies.”

“I’m sure you can make it an outtie again.”

I handed Colby his clothes, and he got dressed as he shivered.

“Let’s get back to the motel and take a shower. A very hot shower,” Colby said.

AFTER OUR very hot shower, Colby and I climbed into bed.

“You know what I’ve been thinking about, big guy?”

"I thought I told you it wasn't good for you to think," Colby teased.

I rolled on top of him and tickled him. He grabbed me, rolled me over, and tickled my sides until I begged him to stop.

"So what were you thinking about?"

"I've dealt with a lot in my life recently. And you've pretty much obliterated most of my rules."

"There are still a few rules I need to take care of. Like number sixteen."

Number sixteen: The clothes in my closet had to be organized—pants together, shirts together. Colby had a completely disorganized and messed-up closet, and it drove me nuts.

"There's another rule you haven't gotten me to break. Rule number one." *No topping.* For as long as I could choose, I'd only been a bottom, always the catcher and never the pitcher. Part of it came from my hustling days and having to fuck guys I hated and despised.

Colby caressed my back. "I know it'll happen when you're ready. And even if it doesn't ever, I'll still be happy as long as I'm with you."

"You told me one time that sex for me was about not having control, and that's why I didn't like to top. And you were right."

"Why are you bringing this up?" he asked.

"Because I'm ready."

"Ready? As in ready to fuck me?"

"Yeah, if you still want that."

"Of course I still want it. I fucking want it bad. When can we do it? I'm ready whenever you are."

I laughed at his excitement.

"I'm ready now too, big guy." I reached down and grabbed my dick. It was hard, and I rubbed it against his asscheeks.

"Hell, yeah, you're ready. Let me grab the lube. There is no way I can take that monster dry." Without rolling off me, he reached over and grabbed the lube. "How do you want to do this?"

"Just like this," I answered.

He smiled and squeezed the slick onto his fingers and onto mine. He reached back and slid his fingers into his ass as I greased up my cock. I was as thrilled as he was to be doing this, and it occurred to me that I had never wanted to fuck someone as much as I wanted to fuck him.

"You have to go slow," he said.

He leaned forward, and I aimed my cock at his slick hole. He pressed back, and I thought for a moment that there was no way it was going to happen. Then his hole relaxed, and the head popped in.

"Oh my ever-loving God!" Colby moaned. "That feels so—"

"Mind-blowingly amazing."

He sank down farther on me, and perfect just got better and better.

The velvet warmth surrounding my shaft was astonishing. He sank all the way down on me, and my body shook like tiny electric shocks were caressing it. The orgasm hit me without warning, and I buried myself in my lover as shot after shot of my seed flowed into him. My body relaxed, and I softened quickly.

He rolled off me. "That was great," Colby said.

"I'm sorry it happened so fast. I didn't think I'd have a hair trigger."

"Baby, I love it that it excited you so much you couldn't control yourself. That was a major turn-on."

I was so tired, I was having trouble keeping my eyes open. "But you didn't come," I murmured.

"It's okay. I can take care of myself. You're exhausted. Go to sleep."

I wanted to offer to help him get off, but I couldn't find the energy to speak. I heard him stroking himself and moaning. I heard the marvelous noises he always made when he came, just before I went to sleep.

My last thought was that everything was just right. I hoped that for once nothing happened to spoil it. But I should've known better.

Chapter 21

THE RINGING of my cell phone woke me from a very deep sleep. Colby was still snoring next to me. The clock on my phone said 3:47 a.m., and the caller ID said it was Lex.

"Fuck." She wasn't calling with good news. "Lex, what's wrong?"

"It's Gabe," she said. "He's in the hospital. It's not good, Cris. He might not make it."

"Fuck! I'll be there as soon as I can." I set down the phone and stopped for a moment so I wouldn't lose it. I shook Colby awake.

"What's going on?" he asked.

"We need to go home. Gabe's in the hospital."

"What happened?" Colby sat up and wiped the sleep from his eyes.

"I don't know, but Lex said he might not make it."

"Shit." He threw his clothes on, and we stuffed everything into our bags. We were out of the motel in twenty minutes and while I drove to Portland, Colby was on his phone getting us airline tickets.

We made it to the airport just in time to board the plane. Before it took off, I called my mom and told her why we had to leave so suddenly. I promised to call as soon as I could. The flight felt maddeningly long, and Colby held my hand the entire time.

Colby had left his car at the Reno airport, so we drove it straight to Renown. Lex was there, and some other people I didn't recognize. One of them was holding Victor, but he wiggled free when he saw me and dashed into my arms.

"Kisstun," he said. "I sad. Mami and Papi got hurt."

"I know, little man." He wrapped his arms around my neck and squeezed, and I hugged him back. "I need to talk to Lex. I'll be back." I set him down, and he returned to the older Hispanic lady who had been holding him.

I approached Lex. "What happened?"

"I don't know everything, Cris. I recognized the address when I heard the call over the radio. It was Gabe and Violet's apartment. They were in the bedroom." She was trying to keep control. "It was horrible, Cris. Blood was everywhere."

"What the hell happened?"

She shook her head. "I don't know. But Violet… she… she was dead when I got there. I thought Gabe was gone too, but I felt a pulse."

"Violet's dead?"

Colby was behind me, and he wrapped his arms around me. I think if he hadn't been there to hold me, I would've fallen.

"Yeah, it looks like they were both stabbed repeatedly. Gabe's in surgery right now. He had major internal bleeding. It's bad, Cris. So bad."

I pulled Lex into my arms and hugged her.

"Victor wasn't there, was he?" I asked.

Lex shook her head. "He was with his grandmother—Violet's mother. That's her family over there."

"Thank God," I said. "Does he know his mom's dead?"

"Yeah, his grandma told him. He's holding up okay for now."

"Cristian," Colby said. "We need clean clothes. Why don't we go home—?"

"No," I interrupted him. "I'm not leaving."

"Okay," Colby said. "I'll go get us clean clothes and come back."

I nodded. "I'm going to stay with Victor." I shuffled over to Violet's mother.

"Excuse me. Can I hold Victor, ma'am?"

"Of course," she said with a strong Hispanic accent. "He likes you very much."

"Trust me, the feeling is mutual." I held my hand out to Victor. He hopped off her lap and took it. "Let's go over here." I went to a quiet part of the room and sat down on the floor with my back against the wall. Victor sat in my lap with his head against my chest.

"How you doing, little man?"

"My mami's dead, Kisstun," he whispered. "That means I don't ever get to see her again. That makes me sad."

"I understand," I replied. "But you know what? It's okay to be sad, and it's okay to cry."

Just like that, the dam burst. The little boy had been holding it in, and he couldn't do it any longer. I held him as he cried, the tears flowed, and he wailed in pain—pain that no one should ever feel, especially a boy so young. Eventually he cried himself to sleep, and soon after I dozed off as well.

LEX SHOOK me awake, and I was scared when Victor wasn't in my lap.

"Relax," she soothed. "He's getting breakfast with his nana."

I stood up and stretched.

"Gabe's out of surgery."

"How is he?"

"Still weak. The doctor said he isn't out of the woods yet. But if he's strong, and we know he is, he has a good chance of making it."

"Can I see him?"

"Yes, but only for a few minutes."

Damn, I was getting tired of hospitals. After talking to the doctor for a minute, I followed him to Gabe's room. The kid looked so weak and tired, I almost cried.

"Hey, kid," I said. "You keep getting yourself hurt and they're going to reserve a permanent room here for you."

"The service is decent," he said softly. "But the food sucks."

"What happened?"

"I don't remember anything from that night," he mumbled. "It's all a blur."

"No memories? Did someone break in? Did you and Violet invite someone over?"

"I don't remember," he repeated. "Violet. How's Violet?"

"Fuck, you don't know? No one told you?"

"Other than the doctor and nurse," he said. "I haven't talked to anyone."

I walked up to him and touched his arm. "I'm sorry, kid. Violet's dead. You guys were both stabbed."

Gabe wailed out unintelligible cries, and before I could comfort him, the room was swarmed with medical personnel who were pushing me out.

Colby was in the waiting area when I came in.

"What happened?" he asked.

"I had to tell Gabe that Violet is dead," I said. His big arms drew me close, and I buried my face in his shoulder.

"Take me home," I said.

BEFORE I returned to the hospital, I made a few phone calls to the first responders. According to Cherry, the CSI, Gabe and Violet had been stabbed by a six-inch serrated blade. She said it was a miracle Gabe had survived, considering the amount of blood he had lost.

When I arrived at Renown, I was told Gabe was asking for me. He didn't look any better, to my dismay.

"Hey, kid. How you doing?"

"I might not make it," Gabe said.

"Knock it off. You're going to survive. Don't think anything else."

"There's a real possibility I'm going to die," he said. "And if I do, I want you to promise me that you'll watch out for Victor. Stay in his life and make sure he doesn't head down the wrong path."

"Gabe, you're not going to die."

"Promise me, Cristian!"

I rubbed my temples. "Okay, I promise."

"Thank you," he said as he closed his eyes and drifted off. A nurse escorted me out of the room. I sat down in the waiting room with Colby. Victor was at his nana's place with the rest of Violet's family. I realized I didn't know much about Gabe's family. I was going to have to contact someone.

Thirty minutes after my visit with Gabe, I heard a hustle of activities and lots of noise coming from down the hallway. I saw nurses and doctors rushing to Gabe's room. I tried to push my way in, but Colby held me back.

It seemed like everyone was in his room for hours, when actually it was only minutes. Slowly and one by one they left the room—some of them were crying. The doctor came out, and I rushed to him.

"What happened?"

"I'm sorry," he said softly. "His heart stopped. He didn't make it."

"Oh fuck. Fuck. Shit. God fucking dammit!"

"Bello," Colby said. "I'm sorry."

"Dammit, I can't lose him, Colby. He can't be gone." I dashed into Gabe's room, and there his lifeless body lay. I took his hand for a moment and held it. I leaned forward and kissed his forehead. "I love ya, kid."

Colby escorted me out and took me home. I took an Ambien, collapsed on the bed, and fell asleep. Colby woke me up a few hours later and handed me a peanut butter and jelly sandwich.

"You need to eat," he said.

I ate it slowly because it had no taste whatsoever.

"I called Lex and everybody I could think of. Violet's parents were notified."

"Victor has to be so messed up," I said.

"Yeah, the grandma said he was asking for Kisstun."

"I need to go see him," I said.

"You have to take care of yourself first, love. You're no good to Victor if you fall apart when he's with you."

"I'll be fine when I see him. I'll fall apart later."

"I'm here for you."

"I know."

VICTOR RAN into my arms when I went to his grandma's house. I carried him into the spare bedroom where he stayed, and we sat on the bed.

"Daddy's gone. Mommy and Daddy are dead. I got no more parents."

"But you have lots of family who love you. And you have me."

"You not gonna die, are you, Kisstun?"

"Not for a long, long time, little man."

"I want you to live fo-ever."

"I'll do my best."

He cried in my arms again, and this time I joined him. I told him everything would be all right, and I wished I believed it.

WHEN I got home, I felt like a zombie. Colby gave me some baked chicken he had made, then pushed me into the shower. I felt so numb, I couldn't even wash myself. Thank God for my man, who washed me, dried me, and tucked me into bed.

I thought about how I had never told Gabe I loved him. I hadn't told him out of some stupid macho pride about real men not showing their emotions. What a fucking stupid waste.

"I love you, Colby."

"Ditto."

"Say the words. I want to hear the words."

"I love you too, Cristian."

Chapter 22

GABE AND Violet's funeral took place Saturday morning. It was sunny and bright, and it seemed wrong. Funerals should always be on rainy and gloomy days.

Lex had managed to find Gabe's mother and two sisters. They hadn't spoken for years and were thrilled to meet Victor.

Lex, Colby, and several others said wonderful and sweet things about Gabe, but when it came time for me to speak, I couldn't do it. Colby held me tight as the casket was lowered into the ground.

We went to a get-together at Violet's mother's home, but I left early because I felt out of place. I went back to the cemetery and sat next to Gabe's gravestone. What I had to say was for his ears alone.

"I loved you, kid. You were one of the very few true friends I've had. I won't ever regret a moment we spent together, but I will always mourn the moments we won't be together. I wish you were here, but you'll always be a part of me. And I won't ever forget you. I'll keep my promise about Victor and visit him often and make sure he doesn't go down the wrong path."

After sitting there for more than an hour, I stood up. I noticed a man in the distance, and for a moment I thought it was Drew. When I looked again, he was gone. I figured if it was Drew, he was just paying his respects to Gabe.

"Good-bye, kid," I said with my hand on the stone.

Chapter 23

THE MONDAY after the funeral, I came to work with a sense of purpose. I was going to find my friend's killer.

"So what's the first step, Lex?" I asked.

"First step in what?" she asked.

"First step in finding the bastard who killed Gabe and Violet, of course."

"That may not be a possibility," she said.

"What the hell are you talking about?"

"The FBI is taking over the case," she said.

"Well, I'm sure I can convince Drew to let me help."

"It's not Drew," she said.

"That's right."

I heard a deep, manly voice behind me and turned around to see a boney older woman.

"Special Agent Phoebe MacIntosh."

She stuck out her hand, and I took it somewhat reluctantly.

"What happened to Drew?" I asked.

"Special Agent Bradley has been reassigned," she said. "I'm in charge of this case."

"How is this a federal matter?" I asked.

"We believe the same person who murdered your friends has also murdered half a dozen other men and women in other states."

"Why do you think the murders are all connected?" Lex asked.

"I'm sorry," MacIntosh said. "I can't disclose that information at this time."

"Listen, lady," I said. "Gabe Vargas was my best friend, and I won't let anyone, including you, stop me from finding his killer."

"I don't give a shit who you think you are, Detective Flesh," she responded. "But you will not be helping me on this case, and you better not interfere." She turned and strode to Brunson's office.

I left the precinct and went to Gabe and Violet's place. I slipped past the police tape and went into the apartment. The blood was contained in only one room—the bedroom. I could picture Gabe and Violet in bed, sleeping soundly when the killer snuck in and attacked them. I wondered what the killer got from sneaking into residences and murdering people. I needed to know his MO in order to do my job.

"What the hell are you doing here?" I recognized Special Agent MacIntosh's deep voice.

"Just having a look around," I replied.

"Do I need to remind you that this is *not* your case?"

"I know that you think this isn't my case. But these were my friends, and I owe it to them to find their killer."

"And that is one of the top reasons you *cannot* help on the investigation, Detective. You are much too personally involved."

"You don't know me very well. I'm at my best when there's a personal stake."

"I'm sorry," she said. "It's not going to happen. Now leave *my* crime scene."

"This conversation isn't over," I said as I left.

LEX AND I were assigned a few other cases, but I didn't let that stop me from attempting to insinuate myself into the investigation of Gabe's death. I used as much free time as possible searching for other murders that could be connected to Gabe's. I didn't have much luck.

"Flesh!" Brunson bellowed from his office. "Get your ass in here. Now!" I looked at Lex, and she shrugged, indicating she didn't know what Brunson was upset about.

"Yes, sir?" I said as I stepped into his office.

"Shut the door," he ordered, and I complied. He got up from behind his desk, stepped around, and stood a few feet from me. "What the hell do you think you are doing?" he said in a very quiet voice. That quiet voice meant he was extremely pissed and trying to hold in his temper.

"Could you be more specific, sir?"

He looked like his blood pressure was sky high. "Why are you trying to interfere with a federal investigation?"

"Chief," I said, "Gabe was my best friend. He saved my life last year. I owe it to him to find his killer."

"I understand, Cristian." His voice lightened up. "But I've had my ass chewed by the mayor and some Feds. And I don't like that happening. I have been commanded to tell you to back off. So this is an official order. Back. The. Fuck. Off!"

"And if I don't?"

"You will be reprimanded, and severely so."

"I don't know if I *can* back off, sir. That would feel like betraying Gabe."

"I will do *whatever* I have to do, Flesh."

"Me too."

I DIDN'T back off. I just covered my tracks better. Then I lost any chance I had at finding Gabe's killer. One day Special Agent MacIntosh was there, and the next she was gone. According to

Brunson, there was no more evidence to be found in Reno, so MacIntosh had returned to the Sacramento office.

I didn't know how I could continue living when Gabe wasn't. I was an empty shell for weeks after his death. Colby was patient and loving with me. We had sex, and it was always good, and it made me feel human again. Though I wanted it, I didn't top Colby for a while.

Every time I felt happiness or joy, I would immediately feel guilty. How could I be living my life while Gabe was in the dirt? I saw Victor often and did my best to get him to smile, but nothing worked.

Colby and I were in bed wearing boxers and T-shirts when he started tickling me—just like old times. I let go for a moment before I stopped it and pushed him off me.

"Goddammit, Cristian. I am so fucking tired of you and your mood swings. You're driving me crazy."

"If I'm such a goddamn burden," I said, "I can leave and go to my apartment."

"You know that is not what I want. Why do you have to be such a dick?"

"It comes naturally," I sneered.

"You walk around like there's nothing in you. We fuck, and it's like I'm screwing a sex doll."

"I'm so sorry I can't be a wildcat in bed because my goddamn fucking best friend died. I will try to make your sex life more enjoyable. Maybe fake a few orgasms. Would that make you happy?"

Colby grabbed my shoulders and made me face him. "Do you think this is what Gabe would've wanted? For you to sit around all sad and depressed? Do you think you're any good at all for Victor like you are? How can you expect him to smile when you won't? How can he start to live his life again if you haven't done it?"

"Just leave me alone," I said and tried to pull away from him.

"No, I will not leave you alone. I'm here for the long haul, Cristian. You've just opened up to me. Don't block me off. Please, bello. I love you."

And finally I let everything go. I leaned into Colby's neck and let myself really and truly grieve. I wept as he held me tight. He pulled me close and continued to hold me tight.

Colby was right. Gabe wouldn't want me to grieve for him forever. He would want me to live my life and be happy. He would want me to smile and laugh and play. He would want me to fuck as often as I could.

Colby and I dozed off in each other's arms. I woke up with a sudden urge to get fucked. I stripped off my shirt and pulled down his boxers enough to get his cock free. I sucked it to life without waking him up, got the lube and slicked my hole, then his cock, and I straddled him and slowly sat on his dick.

"Now that's a nice way to wake up," Colby mumbled as he came to.

"Make love to me, big guy. Pound me. Make me feel it. I haven't felt anything since Gabe died, and I want to feel you in me."

I rode him softly, then hard. Quick, then slow. I ground down onto him, and he lifted his hips to thrust into me. His hands traveled up my chest and cupped my face. One hand ran through my hair, tugging slightly. The tension on my hair created the tiniest bit of pain, and it mixed with the painful pleasure of his shaft thrusting into me. It was glorious. We made love and fucked at the same time, and we did it for close to an hour before I couldn't hold back any longer. I let the wave crash over and felt all the sensations that come from an orgasm—the tingle in my balls, the thrill of my prostate being rubbed, the soft skin of my cock, the feeling of my seed traveling up the tube, the pressure at the head, and the exhilarating feel of my come shooting from my cock. I coated Colby's stomach.

"Oh yeah. That's awesome," Colby moaned.

"Come in me, big guy. That's what I want to feel now."

My prostate continued to tingle with the thrusts of his cock, and I could feel every inch of his length rubbing me, prodding into me. I listened as his soft grunts increased. He spread my asscheeks so he could go as deep as possible. It felt like his dick was bouncing off my heart he was so deep. And finally he came. I relaxed on his chest and listened to his heart beating. My heart was beating the same tune—we were totally in sync.

A CALL from my mother brought good news and bad news. Well, I didn't think it was really bad news, but it's not good to celebrate a death—even if the person who died was a pedophile.

The good news: Glenn Copeland was sentenced to two months in a mental hospital and three years' probation for shooting my father.

The not so bad news: my father was dead. He had recovered enough to spend time in jail. He had been kept in protective segregation but was moved to a general population unit. Apparently other inmates found out what his crime was. I guess even murderers have a code of ethics, and they do not approve of child molesters. While he was out in the recreation yard, he had been attacked by numerous assailants. When the officers found him, he was bloody and barely breathing. The prison medical staff tried to save him, but he didn't make it.

I had to wonder what was worse for him—prison life or the afterlife?

A WEEK later, Colby and I took Victor for the weekend. We went shopping and spoiled him rotten, doing everything he wanted. He finally smiled while we played a racing game on the new game system we bought for Colby's place. And I knew he was starting to get over the death of his parents—well, as much as you can ever get over a thing like that.

"I've been thinking about something," I told Colby in bed on Sunday night after we had dropped Victor back at his new home.

"I thought we agreed you weren't supposed to be thinking without my permission."

"Jerk."

"Asshat. So what were you thinking about?"

"I'm going to get rid of my apartment," I said. "That is, if you still want me to live with you."

"You goof. Of course I want you to live with me. Do you want to find a different place?"

"No, we can stay here. I want to turn one of the extra bedrooms into my office. A place I can go and be alone if the mood ever strikes me."

"We can do that," he said. "I'm so happy."

"Don't be planning a wedding or anything, big guy. I don't think you'd look very good in a wedding dress."

"Who says I'd be the one wearing the dress?"

"It sure as hell wouldn't be me," I said.

"You don't want to marry me?"

"I want to spend the rest of my life with you. I don't need a civil ceremony or whatever to do that. And I certainly don't need some big, huge wedding. If we ever want to do something like that, I say we go to Atlantic City or Vegas and get married in a tacky wedding chapel with a drag-queen minister."

Colby chuckled. "Not a bad idea," he said.

"You remember what we did in Newport?"

"Which thing? Clearing your brother of attempted murder charges? Sex on the beach?"

"No," I said. "Breaking rule number one."

"Aww," he said. "My absolutely favorite rule to break. Even if we only did break it one time."

"You know what they say: rules are made to be broken. You ready to break that rule again?"

"Does RuPaul like makeup? Of course I want to do that again."

"Assume the position, boy," I ordered.

"Ohh, I love it when you order me around."

"On your hands and knees, bare ass in the air."

"Yes, sir!"

He pulled off his pajama pants, scooted to the edge of the bed, and put his ass in the air. I was already naked and stood behind him. I had grabbed the slick and put it next to him on the bed.

I leaned down, buried my face in his ass, and teased his hole with my tongue. I gripped his asscheeks firmly and kneaded them as I slurped and sucked his rim. He moaned and murmured and wiggled against me.

I stood and squeezed some lube directly onto his hole. He shivered at the cold, and I warmed up the lube with my fingers. I slipped one finger into the tightness and slid it in and out for a moment. I slipped two fingers in and scissored them. I pushed in and found his gland. I pressed against it, and a grunt escaped from Colby's mouth. I reached down and gave his cock a couple of quick strokes.

"Feel good?" I asked.

"Yeah, oh yeah," he replied.

I removed my fingers and slicked up my shaft.

"You want it?" I teased his hole with the head—just softly pressed it against him with not enough force to slip in.

"Yes, sir," he moaned. "I want it. I need it."

I didn't think anyone had ever really, truly needed me. And I needed Colby too. At that moment I needed to be inside of him. I pushed in hard, and my dick slid halfway in before I could stop.

"Oh fuck!"

"I'm sorry," I said. "Did I hurt you?"

"Yeah, but it's a good hurt. Damn, I love this."

"Same here," I said. "You're so unbelievably tight. A goddamn vise grip around my cock. And you're so hot inside. Like a furnace."

"You feel huge in me," he murmured. "As if you're going to split me in half. You go so deep. So far in me, I don't know which part is me and which part is you."

"It doesn't matter," I said. "It's just us. Together."

"Fuck me, babe. Fuck me hard."

I pulled my cock all the way out, then slammed back home. My balls slapped against him again and again as I pounded him. It felt so fucking good, I didn't know why I had waited so long to top. But it struck me that if I hadn't waited, it wouldn't have been as special with Colby. I had sucked and been fucked by dozens of men. But this was something special for us.

I pounded him harder, and he kept rhythm by stroking his cock.

"Lord, Cristian. Oh my God!" he moaned, and I felt his tight ring constrict around me. His orgasm spurred mine on, and I drove in one last time. I came and came—shooting loads inside of the man I loved.

I slipped out of him, and he collapsed on the bed. I went into the bathroom and got a rag wet with warm water. I washed myself, then returned to the bedroom and cleaned Colby up. I lay down next to my lover so we were face-to-face.

"That may have been a huge mistake," I said.

"Why?"

"Because it felt so good that I'm going to want to do it again. I am going to wreck that ass of yours. You're going to walk funny from now on."

"Maybe we can take turns?"

"Forget that," I said. "I am fucking you all the time." We both laughed. "I got something to tell you."

"Not more deep, dark secrets?"

"No, you know everything about me."

"So what do you have to tell me?"

"That I love you."

"Ditto."

A FEW weeks later, a letter showed up at work for me. There was no return address, and inside was a handwritten note.

Thanks for keeping your promise
the kid

Keep reading for
an exclusive excerpt from

Blood & Tears

Flesh Series: Book Three

By Ethan Stone

The last thing Gabe Vargas wants to do after nearly dying is to leave his young son. But that's exactly what FBI Agent Drew Bradley is asking him to do. According to Drew, the only way to protect Gabe and find his wife's killer is to fake Gabe's death.

With an already established adversarial relationship, protecting a hothead like Gabe isn't exactly a picnic for Drew either. But Drew lets his guard down and a desire for Gabe leaves him confused. Before the crime can be solved, Drew will have to risk more than his life. He'll also have to risk his heart.

Prologue

Gabe

I DIDN'T know where I was when I woke. Hell, I didn't know *who* I was for an instant. The overwhelming agony when I took a deep breath reminded me and the bitter antiseptic smell confirmed it—I was in the hospital.

The light in my room was off, but a few glimmers of sunlight peeked through the window curtains. Not that there was much to see. A television high on the wall. An IV running into my arm. Nothing worth looking at. Damn, I wasn't sure I had anything worth living for.

Violet was dead. Casey was dead. The only people I'd been in love with were gone. I'd been dealing with Casey's death for over a month but Vi's… her murder was still fresh in my mind. Well, the grief was fresh, but not the actual event. Even though I'd been there when it happened, and been injured myself, I couldn't recall a thing. Not one mother-fucking second of it. No matter how I tried, the memories weren't there.

My best friend, Cristian Flesh, had told me what happened, but it hadn't helped. According to Cristian, a detective with the Reno Police Department, our neighbor had called the police after hearing screams coming from our apartment. Violet, the mother of my son, was dead by the time the authorities arrived, and I wasn't much better off.

I shifted, trying to find a more comfortable position. I lay on my side because my back and ass were bandaged and throbbed with pain. The soreness made me suck in a breath. I closed my eyes and allowed my thoughts to drift. The reality of being a single parent slowly took hold. What if I couldn't be everything Victor needed? A boy needed his mother, right? Tears filled my eyes.

Someone clearing their throat alerted me to the fact that I wasn't alone. I wiped away the signs of my emotions and looked toward the door. The shadows obscured the identity of whoever it was. "Who's there?"

Recognition seized me as the man stepped into the light, and a wave of emotions crashed over me. Fear, anger, grief, and for a moment, unadulterated hate.

"What the fuck are you doing here, Bradley?"

"We need to talk, Vargas." FBI Agent Drew Bradley strode to the middle of the room and stood there with his hands shoved into his coat pockets.

"I got nothing to say to you, *Special* Agent," I snarled. Seeing this man was the last thing I needed. A fresh sense of loss swept over me. How much grief could one man endure?

"You don't have a choice," Drew replied sternly. "I've been assigned to this case. To your case." His back was ramrod straight. I could feel him staring at me, but I didn't meet his gaze.

"Case?" I made eye contact. "What case?"

"It's very likely the attack on you and Violet is linked to an active FBI case." Drew approached my bed.

"I don't give a shit." The only thing I wanted was to see the back of Agent Bradley's head leaving my room.

"You don't want to help find the person who tried to kill you? The person who did kill Violet and almost orphaned your son?" He gestured with his hands as he spoke. "You want to just slink away and hide? That's not what you did when Casey was killed."

Hearing Casey's name spoken aloud wrenched at my heart. I tried to sit up in bed, but the pain held me back. "Don't you fucking say his name, Bradley. It's your fault he's dead."

"I take full responsibility."

His shoulders drooped and his eyes were red. Yeah, the man was sad, but I didn't give a shit.

"I didn't ask to be put on this case. Trust me, I know how much you hate me. I asked—I begged—my boss to assign someone else. He refused. He wants me here because I know you."

"He's a goddamn idiot."

Drew chuckled. "That may be true, but it doesn't change anything. So I'll ask you again—are you going to help, or are you going to run with your tail tucked between your legs?"

I didn't respond right away. I didn't want to deal with Agent Bradley again, but I couldn't let the killer get away with it. I'd gone after justice when Casey died, and I had to do the same for Violet. It was really my only choice.

"You know the answer, Bradley. I'll do whatever it takes to find the fucker who killed Violet. Even if it means putting up with your sorry ass."

"You're a good man, Gabriel." A smug smile crossed his face.

Ignoring the self-satisfaction in his voice, I said, "This isn't about me. It's about Violet. So what do you need me to do?"

He crossed his arms and cocked his head.

"I need you to die."

Don’t miss how the story began!

In the Flesh

Flesh Series: Book One

By Ethan Stone

Reno Detective Cristian Flesh is an out and unashamed cop, but his slutty ways might be his downfall. Cristian lives by a strict set of personal rules, preferring hook-ups and anonymous encounters to committed relationships. His guidelines work for him… until one of his tricks is murdered and he becomes the prime suspect.

Leave it to handsome lawyer Colby Maddox to save Cristian’s life. He takes the case and the attraction between them is quick and undeniable. After several passion-filled encounters with Colby, Cristian unexpectedly wants to break all his rules. However, before they can contemplate a future together, they’ll have to clear Cristian’s name and find the real murderer.

http://www.dsppublications.com

Coming Soon

Closing Ranks

Flesh Series: Book Four

By Ethan Stone

Internal Affairs investigator Jeremy Ranklin is looking into corruption within the Reno Police Department when he's ordered to examine the suspicious death of the Chief of Police. The assignment partners Jeremy with Detective Cristian Flesh. Though they spar at first, Jeremy earns Cristian's trust and they work well together.

Deeply closeted, Jeremy fights an attraction to fellow cop Kipp Mosely. The investigation brings Jeremy and Kipp together, but lies and secrets prevent things from going any further. Jeremy will need both Kipp's and Cristian's help to discover how deep the corruption runs—and to stay alive when the danger hits close to home.

ETHAN STONE is an out-and-proud gay man. Which is fairly new in his life—the out part, not the gay part. He's been queer his whole life, though he tried to deny it for years with a wonderful woman. The years in denial weren't all bad as he has two amazing kids out of it. His son is a teenager and his daughter has made him a grandfather, three times over. A way-too-young grandfather.

Ethan recently returned to Oregon after almost a decade in Nevada. He no longer has a day job and is doing his best to make a living at this writing thing. If he can't make a living, he at least wants to support his Mountain Dew and beef jerky addictions.

Readers can find Ethan online:
Facebook: www.facebook.com/ethan.stone.54
Twitter: @ethanjstone
Google +: https://plus.google.com/u/0/+EthanStone92
Ello: @ethanstone92
Website: www.ethanjstone.com
E-mail: ethanstone.nv@gmail.com

Lightning Source UK Ltd.
Milton Keynes UK
UKOW06f1854260615

254210UK00015B/453/P

9 781632 168801